THE STRANGE TALE OF THE TRILOBITE LIBERATION ARMY

Edward Ringel

Copyright © 2024 Edward Ringel

All rights reserved

The characters and events portrayed in this book are fictitious. Any similarity to real persons, living or dead, is coincidental and not intended by the author.

No part of this book may be reproduced, or stored in a retrieval system, or transmitted in any form or by any means, electronic, mechanical, photocopying, recording, or otherwise, without express written permission of the publisher.

ISBN: 9798320068817
Imprint: Independently published

Cover design by: Ed Ringel
Printed in the United States of America

DEDICATION

This book is dedicated to everyone who ever bucked the system to do the right thing.

FOREWORD

This book is the companion volume to "I Look Forward To Further Collaboration Between Our Species." It continues documentation of the first year of contact between Earth and Lattern, culminating in the world-changing events in the Nevada desert.

I am much more dependent on external sources than in my previous reporting. Regrettably, "facts" are far less grounded in reality than in the past, and documenting events that I did not witness first-hand gives me pause. To the extent possible, I have relied on my most trusted sources and hope they are accurate and complete. In the final analysis, however, I hesitate to describe this volume as a "definitive history" as I did of "I Look Forward…" Please consider these factors when using this book as a primary source; you may wish to do your own research.

Recognizing that some readers may not have read "I Look Forward…" I provide a glossary to help them understand some of the terms and concepts explained in greater detail in the first volume.

Enjoy.

GLOSSARY

Atmospheric Entry Vehicle — **Latternite** ship carried on a quantum communication station, specifically designed for travel within a solar system and planetary landings. Although smaller and carrying less equipment and fewer supplies than a QCS, an AEV is a highly sophisticated vehicle that surpasses similarly purposed Earth technology.

Biobot — vat-grown biological robots, similar in size to a **Latternite** but physically stronger, and their brains are capable of faster and more complex mental processing than either **Latternites** or humans. They can be programmed with the **Neural Profile** of a **Latternite**, creating, in essence, a clone of the individual but with enhanced physical and mental capabilities. Biobots are used for deep space exploration and other dangerous tasks where deploying a "real" **Latternite** would be hazardous or unfeasible. Uploading a neural profile requires careful matching between the neural profile and the biobot. Combining the Neural Profile from one of Lattern's lesser lights with a biobot mind and body can lead to interesting consequences, e.g., Reldap.

Flektan-- another planet in Lattern's solar system, occupying a LaGrange point in the same orbit. Home to Flektanians. It is a dry, dusty planet rich in rare earth metals.

Flektanian — an arthropod-like, semi-intelligent species having a startling resemblance to a one-meter-long Earth dung beetle. Home world is Flektan.

Flek, e-Flek — diminutive for Flektanian. e-Fleks have been enhanced (hence the "e") by their **Latternite** friends, resulting in greater intelligence, more dexterity, and a markedly improved ability to communicate. The enhancement process results in instability of the creature's nervous system and greater vulnerability to exogenous damage, particularly broad-spectrum radiation.

JarVexx — vaccine manufacturer in southern Maine. Because vaccine production depends heavily on cell culture and because of the personal relationships between Drs. Gilner and one of the principals of JarVexx, Dr. Mackowitz, the company became the primary research and production facility for kleptron-related biological research. Developing sophisticated neural tissue cell culture techniques, the company designed and produced kleptron traps and kleptron feeding stations.

KASMA — **K**leptron **A**ssisted **S**elective **M**emory **A**blation — a precise neuropsychiatric procedure that removes thoughts and memories that contribute to psychiatric illness. Unlike a "wild" **klepping**, the target thought is mapped through advanced imaging, and the kleptron is directed to feed on that, and only that, memory. See below for more on **Kleptrons** and **klepping.**

Kleptron — small flying animal, slightly larger than a dragonfly, unique in its feeding habits. After lighting on the head of a human or **Latternite**, the skull is pierced, and the **Kleptron** feeds on neural electrical discharges and tiny amounts of brain matter. In return for this transgression, the kleptron injects a chemical that produces 15 minutes of bliss. Because of differences between human and

Latternite nervous systems, a human-**kleptron** interaction can permanently damage the human's memory. If an individual is **klepped** repeatedly, profound and irreversible damage to the person's memory and intellectual function is possible and even likely. Also referred to as brainsuckers.

(To) Klep, Klepping—the act of feeding by a **kleptron**. Usage: *The brainsucker klepped him as he stood near the tree.* – or-- *The poor fellow just experienced a klepping.* Protection from being klepped is easily afforded by placing a sheet of aluminum foil over the scalp.

Kleppite—an individual who has repeatedly sought to be **klepped**, either for enjoyment or hoping that a noxious memory might be destroyed. Often profoundly neurologically injured, kleppites present a complex rehabilitation and long-term care problem for Earth.

Lattern—Planet 25 light-years from Earth, inhabited by **Latternites**

Latternite—Humanoid species, approximately 2.5m tall, light green/brown skin tone, two thumbs. Their civilization is technologically more advanced than ours and capable of interstellar flight. Are they socially more advanced? Make your own decision.

Neural Profile—akin to the memory dump from a computer. Skills, memories, biases, knowledge, opinions, and everything else that defines an intelligent creature can be downloaded from a **Latternite**. With the proper connection, the Neural Profile can be uploaded into a **Latternite** biobot, effectively creating a super-powered clone of the individual. Artificial, purpose-built neural profiles may also be developed and uploaded. Such profiles may be used to effectively create a biological robot rather than the clone of a **Latternite**. **e-Fleks** can also be programmed at an immature stage of development. Typically, **e-Flek** artificial neural profiles include "memories" that give the creatures background information that presumably will help the **e-Flek** adapt to their environment and carry out their intended tasks. Sometimes this is a good idea, and sometimes it isn't.

Particle Defense Mechanisms—a group of technologies designed to protect spacecraft traveling at high speed (e.g., 50% light speed). Because of Newtonian and relativistic physics, a high-speed collision with a particle the size of a grain of sand could punch a fist-sized hole in a hull. Particle defense mechanisms deflect or destroy these potential hazards. The details of these technologies have not yet been disclosed to human civilization.

Personal Digital Device (PDD)—smartphone on steroids

Pronouncement—the closest human approximation is a dueling challenge combined with an oath, short of physical combat. **Latternite** 'A' demands that **Latternite** 'B' undertake a task or behave in some manner. If **Latternite** 'B' fails to comply with the demand, **Latternite** 'B' is cast out of society. Pronouncements are made rarely; although the consequences of **Latternite** 'B''s failure can be enormous, it can be equally damaging to **Latternite** 'A' to be seen as issuing a pronouncement injudiciously. Often seen (as was the case with Reldap and Zeftan) in the context of a parent's frustration with an adolescent or young adult offspring and issued in the heat of the moment.

Quantum communication—instantaneous communication over interstellar distances based on quantum entanglement.

Quantum Communication Station—so termed by the **Latternite**s, a better description is that of a mother ship.

Once **Lattern** decides to contact a civilization, the QCS is sent to orbit the star of the civilization's home world, but well distant from that planet. The ship carries **Atmospheric Entry Vehicles** (usually two), **biobots** in stasis, advanced communication capabilities, specialized laboratories, and numerous other specialized materials and equipment. Other living things may also be carried; in the case of the Earth contact, six **e-Fleks** were in stasis as well as kleptrons. Using the mother ship model (rather than simply landing on the planet in question) affords the **Latternites** greater control over disseminating their technology. If a contact becomes untenable, the QCS can withdraw or self-destruct, denying **Latternite** technology to that species.

Smek — intoxicant chemical used by **Latternites**. It has no effect on humans. For **Latternite**s, it is similar to the effect on a human of a mildly sedating strain of cannabis. Although fully legal, there is some social stigma associated with use.

PROLOGUE

Jack Flannery, a detective with the Falmouth police, pulled up to the JarVexx lab. Flannery was a good cop. Fifteen years on the force, five as a detective. Solved the occasional burglary and vehicle theft. Even tackled that nasty armed robbery two years ago; got a commendation from the Governor for that one.

But this was different. The call had come in half an hour ago, a break-in and theft at the JarVexx kleptron containment facility. The door had been forced open but was still on its hinges. He showed his badge to the chief technologist, Jen Doyle, and her boss, Dave Mackowitz, the company's CEO. Led by them, Flannery walked through the building, occasionally stopping to take note of a potential clue. They finally got to the actual kleptron containment module. *Jesus, what a mess*, thought the detective. The electronic control panel had been ripped from the wall. Backup batteries had been removed from all the control and sensor modules and were strewn everywhere. The lock on the door to the kleptrons' storage room had been smashed and drilled, and the door was wide open. Inside, the paper checklists and cage liners were all over the floor.

All the breeding pairs were gone, and about half of the other male and female kleptrons were also missing. A note was taped to one of the shelves. "Thanks!" Worst of all, every video camera in the facility had been pulverized. As he looked around the containment room, the seriousness of the crime became more and more apparent.

"This is a pretty big deal, isn't it?" said Flannery. "I mean, this is serious stuff. Stealing alien critters? Somebody was crazy enough to steal kleptrons?"

"Regrettably, you are correct," said Mackowitz.

"Okay, let me get this straight," Jack said. "Give me the lay of the land. This is where the kleptrons were stored, right? We're talking about the brainsuckers that caused all that havoc."

"Correct," said Mackowitz.

"These are the animals let loose by the aliens and finally recaptured."

"Right again," said the CEO.

Flannery unconsciously rubbed his head. "The ones that drilled into peoples' skulls and ate their memories and left a couple of thousand people blotto.., and the stuff about the aluminum foil on your head protecting you?"

"Well, it's more complicated than that, but yes," said Mackowitz.

"And that rocket fuel guy, whatshisname Jackner, went around telling everyone it was safe to get klepped. What did he say? 'Your brain, your choice.' And he got into a physical tussle with the President. That whole Latternite alien landing and kleptron thing. What a story."

"Yeah, it could fill a book," said Mackowitz.

"Huh. And I'm in the middle of it," Flannery mused. "Okay. Let me keep going. So they finally recaptured the animals, but the Latternites wouldn't let you put them down — that's why we have this containment facility."

"Yup," said Dave.

So making the best of it, you guys and a bunch of scientists and doctors started doing experiments to see if the brainsuckers could be used somehow to treat psychiatric disease 'cause they could mess with people's memories."

" The experiments started before all the kleptrons were caught, but yes. You are correct about the research," said Doyle.

"Yeah, I saw that on the vids. Fascinating." Flannery looked thoughtful and didn't say anything for a minute. "Okay, I think I got the background I need. Let's get down to specifics. Did this containment facility house all the kleptrons?"

"Well, some of them," answered Doyle. "We had already shipped some kleptrons to other research sites."

Flannery nodded in acknowledgment. "Makes sense if there's all kind of experimenting going on. Are there sites all over the country?"

Jen nodded yes.

Flannery crouched down and looked around. Whoever had done the job knew the facility. At first inspection, the control panel looked like it had been ripped from the wall, but the wires had been carefully cut. The lock had been expertly drilled. None of the sodium-bromine batteries were damaged despite their notorious fragility. The mess was staged, he thought.

He rose to his feet. "Okay, make sure your remaining animals are safe, contained, and properly cared for. Then leave and touch nothing else. Crime Scene Investigation from the Portland police will be here shortly, and they'll contact your security people. We're also gonna get some help from our State Police and FBI friends. Dealing with this is way above my pay grade. I'm a small-town cop and I solve small-town crimes. We're a small bedroom community. Yours is the only large business here. We don't have the resources to investigate a crime like this."

"You realize our fingerprints and DNA are all over this room and this facility, don't you?" asked Doyle.

"We'll fingerprint and take a DNA sample tomorrow from everyone who works here for elimination purposes. Don't worry about it," said Flannery.

Doyle and Mackowitz both nodded.

Mackowitz turned to Jen. "Are you all set?"

She nodded. "Then I'm off," said Mackowitz. "I gotta get the insurance adjusters, and the security guys, and the repair guys..."

"Don't worry, boss. I'll tend to the critters. You take care of your end of things." Mackowitz thanked her and left.

Jen quickly looked around the room, made a few adjustments to the autofeeders, confirmed that the remaining bugs were securely in their cages, and then departed.

What the hell would somebody want with a couple of hundred brainsuckers, thought Flannery. He walked back out to his vehicle and started making some calls.

CHAPTER 1

Reldap, the alien biobot emissary from Lattern, was due for his weekly check-in with Mission Control. Sent to initiate a cultural exchange between the two civilizations, he had now been on Earth for almost a full Earth year, learning about the humans, their culture, and their technology. He had been largely pleased with what he had seen and learned. Comfortable chairs, delightful food and drink, and truly magnificent rocket fuel were the early gifts from Earth.

Lattern, in turn, had provided, well... What exactly had Lattern given the humans? Not a whole lot. Latternites were obligate omnivores (a fully vegan diet was not an option, and they were nutritionally obligated to eat some meat regularly) who claimed they hated to kill anything. They had developed advanced cell culture techniques to replace animal slaughter, but for Earth the delicious synthetic meat grown using Latternite techniques was still a good year away. How about quantum communication for instantaneous interstellar data transmissions? After all, it was the mainstay of Latternite space exploration and would open the galaxy to humans. Nope, off-limits to Earth folks. As far as Lattern was concerned, we were just too damn crazy to trust with that technology. We'd just spread conspiratorial rubbish all over the known galaxy. Particle defense mechanisms and force field shields, so important to space travel? No way-- too easy to militarize. Can't give them that, either.

So what gift had Lattern bestowed on Earth? Kleptrons. Brainsuckers. Little critters slightly larger than a dragonfly that fed on neural energy in exchange for 15 minutes of bliss. An annoyance and a distraction for Latternites, but they could be highly destructive to human nervous systems. Human memory could not withstand their assaults—if a kleptron hit the right place in your brain, you could permanently lose a memory. Or two. Or fifty. All you needed to do was put some aluminum foil under your hat, and you were protected. That is if you wanted the protection and believed the threat was real. The struggle over the narrative, over what to do about the kleptron threat, was a story in itself.

And they hadn't really been gifts, had they? Several thousand had been released onto Earth in a drug-fueled haze by our heroic emissary. A combination of ignorance, human stubbornness, and incompetence had created a short-lived plague where thousands of bareheaded people got their brains zapped. Thanks to the combined efforts of the Latternites and humans, effective traps were devised, and the little devils were captured. However, the kleptrons had done quite a bit of damage before they were corralled and controlled.

Still, there was an upside. The humans, ever ingenious, had figured out that if kleptrons were used judiciously to damage intrusive memories selectively, certain kinds of mental illness could be treated with unprecedented efficacy. KASMA, Kleptron Assisted Selective Memory Ablation, was under active investigation and development at centers of excellence worldwide, and there were already almost a thousand grateful patients.

And then the kicker: six months after the brainsuckers had been caught and caged, when everyone was finally calming down and breathing a sigh of relief, someone broke into the kleptron storage facility at JarVexx (the famous cell culture and vaccine lab just outside Portland, Maine) and made off with a couple hundred of the little buggers, including mating pairs. They were gone. Disappeared. No one had a clue where they were or who had them. Every three-letter agency in the world was on it, to no avail.

Over time, we learned why the kleptrons had been stolen. Some ingenious but less principled humans had figured out that kleptrons could be used to perform all sorts of mischief. The dark web regularly advertised klepping parlors where, for a hefty sum, supplicants could get their 15 minutes of bliss, and there continued to be a steady stream of new kleppites, who, as the saying goes, couldn't tell a chocolate éclair from a dog turd.

The kleptrons had also been put to more nefarious uses. Valentin Rusov, the capo in the Russian mafia that had turned state's evidence, could no longer remember critical details of the gang's inner workings after a "vacation." Then there was the story of Hideki Hayoshi, the brilliant engineer for Sartaru Motors, on the cusp of a design change for his company's hydrogen fuel cell that would have increased efficiency by 30%. Kidnapped, he was released 3 days later, intellectual capabilities reduced to drawing stick figures and sucking his thumb. The share price for Sartaru Motors dropped by 50%, to the delight of a consortium of short sellers who had somehow decided to invest just a few days before the kidnapping.

Something had to be done; the sooner, the better.

*****

Reldap was a biobot imprinted with the neural profile of the son of a prominent Latternite. The original Reldap, "Lattern Reldap," was a lazy ne'er-do-well, a star example of an intergalactic slacker. His biobot clone, "Earth Reldap," had grown into his job and had matured considerably. He (mostly) took his work seriously and had come to love Earth and his friends. By misadventure, his ship had landed in Waterville, Maine, and he had befriended a host of interesting folk. Reldap was particularly enamored of Earth food, and he had settled in Portland, Maine, because of the restaurant and craft brewery scene. He lived there with Penfor, a Latternite biobot who carried the neural profile of one of Reldap's schoolmates. Activated and sent to Earth to support Reldap when his initial forays on Earth were on the verge of failure, she had steadied Reldap, was working to get the cultural exchange off the ground, and generally functioned as the adult in the room. A common sight in downtown Portland, the 2.5-meter tall green aliens with two-thumbed hands were gentle, friendly folk, well-loved by their neighbors and friends. Despite living in Portland, Reldap and Penfor insisted on keeping their ships at the Robert LaFleur Airport in Waterville, which had become Earth's de facto intergalactic spaceport. Although he and Penfor would not acknowledge this to Earth authorities, his primary reason for leaving his ship in Waterville was to always have an excuse to visit his friends, Ed and Helen Gilner, the physician couple that had helped him when he had first landed.

His ship was equipped with a quantum communicator, allowing instantaneous data exchange with Lattern. He couldn't put it off any longer; it was time to contact Mission Control despite his dread of the conversation. He had not solved the kleptron problem, and Mission Control was becoming impatient. Reldap activated the car that had been modified to accommodate his large frame and programmed it north.

Traffic was light, and the car directed itself to the airport without any delays. He greeted the guards at the airport and made his way to his ship. Reaching into his shoulder bag, he took out a small box. Speaking to it in Lattern, he inserted his finger in its side port. The intrusion systems shut down, and a barely visible door on the hull opened. Steps descended, and Reldap bounded up into his ship. Although he loved Earth, his ship was a refuge from the strangeness of Earth, and he could return, at least for the moment, to a Latternite environment.

He sat for a few moments in silence and composed himself. Reluctantly, he turned on the communicator. The image of Ventak, the Mission Control specialist in charge of the Earth initiative, appeared. Sitting next to him was Zeftan, the "real" Reldap's father, the nobleman sponsoring the mission. After pleasantries were exchanged, Ventak spoke.

"Reldap," he said, "what is the status of the missing kleptrons?"

Reldap thought before he answered. "Ventak, the situation is not desirable. The humans have many agencies specializing in solving crimes and maintaining order…"

"They need them," grumbled Zeftan.

"Yes, my lord and father," continued Reldap. "However, they have made no progress. The perpetrators of the original theft have not been caught. We do not know who else may now have possession of the creatures. We cannot locate the stolen kleptrons."

The three Latternites sat in silence. At length, Zeftan spoke. "We must consider the biological option."

Shocked, Ventak looked up but said nothing. Reldap said, "My lord, do you truly wish to take that approach?"

"Yes. It is time. This has gone on long enough. We have inflicted this plague on the humans, and we must end it. Use the biological option."

Ventak spoke. "Very well, my lord. Do we activate the enhanced or natural option?"

"Enhanced. We must use every means at our disposal."

Reldap, despite misgivings about disagreeing with his irritable parent, persisted. "The enhanced biologics have not been fully tested…"

"They have been tested enough. This is my decision."

Reldap and Ventak spoke almost simultaneously. "Yes, my lord. As you wish."

Zeftan spoke again. "You are in the Waterville commune, yes?"

Reldap nodded yes on screen.

"Good. Go tell your Gilner human friends. They will help you again."

"My lord, they have no experience in detective work or law enforcement."

"I don't care."

Ventak and Reldap together: "Yes, my lord."

The three Latternites bid each other farewell and shut down the comm link. Reldap looked around his ship again and then descended the stairs, reactivating the anti-intrusion systems. The stairs withdrew into the ship, and the door closed. Sputtering in Latternite that this was "Not a good idea, not a good idea at all," he got into his car, and instructed the vehicle's AI to head to the Gilners'.

CHAPTER 2

I saw Reldap's car come up the driveway. Helen and I expected him, as this was his check-in day with Lattern mission control, and he almost always stopped by after he chatted with his home world. He came up the stairs and knocked on the door.

"Reldap," I said. "How good to see you."

Helen welcomed him as well. "Hi, Reldap. Stay for dinner? We're having pizza from the Korner Store tonight."

Reldap smiled as our two cats, Tigress and Euphrates, came over to say hello. "Hello, my human and cat friends. It is good to see you. Thank you for the dinner invitation, but I cannot stay." He paused, looking at the floor. From previous experience, I knew that the "floor stare" was not a good sign.

"I must speak with you about today's communication with Lattern."

"Yes," I said, keeping my voice neutral. "I'm always curious to know how those conversations go."

"My father is concerned about the continuing problems with the kleptrons." I nodded, and Reldap continued. "He has grown frustrated with the lack of progress and wishes to bring the kleptron issue to a close." Again, I nodded, urging him to continue.

"I have not been fully forthright with you as to some of the contents of the quantum communication ship and the inhabitants of my home world."

Oh shit. Zeftan is irritable and impatient, and Reldap is not being fully forthright. Not a good combination.

"You mean the large base station ship orbiting between Earth and Venus?" asked Helen. "I know that the ship contains all sorts of equipment and materials that you are reluctant to bring to Earth and that the communications capabilities are far beyond those of the ships you used to get from the base station to Earth."

"Yes, human Helen. That vessel. In addition to equipment, there are other dormant life forms on the spacecraft."

"Of course," I said. "You still have other biobots in stasis that can be reactivated if needed. Are you referring to them?"

Reldap looked at the floor again. "No, Edward. I am referring to enhanced Flektanian eggs."

I cleared my throat and looked at Helen. Enhanced Flektanian eggs. I put on my bravest face. "Well, that's interesting. Can you tell us about enhanced Flektanian eggs?"

Reldap smiled brightly. "Of course, my human friends. There are other sentient creatures in my home solar system. The Flektanians are a semi-intelligent species living on another planet in orbit around our home sun. We collaborate with them at times. We mine their planet for rare earth metals and share our technology in return."

"Well, that sounds reasonable," said Helen. I nodded.

"However, they do not fit completely with the Latternite way of life," said Reldap. "They still hunt and eat live meat. They have no culture or love of literature and music. Nonetheless, they are useful for some tasks, and we have helped them."

"Just how did you help them?" I asked.

"That is very easy to explain," said Reldap. "We, uh, invited several Flektanians to Lattern. After discussing options with them, we enhanced the intellectual capabilities of these creatures from semi-intelligent to the equivalent of a human in 8th or 9th grade. We also improved other aspects of their physiology, including the ability to detect kleptrons. We also, uh, rearranged things in their nervous systems so that kleptrons are perceived as a tasty treat. Most Latternites, and the enhanced Flektanians themselves, call themselves e-Fleks. I think it is a good name. I think you humans might want to use that term as well."

"Rearranged things?" asked Helen.

"Yes, human Helen. Rearranged things."

"How did you rearrange and enhance them?" I asked.

"I cannot discuss that with you." Reldap smiled brightly and continued. "The important point is that the enhanced Flektanians have a unique ability to find kleptrons. Sometimes, on our home planet, a kleptron infestation will be too much, even for us. We bring several enhanced Flektanians to the afflicted area and let them loose. In a few days, the infestation is resolved."

"Wait a second," I countered. "That makes no sense. You wouldn't let us destroy the escaped kleptrons we caught on Earth. You made us warehouse them. That's why we are in our current predicament!"

"Calm down, human Gilner," said Reldap. "This is different. We are just letting the natural order of things play out. This is a normal predator-prey relationship…"

"Wait a second," I said. "Rearranged things? Improved other aspects of their physiology? Just what did you people do to these creatures? And you say that they have a natural predator-prey relationship? How is this a natural relationship if the two species arose and evolved on different planets? The e-Fleks prey on the kleptrons only because you altered them to do so!" I was fuming.

"Well, it is of no matter." Reldap smiled. "I think they will help us find the hidden kleptrons on Earth."

"Wait, wait, wait," I said. "Did these creatures give permission for all this 'rearranging'?"

"That is a difficult topic I would prefer not to discuss."

I sighed. "All right," I said. "Please finish telling us your plans."

"Certainly," smiled Reldap. I will return to my base station using the excellent rocket fuel produced here on Earth. I will take several e-Flek eggs out of stasis and activate them. After they hatch and are in the pupal stage, we will upload information about Earth so they may hit the ground running, as you say. They will have keen insight into your culture, your history, and everything else. It will be almost as though they were brought up on your planet watching Earth vids. After they are conditioned, we will bring them to Earth, and you will use them to help find and control the kleptrons."

More alarms screaming and red lights blinking from the bullshit detectors. "This is tested, safe, working? Are they emotionally stable? Have you Latternites ever done this before?" I asked.

"Oh yes," replied Reldap. "I am sure everything will be fine. Our finest scientists say this is a good plan."

"Reldap, you are not answering my question…"

"Edward, let us say that we will be exploring new frontiers with this approach to the problem."

I had to admit that given the threat posed by the kleptrons, almost anything that would or could work would be worth a try. The other problem was that for all their obsequious smiling and statements of good will, their technical capabilities outstripped us by leaps and bounds, and they were going to damn well do what they wanted to do. "OK," I said. "I'm just curious. You've mentioned eggs, and you've mentioned a pupal stage. Just what exactly do the Flektanians look like?"

"Oh, that is easy to describe. They are meter-long creatures that look remarkably like dung beetles."

Euphrates hissed at me as my mouthful of coffee sprayed out of my nose and hit the cat.

CHAPTER 3

I cleaned up the mess on the floor while Euphrates stalked off, indignant. "Reldap," Helen said, "why don't you stay for dinner? As I said, we're having Korner Store pizza. You are going to be very busy for a while. Relax, tell Penfor what's happening, and get your ship fueled and ready. You can leave in the morning. You don't have to leave tonight."

"This is true," said Reldap. "That is a good plan."

He went into another room, and I heard him speaking first to the airport and then to Penfor in Lattern over his communicator. He brought his friend up to date. The conversations were longer than I expected.

"Is everything all right?" I asked.

"Oh yes," said Reldap. He smiled. "Let us discuss pizza toppings."

As planned, we had pizza from one of central Maine's iconic institutions, the Korner Store. It was delicious, as usual. Enjoyed with a beer or three (alcohol just didn't affect Reldap the way it did humans), his smile at the end of the meal was genuine. We had renovated one of our kids' unused bedrooms with a custom-made Latternite-sized bed, and Reldap excused himself for the rest of the night. In the morning, we had a simple breakfast. We said our goodbyes, and Helen and I wished him a safe journey.

He directed his car over to the airport. His ship had been fueled and fitted with wing tanks; extra fuel meant extra speed. He identified himself to his ship using his communicator, the usual speech and finger routine. The hull door opened, and stairs dropped to the ground. He ascended the stairs and, after taking a quick look around, entered his ship. The stairs retracted into the vessel, and the hull door closed, nearly invisible.

He made his way to the bridge and sat down in the master control chair. He quickly reviewed the ship's dashboard; all systems were healthy, and all fuel tanks, including the outboard tanks, were topped off. "Ship," he said, "Set course and arrange for departure to the quantum communication station."

"Please confirm identity and authorization," replied the ship's AI.

Reldap placed his finger in a small port on the instrument console. A few seconds later, the ship spoke. "Identity and authorization confirmed. Please confirm destination and departure time."

"Quantum communication station in this solar system. Depart as soon as feasible."

"Understood. Ship will contact necessary traffic control and space defense agencies to secure launch clearance. Please acknowledge and stand by."

"Acknowledged."

The instrument console lights dimmed, and a small light at the lower right of the console started blinking slowly. About 15 minutes later, the red light stopped blinking, and the instrument panel brightened.

"Ship has secured all necessary clearances. You may depart immediately without concern for human interference. When this vessel is beyond local space, Ship will modify hull and wing structure and accelerate for interplanetary travel."

"Acknowledged." Reldap, now used to interacting with humans, found the dry tone increasingly dull. "Ship, could we not just accelerate immediately and buzz a couple of human cities?"

"That is not advisable. Ship has monitored human communication activity to assist in Latternite analysis of human behavior. Ship identifies your comment as an attempt at human humor. It is not effective. Please sit in your chair and prepare for launch."

Shut up and sit down, thought Reldap. *OK, let's go.* He settled in his seat and strapped in. He felt the ship start moving. It moved out to the runway to avoid other aircraft and human activity, and then he felt it lift. At 2 km altitude, the ship accelerated sharply, flying west and gaining altitude. It rose rapidly until 1000 km above the Earth. Beyond the atmosphere and no longer needing wings, the ship adjusted for interplanetary flight. The craft orbited the planet once and then slingshotted off into space.

The ship flew itself, requiring nothing from our Latternite friend. Rather than get into trouble with smek (the Latternite equivalent of a well-cultivated Indica strain) while twiddling his four thumbs, he decided to go into stasis. He spoke to the ship.

"Ship," he said, "I should enter stasis until we reach the quantum communication station."

"Ship agrees. You do not make good judgments when alone and idle."

Reldap grimaced but inwardly acknowledged the accuracy of the observation. "Here are my instructions. Stasis for the remainder of the trip. Auto-dock upon arrival. The quantum communication ship should open the Flektanian egg chamber four gorts [author: about six days] before my arrival and initiate the accelerated maturation sequence."

"You are certain of this?" asked Ship.

"Yes."

"No deviation?"

"None. No deviation."

"Very well," said Ship. "No emergency…"

Reldap, already irritated by Ship's observations, showed a bit of temper and interrupted Ship. "No. No emergency, nothing. Just do what I say."

"Very well," said Ship. "As you say. Please proceed to your stasis container."

Reldap walked over to the container and got in. There was a painful but quick pinch as the IV and monitoring systems inserted themselves into his thigh. He relaxed, allowed the warm blue liquid to flow over him like a blanket, and closed his eyes.

The trip to the quantum communication station proceeded without incident until four days prior to arrival when there was a significant solar coronal mass ejection. A coronal mass ejection, for the uninitiated, is when a chunk of the sun's surface gets thrown out into space, an event associated with the release of massive amounts of broad-spectrum ionizing radiation.

Protected by the Earth's magnetic field, such an event on Earth is associated with the aurora borealis and disrupted radio communication but poses little or no risk to life or health. Out in space, though, it can be a bitch. Reldap, fortunately well shielded by his ship and his stasis tank, suffered no harm.

The same cannot be said for the e-Flek eggs, handled by the communication station precisely as prescribed by Reldap. Removed on schedule from their well-shielded shipment container, and with their cells dividing at a prodigious rate, the alien DNA was hammered.

Reldap's ship decelerated as it approached the quantum communication station and docked smoothly. The light blue liquid drained from his stasis tank, and he was injected with a mild stimulant. In a few minutes, he awakened and roused himself. The tank withdrew the IV and monitor bundle and sealed the wound. Reldap stood, at first unsteadily, but then made his way to the recovery shower, where the last of the stasis bath was flushed away. He dressed and made his way to the quantum communication station bridge.

He was greeted with multiple alarms indicating that the station had experienced a significant energy pulse, and he quickly determined that this was due to a coronal mass ejection. An interstellar Latternite ship was designed to shake off the effects of such a radiation dose like an Earth dog might shake off water after a romp in a local lake. For the most part, that was true. Reldap reviewed the readouts. There had been a short (10 Earth minutes) interruption in quantum communication with Lattern. Several systems had needed to deploy self-repair protocols, but they had all been successful. Life support was fine. The e-Flek eggs were not.

He directed the information console to provide more information about the eggs. All eggs had been taken out of stasis and had received a hefty dose of radiation. However, they were continuing to grow and mature. He reviewed the readouts for each individual egg. All eggs demonstrated a DNA disruption index between 5 and 6 percent. *Hmmm,* thought Reldap. *Is this OK?*

He queried the quantum communication station's main computer, recalling that there was precedent for such an event.

"...in the incident relating to the transport of Flektanian eggs in an unshielded container exposed to a coronal mass ejection..." blah blah blah "...the eggs experienced a range of radiation and DNA disruption..." blah blah blah—*Ah, OK* thought Reldap. *Here we go.* "...all eggs with a DNA disruption index above 5% produced Fleks with significant abnormalities of comprehension, processing, and emotional stability...the higher the disruption index, the more pronounced the deviation from expected behavior..."

All the eggs had been toasted. There were no remaining, unaffected eggs. Deploying these creatures once mature might be unpredictable and cause their own set of problems. On the other hand, he was under strict instructions to get the bugs to Earth and clean up the kleptron mess. Not doing so risked another Pronouncement, where his father would publicly shame him if he did not meet the terms of the edict.

They are only a little bit above 5%. It will be fine. Why make a fuss over such a minor issue? And after all, all they are going to be doing is finding and eating kleptrons. They do not need a lot of smarts for that. Yes, it will be fine.

Oh, Reldap…

CHAPTER 4

In retrospect, I should not have been surprised when the black SUV rolled up our driveway. The big vehicle gently braked to a stop, and our old friends Joe Stein and Maria Labrador stepped out. Two very connected Federal agents, Helen and I had never been able to identify their organization or their precise location in the Federal food chain. Assigned to "assist" us when Reldap first landed, they were now friends and would help Reldap (and us) when the various government bureaucracies decided to "exercise leadership" in the Earth-Lattern cultural exchange.

"I guess I should have been expecting you," I said as I hugged Maria. I shook hands with Joe and invited them in. "What's that big rock doing on your finger?" asked Helen. Maria grinned and pointed at Joe. "Really? That's fantastic! I…"

Joe interrupted. "Sorry to break up the party, but we'd kinda like to understand why one of the alien spaceships requested orbital clearance and now seems to be headed toward the quantum communication station. We aren't going to deny our friends launch rights, but this wasn't on anyone's radar."

"Yeah," I said. "That is an interesting question. Come in and sit down."

We went back inside the house. Tigress loved Maria, and there was an obligate half a minute of purring, head bumping, and strutting about before we could get down to business. I relayed Reldap's story as best I could. Joe sat for a moment, scratching his head. "I suppose I should call some people," he said. "What the hell was he thinking? Bringing another alien life form here without human permission? He didn't even talk to you?" Helen shook her head no.

"Presented as a fait accompli," she said.

"As always. Shit." I looked up, surprised at Joe's language. He and Maria were always so LC (linguistically correct). "All right, give me a few minutes to make some calls. The Prez is not going to like this." Joe opened his PDD (personal digital device) and left the room.

It was a difficult situation. The relationship with Lattern was not one of equals. The Latternites were relentlessly friendly and allegedly abhorred violence. The ships did not bristle with weapons, and except for a couple of diplomatic faux pas early on, personal relationships had always been smooth. On the other hand, they had some crazy powerful machines.

The ships' force fields and megawatt lasers protected Latternites and their spacecraft from interstellar debris and ground intrusion by non-intelligent species. However, we'd seen several instances when the ships' particle defense systems had handily taken out advanced earth weaponry. I watched what happened when a brash federal agent decided to try to enter Reldap's ship without the ship's or Reldap's permission. No lasting damage, but he certainly wasn't going to try that again. We had "guards" at the Waterville airport, but they were there because Reldap and Penfor allowed them to be there.

The Latternites would do what they wanted, with big smiles on their happy faces as they told us it was all for our own good. There were going to be e-Fleks on Earth.

After a few minutes, Joe came back into the room. "I've been instructed to put the best face on this that we can. We're thrilled that our Latternite friends are pulling out all stops to help resolve the kleptron issue. We look forward to meeting the representatives of another civilization. We will warmly greet our visitors with the respect and celebration they deserve. Contact Penfor. Find out when Reldap is returning and how we can best welcome our new visitors."

"On it," I said.

Sounds good, but you had to be in the room. The look on the poor guy's face as he spoke could turn Medusa to stone.

Joe and Maria left shortly after the conversation ended. I called Penfor, as requested. Our talk was brief. She promised she'd call Reldap in two or three weeks. By that point, he'd have gotten to the quantum station, started maturing the eggs, and would have an accurate time and date for when he would return to Earth. Concerned that Earthside fuss would distract Reldap from preparing and conditioning the e-Fleks, she didn't want to call quite yet. It sounded pretty reasonable to me.

CHAPTER 5

Reldap was dozing when the maturation alarm sounded. The eggs had hatched several Earth days ago, and the e-Fleks were in the pupal stage. Reldap needed to intercept their growth just as they emerged from their cocoons to insert the programming interface.

He roused himself and walked over to the incubator. He had already prepared the instruments and work table necessary for the procedures. Six e-Fleks; he'd need to work fast.

He looked in the warmer and saw six hand-sized creatures milling about aimlessly. As expected, one was about two cm. longer than the others. Eggs and pupae maturing in clutches often had a dominant individual. He drew out the largest. As Reldap had said previously, they looked remarkably like dung beetles. He rolled the animal onto its back and felt for the space between the head and the thorax. He quickly inserted the interface, gluing it in place. The interface seemed oddly large and clumsy, given the size of the bug, but it would be suitable for the fully mature critter. He returned the e-Flek to the warmer. He repeated the procedure with the other five beasts. He'd give them a day to recover from the procedure and then connect them to the conditioning system. He continued with other housekeeping tasks and snoozed on and off for the rest of the day.

He got up the following day and linked the animals to the conditioning system. The Flektanian nervous system was typical for an arthropod, with a brain (of sorts) divided into three sections, a long ventral nerve cord, and multiple other ganglia chains. However, unlike Earth arthropods, the brain sections were more developed and complex and capable of some limited abstract thought. In their travels, the Latternites had found this common for highly evolved arthropodal forms. The Latternites, though, never leaving well enough alone, had fiddled with the Flektanians. Experimenting with DNA manipulation, they increased Flektanian total nervous system tissue volume by approximately 30 percent. With a few more tweaks, the number and complexity of synaptic connections were boosted by a similar fraction. An alert Latternite researcher also observed that increased neural complexity permitted programming similar to that possible with a Latternite biobot. These were the creatures that Reldap had referred to as e-Fleks, enhanced Fleks.

Reldap started the downloads, loading the creatures with multiple further enhancements to vision, hearing, and smell. Mandibular structures were re-wired to permit slow, croaking speech. Knowledge of Earth—history, current conditions, customs and mores, and technological skills—were pumped into the critters. Reldap, trusting the quantum communication station's AI, largely ignored the process and went about his business. Time passed as the e-Fleks (this quickly became their Earth name) were pumped full of information, some of limited relevance to solving the kleptron problem. They grew and molted several times, quietly feeding as they matured.

After three days, they were too large for the warmer. Reldap cordoned off the lab and changed the programming interface to wireless mode. He removed the bugs from the warmer and allowed the e-Fleks to roam the lab. He closed the door and started his 45th game of rumaka, a complex strategy game popular on Lattern.

Three more days passed. His communicator chimed and informed him that e-Flek maturation was complete, and the upload was finished. The ship was large, and the e-Flek lab was nearly 100 meters from Reldap's quarters. As he neared the laboratory, the croaking and chittering coming from the lab became uncomfortably loud. Reldap had no direct prior experience with Fleks or e-Fleks and had never previously conducted an M/U (maturation/upload). From everything he understood about the process, however, he had not expected a raucous awakening.

He reached the lab and opened the door. The largest e-Flek, now a full meter long and half a meter wide, had somehow hoisted himself onto a table a meter off the floor. He had fashioned a crude cape out of lab wipes that he had draped over his carapace. He was tilted up, resting his middle legs on some equipment so that he had the appearance of speaking in front of a podium. He croaked and swung his front legs around as if punctuating each sentence. The other five smaller animals, each about 75 cm long, ran around aimlessly, occasionally chittering as the big bug emphasized some point.

Shaken, Reldap closed the door and returned to his quarters, where he grabbed his translator. He walked quickly back to the lab, dialing the proper settings for Flektanian into his translator as he made his way there. He opened the door and entered the room. The largest bug's harangue was still in progress.

"Greetings, Flektanian comrades," said Reldap. He used the Flektanian form of semi-formal address. "I am Reldap, a Latternite biobot. It is good to see you awake and well. How may I be of assistance?"

The e-Flek on the table looked up at Reldap and spat a black-brown juice on the floor. Reldap recalled that this was a greeting among Flektanians and forced himself not to react badly. Reldap spat as well. "Greetings, Latternite Reldap," croaked the e-Flek. Reldap's translator swung into action. "I am Klak, leader of the Flektanian Earth Expeditionary Force…"

He tried to keep his face neutral. "I was unaware there was a Flektanian Earth Expeditionary Force," interrupted Reldap. "I…"

Klak seemed to take offense at being interrupted by Reldap's lack of knowledge about the Expeditionary Force. It started waving its front legs again, and its antennae twitched like mad. "Silence, Latternite dog! I represent the Galactic Arthropodal Council. We travel to Earth to liberate our chitinous brethren, long subjugated, exterminated, and eaten. So-called evolutionary forces have oppressed them for hundreds of millions of years. We will resurrect the reign of the trilobites! We will make arthropods great again!"

He nattered on and on while Reldap tried to make sense of these events. Latternite dog? WTF? Lattern didn't even have dogs. Galactic Arthropodal Council? Granted, many arthropods were more developed than those seen on Earth. But Flektanians represented the highest level of function among all the arthropodal races encountered by Lattern. There was no Galactic Arthropodal Council.

At a loss for what to do next, it was time for a call home. Reldap left the lab and returned to the communication bay. He activated the quantum communicator and asked for Ventak, the Latternite Mission Control expert. After a quick exchange of greetings, Reldap described the bizarre tableau. Ventak nodded as Reldap spoke, his face looking graver and graver.

"You say all the eggs were exposed to the coronal ejection?" asked Ventak.

"Regrettably, that is correct. All eggs were damaged. We cannot start again. We have no reserve." answered Reldap.

Ventak sighed. "I have heard of this before. This condition is FDS, Flektanian Delusional Syndrome. It happens about 10% of the time that an e-Flek with DNA damage is conditioned. The creature develops an unshakable delusional system, often centered around the task for which the animals are being prepared. Almost invariably, the e-Fleks are highly impaired in addition to being crazy. Do you think Zeftan will still insist that the bugs be used on Earth?"

"Regrettably, I believe he will."

"Amazing. I have not encountered a situation where all the e-Fleks or Fleks intended for a task were damaged. And they've developed this bizarre hierarchy. I will be interested to see how the humans handle this." Ventak stopped speaking, but from the image on the communicator, it was evident he was thinking. After a few moments, he resumed talking. "I am sorry, but I have no advice. I will inform Zeftan of these developments. As you say, I doubt he will change his mind, but I will check. What do the humans say? Keep me posted? I will enjoy this." Ventak laughed as he reached for the terminal's controls.

They disconnected. Reldap left his quarters again and stood outside the lab where Klak held forth. He was ranting about shrimp and spiders and predatory fish.

Reldap listened for a moment, sighed, and returned to his living area.

CHAPTER 6

Reldap prepared to return to Earth. He gathered and transferred his personal belongings from the quantum communication station to his AEV, the atmospheric entry vehicle that had brought him to the large orbiting ship. He could not stand the thought of listening to eight days of demented chattering by Klak on the return trip. He prepared stasis chambers for the e-Fleks on his AEV and returned to the QCS.

The Latternites, despite their professed nonviolence and dedication to peaceful interactions with other species, were also realistic, protective of their technology, and not stupid. The communication station had defense mechanisms, albeit nonlethal. Reldap brought up the anti-intrusion system app on his control console. He flagged the e-Flek-filled lab as breached by an arthropodal species, pressed the "SUPPRESS" button, and turned on the video monitor.

Reldap watched as a pink mist floated down from recessed vents in the lab's ceiling. After a few minutes, the noise tapered off, and the smaller bugs stopped their purposeless roaming. Finally, Klak's antennae stopped moving, and his front legs fell still. Reldap pushed the "CONTAINED" button; the pink mist stopped, and an exhaust fan started. He had about 45 minutes to put the animals in stasis, which was more than enough time.

He brought a dolly to the lab and opened the door. There was a faint, sickly-sweet odor, a remnant of the sedative gas. Designed to slow down an arthropod nervous system, Reldap was unaffected and gently moved the e-Fleks onto the cart. He wheeled the e-Fleks to his AEV and put each e-Flek into a chamber. He attached the life support and telemetry cables, closed the chambers, and initiated stasis.

He exited the AEV and returned to the QCS's bridge. He took a final look around and checked system health readouts. The station was fine. He reset the station's status to autonomous function and returned to his ship.

"Ship, plot a course for Earth, LaFleur airport. Determine flight time and obtain orbital clearance. Report when ready to launch."

"Noted. Please stand by."

After half an hour, the Ship spoke. "Course ready. Fuel consumption plotted. Orbital clearance is on standby. I am waiting for your approval of the flight plan."

Reldap reviewed the information on the screen. The trip would take eight days, and he would land with a safe fuel reserve. "Flight plan approved. Obtain orbital clearance."

"Wait," said Ship.

Ten minutes later, Ship spoke again. "Orbital clearance obtained. Should Ship initiate launch sequence?"

"Yes," said Reldap. "Separate from the QCS and launch."

"Acknowledged. Launch initiated. Ship has a request."

A request was unexpected. "Yes?"

"Please allow Ship to control atmospheric reentry. Ship does not wish to undergo further repairs. Ship experienced our first landing as traumatic."

Reldap grimaced. *Wiseass Ship. How the hell did Ship experience trauma? The damn thing is spending too much time thinking and not enough time flying.* "Ship, I will not try to land you manually again. I am not under the influence of smek, and this time I am not anxious about meeting the humans. It will be fine. What can I do to assure you of my intentions?"

"Apologize," said Ship. "Launch sequence does not start until you apologize."

Apologize to an AI while carrying a cargo of demented giant beetles to catch and devour little creatures that feed on the thoughts of humans. Fine. "Ship, I apologize. I will not try to land you manually. I will not take smek during reentry. I will allow you to control the entire flight."

"Apology accepted. Launch initiated."

Reldap strapped into his acceleration couch. He heard the docking clamps release, and the atmosphere recycling system cleared the airlock of the precious gas. The ship drifted briefly, and small maneuvering jets pushed the AEV away from the quantum communication station. The main rockets fired when the craft was safely clear, accelerating the ship toward Earth.

The acceleration couch was very comfortable, and Reldap soon dozed off. By the time he awoke, Ship had already released his safety harness. *Now what?* His choices for what to do when he reached Earth were not great.

It was clear that he would need to use the e-Fleks; tossing them out an airlock was, at this point, an uncomfortably attractive option, but he couldn't do that; Daddy would have a fit, and it just wasn't the right thing to do. Play dumb? That held some promise. *Holy mackerel, as you humans say, I have no idea what happened to them...* No, even if some humans might fall for it, the Gilners and Penfor would smell a rat. Change the narrative? *Oh yeah, they're a little kooky this way. Let's just humor them and get the job done...* The more Reldap thought about it, the more the last option appealed.

Reldap asked Ship to set up a conference call among Lattern, Penfor, and him. Ship summoned him after a couple of minutes. "Call is ready."

"Thank you, Ship."

"Ship likes that more collegial tone. Sit at your communication console, and I will start the discussion."

Doing as he was told, Reldap walked over to the communication console and sat down. The screen was split, with Penfor sitting in her AEV at LaFleur and Ventak and Zeftan sitting together in Lattern Mission Control. Penfor looked uncertain. Ventak was laughing while talking to Zeftan; Zeftan was smirking. Zeftan started. "Flektanian Delusional Syndrome? Flektanian Earth Expeditionary Force? Make arthropods great again? That's precious! I love it! We've been monitoring this nonsense the whole time. All right, Mr. Smart Guy, how will you get out of this one? And yeah, like I said before, you need to use the e-Fleks."

Even Penfor started giggling. "Reldap, what happened?"

Reldap sheepishly relayed the story.

Penfor thought for a moment. "So, you have six profoundly damaged, delusional giant beetles who believe they are coming to Earth on a crusade to free arthropods from persecution and from ending up as someone's dinner. Even crazier, they are ranting about resurrecting the reign of the trilobites, creatures that went extinct 250 million years ago."

"Right."

"And you expect the humans to accept this conduct as normal Flektanian behavior, and they should just humor them?"

"Correct again."

"You are insane! You have been living with the humans for too long!"

Ventak couldn't help himself and started giggling. "All right, let's not get overwrought. Reldap may be right. The humans have an astonishing capacity for self-deception. This may be of use to us."

Zeftan nodded. "It might be quite amusing as well…" His voice trailed off, and he smiled.

"My lord," said Reldap, "there is an old Earth story called The Emperor has no clothes. The Emperor seeks a new set of robes, but his tailor is a swindler. The tailor pretends he is fitting the king with an elaborate, expensive suit. In reality, he is just going through the motions in thin air. There is no cloth, and the king remains undressed save for his skivvies. The king, afraid of looking like a fool for challenging this putatively well-known, expensive tailor, agrees that the suit is beautiful and proceeds to leave the castle in nothing but his underclothes. His subjects, fearful of criticizing the Emperor, praise the beauty of his new raiment. It falls to a little boy to speak truth to power and state the obvious." He paused, and Ventak and Zeftan nodded for him to continue.

"My lord," continued Reldap, "there are very few little boys left on Earth. We will be fine."

Penfor looked apoplectic, but she tempered her comments. "I participate in this unprincipled scheme under protest."

"Noted," said Zeftan. "Please arrange for an appropriate, high-level diplomatic greeting and reception."

"Yes, my lord," replied Penfor.

The call ended. Reldap checked the stasis chambers; all was fine. He returned to the bridge, settled into the acceleration couch, and took a nap.

CHAPTER 7

Earth Penfor was also a biobot. She was based on the neural profile of Lattern Penfor, a friend of Reldap's from university. She was bright, pragmatic, and mature. Ostensibly, she was Reldap's assistant and collaborator. Operationally, "adult in the room" was a more apt job description. It was true that biobot Reldap seemed to have matured considerably. However, he was still prone to fanciful interpretations of Earth's politics and commerce and had unjustified confidence in his ability to control events. Penfor, suffering from no such delusions, would provide the occasional needed verbal or physical slap on the side of the head and appropriate redirection.

On the issue of the e-Fleks, however, her hands were tied. Directions from Lattern were straightforward about the narrative. The Fleks, especially the e-Fleks, were an evolved, vibrant species with much to offer Earth if its inhabitants could all get past their quirks. After all, Earth had been served by many effective leaders who had suffered from character flaws. The e-Fleks will finish the Kleptron cleanup, and Earth would move on.

She hated lying. She hated misdirection. She wasn't very good at either, but she'd need to step up. She called Maria Labrador.

"Maria," said Penfor, "we have word from Reldap and Lattern Mission Control."

"Hang on," said Maria. "Let me start recording and take some notes."

Penfor relayed the technical details—time and place of the landing, basic needs of the e-Fleks such as diet, and how to transport the creatures if they needed to be moved. Then she took a deep breath and plunged ahead with the party line.

"Maria," continued Penfor, "these creatures are quirky. As Reldap told you, they function at the intellectual level of human 8th or 9th graders. They fantasize, and they play games. You know how children can get when playing a vid game. It's all harmless, but sometimes it can get intense. The e-Fleks don't have much self-confidence. They love role-playing. They will say and do strange things. So please, humor them."

"Penfor," Maria answered slowly. Something wasn't right, but she couldn't quite put her finger on it. "I don't understand everything you just said, but I will take it at face value and pass those recommendations along. As to a welcoming committee, who should be there?"

"The more senior, the better. The e-Fleks will respond well to being feted."

"Got it. Let me get things rolling."

The call disconnected. Penfor shuddered at what she had just done.

Chapter 8

The Prez, as he liked to call himself, stood up and smiled at his advisors. He was a little shaky but gripped the table edge to steady himself. There was just the faintest whiff of cannabis smoke in the air.

"So, fellas, let me get this straight. My buddy Relly went up to that friggin' spaceship they have circling us and is bringing back a bunch of giant bugs to help catch the brainsuckers?"

"That is correct, Mr. President," answered one of his advisors.

"And those bugs want me to make it like this is a big deal?"

"Yes, Mr. President."

"Jesus, I gotta cut down on this shit." He took a long hit and stubbed out his blunt. "Alright, what do I do?"

President Albert Moorehead, the first US president from the New Independent party, was not in a good place. His legacy was deeply jeopardized by the notorious refueling incident and physical altercation with his rival. He was struggling to keep his political ship afloat. He looked weak and vulnerable. The government's response to the initial landing had been a mess. Following one of Congress' most cherished traditions (distracting the public with investigative hearings and then going back to doing nothing), the House Un-Human Activities Committee had been convened by Moorehead's rivals to investigate the debacle. Derisively referred to as the HUHA committee (pronounced hoo-ha), it had nevertheless uncovered jaw-dropping levels of incompetence and governmental overreach in response to the alien contact and kleptron fiasco. Accused by his detractors of nearly tanking the first contact between an alien species and humans, he fought to regain his political footing.

"Optics, Mr. President, optics. We use the landing of this new alien species as a pivot, a new muscular approach. These poor animals are being exploited to fix a problem the Latternites could not. We sympathize with and support this exploited species. Americans love an underdog. You champion self-determination and fair treatment of all sentient beings."

"Fuck, yeah! I love it! Let's do it. Do what it takes. We haven't been up to Waterville in a while. Bring the Marine Corps band, the whole thing. This is not going to be a shit-show like the last time."

"Yes, Mr. President."

Another aide spoke up. "Mr. President, any guardrails here? Any limits on what we do or say? We really don't know what we are going to be dealing with. It could get a little crazy."

The Prez shook his head. "No. This will change everything. Pull out all the stops. We gotta get ahead of this. We gotta own it. We gotta be the drivers."

I have absolutely no idea of what he is talking about. *"Yes, Mr. President."*

CHAPTER 9

I saw the two black SUVs come up the driveway and felt the now-familiar sinking feeling in my gut. What now? The doorbell rang, and I opened the door. There stood Beefy Guy A (BGA), whom I hadn't seen since the refueling debacle. Beefy Guy B (BGB) stood behind him. They were members of The Prez's security team.

"Good morning, Dr. Gilner. May we come in? We'd like to talk to you about the upcoming landing of Reldap and the Flektanians."

Wow, a little change here. Polite this morning. "Good morning. Certainly, gentlemen, come in."

The two men came in, and I closed the door. The cats were not impressed and slunk down the basement stairs. Helen joined us, and we all sat down. BGA started. "Reldap will be landing in about 48 hours with a contingent of Flektanians, and I believe they are e-Fleks, to assist in the kleptron cleanup. We want to give the e-Fleks a better greeting than Reldap's."

"Sounds good," said Helen.

"Right," said BGB. "We'd like you two to be part of the welcome. Both of you have considerable insight into our Latternite visitors, and any assistance would be gratefully appreciated."

"Go on," I said.

BGB continued. "The President will make a few introductory remarks. We'd appreciate your reviewing his proposed comments and ensuring we do not offend Latternite sensibilities. We'd also appreciate it if you participate in the welcome. Despite your unofficial status, you remain vitally important to human-Latternite relations."

Knock me over with a feather. I looked at Helen. She nodded. "Okay," I said.

BGA spoke. "Great!" he said brightly. "I'll send you both the speech. We think it's fine, but we want another set of eyeballs on it, just in case. Let us know if anything doesn't sound right. We'll pick up you folks Wednesday morning at 9. Penfor will meet us at the airfield."

We chatted for a few more minutes, and then BGA and BGB left. When the door closed, I saw two small heads appear at the door to the basement. "Yeah, guys, come on up. They're gone," said Helen. Tigress and Euphrates returned to the family room, settled on opposite ends of the couch, and promptly went to sleep.

"Something has changed," I said.

Helen smirked at me. "Do ya think? You are perceptive this morning, aren't you?"

"Okay, wiseguy. What do you think's going on?"

Helen got serious. "I don't really know. I strongly suspect this has more to do with US politics than interstellar relations."

"Agreed."

"Ed," she said, "we won't get anywhere with the cultural and technical exchange until we resolve the kleptron problem. Let's stay focused. If The Prez wants to make a big fuss, we help him make a big fuss. I can't see how he could muck it up."

I agreed with Helen's assessment of the kleptron problem, but any time The Prez opened his mouth, there was a 50/50 chance it wasn't harmless. "Are you sure?" I asked. "He's elevated incompetence to an art form."

"All right, all right. Point taken. My anticipatory, blanket approval of Wednesday's proceedings is officially withdrawn. But give it a chance, will you?"

"Fair enough."

"Come. It's sunny and warm out. It will only get hotter later in the day. Let's go for a walk."

"Let me put on my sneakers."

CHAPTER 10

Helen and I drove out to the airport to see the preparations underway. Reldap had insisted on using LaFleur as his official transportation center (or whatever it was called.) Every time he flew to Paris or Nairobi or Perth on some mission or another (really, it was sightseeing and food tourism mainly), he left from LaFleur on his own ship. The FAA had needed to put in a control tower, and the ILOA (International Low Orbit Agency) also had a rep at the airport to manage the orbital and suborbital launches and landings. Multiple self-important types (national and international) had insisted on flying in since Reldap's landing, so staging, seats, podiums, audiovisual equipment, and all the other trappings of 22nd-century officialdom were set and in place. Worker bees dispatched by The Prez were busy making everything just right. It wasn't terribly interesting, and we only hung around for a few minutes.

******

Reldap, about 10 hours from landing, faced a more difficult task. Resigned to several hours of e-Flek chatter once the critters were awake, he reversed Klak's and his minions' stasis. The process went smoothly, and a low chime indicated the process was complete.

He returned to the storage room and opened the stasis chambers. They moved sluggishly at first, but all six e-

Fleks were fine. Reldap firmly took hold of Klak and put him up on a table; he was only a few kilos and carrying him was more awkward than heavy. He put on his translator and turned Klak toward him.

"Klak," started Reldap, "we need to talk about what you will say to the humans."

"Yes," said Klak. "We need to talk about what I will say to the humans," and stopped. There was an uncomfortable silence.

"Well," said Reldap, "do you have any ideas?"

At length, Klak spoke. "I am a proud arthropod. My team members are proud arthropods. We are landing in America, yes?" Reldap nodded. "I have studied the slights and aggressions of American humans against our arthropod brothers and sisters. We have discussed this among ourselves. We must strike the first blow and be relentless. I will present our demands and grievances."

"What demands and grievances?"

"We cannot discuss that with you. We have suffered enough at the hands of your countrymen, and you cannot be trusted."

Oh shit, thought Reldap. This might get complicated.

"Latternite, where is my cape?"

Yes, this will definitely get complicated.

CHAPTER 11

Helen and I arrived at the airfield, and Beefy Guy A ushered us to reserved seating at the front of the audience; we didn't quite make the cut for the sitting with The Prez and Reldap. The media types set up their stuff in front of the VIP dais. The President's motorcade rolled in as we seated ourselves.

"Mr. President, I've just gotten word that the Latternite ship will land shortly."

"Good, good. Can't wait to see Relly and his pet bugs," said The Prez.

"Mr. President, I want to confirm our approach to the Flektanians. We are grateful for their help. We understand there is a history between the Flektanians and the Latternites and that, by our standards, the Latternites have often treated the Flektanians poorly. While we respect and acknowledge the ways and traditions of our Latternite friends, we are committed to independence and self-determination for all. We are wholly supportive, welcoming, unquestioning…"

The Prez cut him off. "Okay, stop shoveling the shit. We're good."

"Yes, Mr. President."

Moorehead left his car along with his security detail and an aide. The Prez ducked behind a curtain for a minute, and I smelled cannabis smoke. He emerged smiling and headed for the dais. Moorehead was a little unsteady on the steps but didn't need any help. He navigated to his seat and settled himself, still smiling.

"Okay, while we're waiting for the space patrol, do I gotta solve any international crises? Make an emergency declaration? You know, any presidential kinda stuff, or do I just sit here on my ass?"

"Mr. President, this is an excellent opportunity to rest and regroup as we await the arrival of our alien friends."

"Yeah, that sounds good." He leaned back in his chair and closed his eyes. Several minutes passed.

"Look!" someone shouted.

A speck was visible in the eastern sky. Soon, we saw the familiar shape of the Latternite atmospheric entry vehicle and heard the soft whoosh of its atmospheric flight engines. The aircraft slowed and approached the honor guard formed at the AEV's reserved tiedown. The ship's spindly legs extended, and the craft gently touched down.

After a few moments, a hatch opened on the ship, and steps extended to the ground. A second hatch opened, and a small platform extended from the hull. A black, shiny creature looking for all the world like a giant dung beetle wearing a cape scuttled out onto the landing. Five other, slightly smaller e-Fleks crowded onto the stand. Its function as an elevator now apparent, the lift slowly started toward the ground. Reldap appeared at the top of the stairs, smiled, and waved to the audience's applause.

After all the aliens were safely on the tarmac, Reldap took out his ship controller and stuck his finger in the side port while talking to the small box in his native language. The elevator returned to ship level and withdrew into the craft as the stairs did the same. Both hatches closed. Reldap then activated the anti-intrusion systems. Penfor walked out to him, and they conversed briefly before both headed for the dais. He left his rolling cart at the side of the platform and picked up the largest e-Flek before mounting the stairs to the seating. The five smaller e-Fleks quickly arranged themselves on the ground, between the first row of the audience seats and the stage.

The VIP seating was not set up for a giant bug. Reldap stood holding Klak while there was a hurried conference among the reception's organizers. An assistant quickly returned with a board and a couple of sawhorses. She set up the small platform alongside the other seats. Reldap placed Klak on the board, but Klak's squawking stopped him from taking his seat. Reldap nodded.

"Klak wishes to have a podium," said Reldap. He quickly explained what was needed, and a short time later, a half-meter long piece of six by six (why did we still use inches for dimensional lumber when the U.S. finally switched officially to metric in 2061?) appeared. Reldap slipped the piece of wood under Klak's middle set of legs, and the e-Flek expressed his satisfaction with the arrangement. All was ready.

Vicki Nguyen, assistant director of the Office of Alien Relations (OAR), stood up. Just a couple of years out of college, a combination of legitimate competence, an agreeable disposition, and her father's financial largesse had landed her the plum position.

Despite the word "director" in the title, she was still a political ingénue, and giving the introductory remarks at the landing was punching above her weight. However, she had no alternative. Her boss, who was even more connected despite being less competent and less agreeable, was off on one of his "fact-finding" tours in the French countryside and couldn't be disturbed, even for the landing of a new alien race.

She took a deep breath and started. "Good afternoon, everyone. On behalf of the Office of Alien Relations, I welcome you all here…"

Ms. Nguyen was interrupted by loud sounds coming from Klak.

Reldap spoke up. "He says she is noisy and rambling," he said. "I am sorry, he does not understand human ways. Give me a moment."

The Prez shifted uncomfortably. "Hey, this is supposed to be about me. Well, I mean, not about me, but you know, about me. What is this crap?"

Vicki spoke. "I'm sure we'll get this straightened out momentarily."

"You better, kiddo," said The Prez. "Otherwise, I don't care how much money your daddy gave me. I mean, gave my campaign."

The poor woman looked like she had been slapped but said nothing. While all this was happening, Reldap opened his ever-present shoulder bag and took out another translator unit. He powered it up and fiddled with the settings. After a couple of minutes, he walked over to Klak's table. He spoke briefly with Klak. The beetle replied, and Reldap looped the translator's lanyard over Klak's head.

"I apologize," said Reldap. "I did not prepare Klak fully for this ceremony. We have talked, and I have explained this human custom to Klak. I have also provided him with a translator that will allow him to understand human

American speech and translate his statements into English. I think things will go more smoothly now."

Moorehead gave Reldap a dirty look but said nothing. "May I continue?" said Vicki. The Prez nodded.

The assistant director spoke. "Well," she said as she put on her best customer relations smile, "now that we are all settled, let me be the first to welcome Reldap back to Earth and offer my personal warmest and heartiest welcome to our Flektanian visitors. This is a great day for Earth, Lattern, and our new Flektanian friends. Without further delay, let me give the floor to Albert Moorehead, President of the United States of America!"

The audience applauded. The Prez got to his feet and wobbled to the speaker's podium. He gripped both sides of the stand, steadied himself, and smiled.

"My fellow Americans and other critters," he started. Several in the audience cringed. "Last September, my buddy Relly popped off his spaceship and into our hearts." He grinned. "What a wild ride. He helped expose that jerk Phil Jackner for what he is, a low-down dirty…"

An aide quickly got up and whispered in The Prez's ear.

"Yeah, sorry, right. Getting a little off-topic. Sorry about that. Listen, we've been having terrible problems with those brainsuckers. I'm glad Reldap and his people are finally doing something about it. I've never seen anything quite like it. A giant friggin' beetle that eats brainsuckers. Just what we need!

"But I got one question. Are we sure that it's OK with these bugs? I mean, are they OK with being here and helping us? Anyway, who cares, right? They're just bugs, and our friend Relly and his crew wouldn't exploit these things, would they?" He looked pointedly at Reldap and Penfor.

This is strange, *I thought.* Since when did Albert Moorehead develop a conscience? There has to be another agenda.

"...so it's all good. They should help. Welcome to America. I mean Earth. Whatever. And we stand in solidarity with our new alien friends." He wobbled back to behind the curtain.

The field was utterly silent. Vicki Nguyen went to the podium. Big customer service smile.

"Thank you, Mr. President. Reldap has indicated that Klak would like to make some remarks."

Reldap walked over to the flek's table. Klak's antennae started moving, and his front legs began waving.

"Latternite, is this safe?"

"Yes, Klak."

"No raptopods?"

"No."

"No nestodons?"

"No. It's fine, really."

"No lapenths?"

"No, certainly no lapenths. We are not on your home planet. There are no native predators here."

"What is this help with brainsuckers? What are brainsuckers? I am to help these mammals? Who said anything about helping mammals?"

I was observing this carefully. Looked like Reldap hadn't told our new guest about our plans.

"Klak, brainsucker is the Earth's name for kleptron. There are free kleptrons on this planet."

"What is wrong with that? You Latternites love getting bitten by a kleptron."

"For humans, it is not a good thing. We must help them get rid of the kleptrons."

The e-Flek paused. "If I find one, can I eat it?"

"We'll see."

"Latternite dog, what do you mean we'll see? They are tasty. I will not help if I cannot eat the kleptrons."

The other five e-Fleks started moving around quickly but aimlessly. They looked agitated.

Reldap looked imploringly at me. What was I supposed to do? I shrugged my shoulders.

Reldap finally spoke. "Yes, I suppose you can eat the kleptrons."

"Good."

"It is customary in human situations like this one for the guest of honor to make some remarks," said Reldap.

"I am the guest of honor?"

"Yes."

Klak paused. It was hard for the beetle to turn because he was propped on his podium, but he managed to look around. "All right," he said.

"Mammals," he started and then paused. *Oh shit*, I thought.

"Mammals, I do not spit in your presence," he said. Reldap was shocked. There was no greater insult among Fleks. "I have studied Earth. Your history. Your evolution. Shame on you! I am here to right a great wrong. I stand with the arthropods of Earth. Their cause is my cause. My legs are their swords. My exoskeleton is their shield. My voice is their call for justice. For millions of years, you have oppressed us. For millions of years, you have eaten us, exterminated us, and treated us as pests. You have ignored our rightful place in evolution.

"Our ancestors were here hundreds of millions of years before you were. We ruled the seas before the fishes. Our dragonfly brothers and sisters, who live to this day, flew above the dinosaurs. And yet, despite all of our contributions to Earth, change continued, and we were left behind.

"Yes, change continued. Amphibians. Reptiles. Those vile birds. And then you, the mammals. So proud of your thermal homeostasis. So proud of your fur. So proud of your milk." I could not believe what I was hearing. This was crazy. Was this thing going to help solve the kleptron problem?

Klak continued. "What do you do to us? Raccoons eat crayfish. Chimpanzees eat termites." He paused. "And then we come to you. The humans. The highest form of life. The pinnacle of biology. Ha! You humans, you humans are the worst. You wrest lobsters from the sea bottom. You farm shrimp to be eaten. You enslave and exploit the bees. You put pins through butterflies. You have spent endless billions of dollars on insecticide. Ant traps. Flypaper. Crop dusters. You have made common cause with the Latternite dogs, who have exploited us for hundreds of your years."

Penfor, who until this point had said nothing, seemed to finally lose her cool and started to speak. Reldap said something in Lattern and shushed her.

Klak continued to speak. "We have fought back. We bite you. Mosquito patriots infect you. My scorpion allies sting you. Bedbugs bedevil you, yet you persist.

"Now, I know some mammals don't do these things. There are some humans who are very fine people. But this must end. I am the only one who can help. I will undo the lie of evolution. I will topple this fiendish hierarchy. I lead the Flektanian Earth Expeditionary Force! I will make arthropods great again!" Klak rambled on and on.

An aide sidled up to Moorehead. "Sir, I realize that we were told to expect some odd behavior and outlandish statements, but this? Isn't this a bit overboard? Can we really work with this?"

"Kid, trust the plan."

"Yes, sir."

CHAPTER 12

Things always seemed to fray at the edges and unravel when The Prez was involved. I'm glad this was all recorded because it was so disorienting, so bizarre that I lost track of three-quarters of what was said.

Vicki Nguyen, much to her credit, finally stood up and interrupted. She thanked Klak for his insightful remarks and announced that The Prez was meeting with the British ambassador in three hours in Washington and needed to return. She regretted that this fascinating discourse needed to be put on hold, but it would surely continue after the kleptron problem was resolved. Reldap took the cue and took Klak down from his perch. Slowly, the crowd dispersed. The Prez and his entourage departed. Helen and I were left standing with Reldap, Klak, and his followers.

"What do e-Fleks eat?" asked Helen.

"Almost anything," said Reldap. "They are the archetypal omnivore. They have been modified to eat sources from many planets, including Earth."

"Well," said Helen, "perhaps Ed and I can host them at our house. Looks like some bridge building and de-escalation is in order."

"That is a kind offer," said Reldap.

Klak spoke up. "I will spit on your floor, human."

Helen was taken aback. "No, no, that's a good thing," said Reldap.

I wasn't sure a home-hosted meal was a good idea, but I agreed. The powers that be had left a flatbed-covered truck to transport the e-Fleks. We hoisted the critters into the back. Helen drove the truck, and I took our car with Reldap.

We arrived at our house without incident. We unloaded the e-Fleks, and they trundled into the house.

Chaos ensued. The six animals formed a circle, spat a foul-smelling brown liquid onto our foyer, and looked at us expectantly. "Go ahead," said Reldap. "It is expected that you will spit as well." Reldap proceeded to spit on the floor into the same disgusting pool of liquid the e-Fleks had created.

Helen and I looked at each other. Helen pulled her hair out of the way and daintily spat. A glob of her saliva landed on the floor. I decided, what the heck—if I gotta do it, let me make it a good one, and launched a goober into the mess.

"Ah, humans, we are now friends," said Klak. Great, *I thought.* Just what I wanted. Friends with monster spitting bugs.

"Helen," said Reldap quietly, "both Latternites and humans value cleanliness and tidiness. However, the e-Fleks would consider it a great insult if you cleaned up before they left."

I wasn't sure if Reldap was pulling my leg, but I nodded. Helen did as well.

At that point, all hell broke loose. If things hadn't been bad enough, Tigress and Euphrates came up from the basement to investigate.

The cats were Maine Coons, huge, weighing 8 or 9 kg apiece, in the prime of their lives, and all muscle. While Maine Coons are often described as "gentle giants" in cat books, this does not apply to interactions with species other than humans and Latternites. Proud members of the genus *Felis,* sturdy cousins of *Panthera leo* and *Panthera tigris,* they were not going to put up with this shit. First arching their backs and hissing, their ears went flat, and they started circling one of the smaller e-Fleks. I feared we were about to witness an interplanetary incident in our foyer.

The bugs, however, were used to more passive fare on their home planet. Unaware of our creatures' potential lethality, they saw the cats as lunch. "Thank you," said Klak. "We enjoy fresh meals."

With surprising speed, the bugs tried to circle Tigress. The bugs' agility notwithstanding, she was much faster and handily out of harm's way in a second. The e-Flek that had been initially targeted now realized that it was in danger. Looking for the fastest exit, it shot down the basement stairs.

At considerable personal risk, Helen and I picked up the two snarling, hissing cats, took them upstairs, and locked them in a bedroom. Per standard cat protocol, they immediately started mewling like kittens, demanding release from prison. Ignoring them, we went back downstairs.

"We'd better check the basement," said Helen. I agreed. We went downstairs and found the smaller e-Flek on its back, legs wiggling in the air. Helen giggled, and I lost it as well. I heard the heavier steps of Reldap on the steps, and he looked at the bug and then at us.

He snorted a couple of times, clearly trying to keep his laughing under control. "We must not let the other e-Fleks see this," he said. "This is a great humiliation."

"Yeah, I could see that," I said. I forced myself to stop laughing. "Reldap, fiddle your translator so he can understand me." He nodded and did as he was asked. I reached down and gently put the creature back on his feet.

"I am sorry," I said. "I know this is a terrible embarrassment and dishonor. No one outside of this basement will ever know what happened. We will tell everyone how amazed we were that you landed on your feet after such a tumble."

"Thank you," said the bug.

"What is your name," I asked.

"Sek."

"Welcome to Earth, Sek."

"Thank you, human Gilner."

"Stairs are hard for e-Fleks, Sek. Let me carry you back up."

"That would be most helpful." I picked the little guy up, and we all went upstairs. Sek rejoined his pod (or whatever you call a grouping of giant, semi-intelligent alien beetles), and they spoke. We still had to deal with feeding these things, but I did not want to share a table with these guys. When everyone looked settled, I spoke.

"Klak," I said, "you and your friends have been living on space rations. I see that you are skilled hunters and like your meals fresh."

"This is true, human," he answered.

"We have much land behind our house. There are many plants and small animals there. Perhaps you would prefer to hunt and graze and take your leave of us for a few hours?"

Klak turned to the others, and they spoke in their harsh, clicking language. "An excellent plan, human Gilner. We thank you."

"That was inspired," whispered Helen.

"Thank you, human Gilner," I said. She swatted me.

We led the creatures out of the house and into the backyard with the woods beyond. With everyone more relaxed, Reldap explained the concepts of ornamental plants, gardens, and pets and how they were not fair game. He told them to avoid mushrooms.

"This will be fine," said Reldap. "I think things will go more smoothly."

"I sure hope so," I said. We watched the e-Fleks slowly wander through the garden, cropping various plants and nailing the occasional bird or chipmunk as they approached the tree line. Interestingly, despite all of Klak's speechifying, I did see the occasional grasshopper or beetle get consumed as well.

Helen, Reldap, and I had a more conventional lunch and a beer (or three, in Reldap's case) while we considered our next steps.

CHAPTER 13

"This is not going to be easy," I said. "I think…"

At that moment, the e-Fleks scurried back into the house. "What are you doing?" asked Klak.

"We were starting to discuss our options," said Reldap. "We must decide how to find and capture the Kleptrons."

"All discussions must include me and the rest of the Expeditionary Force."

Heaven help me, I thought. "Certainly. Do you have any thoughts on the matter?"

"Yes," said Klak. "I have reviewed Earth data that was downloaded into me when I was just a larva. I have already considered this in detail. I have studied many human detective shows. The detective shows are more complete and much more interesting than police reports. We will approach the problem in the manner of the British police procedural dramas of the early 21st century. The Senior Investigating Officer must be female and have an upper-class London accent. It will be enjoyable to keep calling them 'ma'am.' At least one junior officer must have an accent from Scotland or the north of England. There must be sexual tension between the SIO and at least one subordinate.

"The detectives are almost always successful in locating and catching the criminal when these conditions are met. It is also acceptable if the Senior Investigating Officer is male and from Scotland if there is at least one female junior officer with a posh accent. Can we arrange this?"

Helen and I looked at each other. "Klak," said Helen, "humans love stories about complicated and dangerous situations. But they are not real. They are not representations of true events."

"Then why do you show such things? It is misleading. And I am not sure I believe you. Are you profiting from the kleptrons? Are you, as they say in the early 21st-century British police procedural dramas, bent?"

Helen was a neurologist. While many of her patients had intact thought processes, a sizable minority had a couple of cognitive screws loose due to their various illnesses. She didn't miss a beat. "No, I am not bent, and I am not lying. I agree that we will need help in our investigation. We will find the most qualified individuals to help us. If they have any or all of the characteristics you have outlined, so much the better. However, they will not drive our search. Do you understand?"

"Human, I believe you are making a grave error…"

Klak was interrupted by Sek. There was an intense back-and-forth of grating noises. At length, Klak spoke through the translator. "My sergeant has informed me that this is an acceptable approach. For the moment, we will go forward with your plan."

"Good," I said. "I will call Joe and Maria. They will find a working space for us and help us find the right people to help us."

"Excellent," said Klak. "A command center and subordinate investigators."

I sighed and got out my PDD. Maria responded promptly, and I relayed what had transpired. I could see her roll her eyes, but she said she and Joe would get right on it and we should stay put for the moment. I wanted these things out of my house ASAP but agreed to Maria's request.

Joe called me back about 30 minutes later. Impressively, in that short time, they had already lined up the old Oakland Grange Hall to use as the command center and house the bugs. Used only occasionally for decades, it was still in pretty good shape. Equipment would arrive shortly, and he thought it would be easy to find a couple of investigators who were both competent and able to keep a straight face. Best of all, behind the building was a large, overgrown field full of mice, chipmunks, voles, and other tasty critters.

We herded the e-Fleks onto the flatbed truck and drove to the Grange. As promised, there was a nice big field behind the hall. The front door was open, and George Fielding, the assistant town manager, stood before the steps. He just stared.

"Hi, George," I said. "How's things?" George and I knew each other from some reporting I'd done on phosphorus abatement in one of the Oakland lakes.

"Just fine, Mr. Gilner," he said. "I got a call from Homeland Security asking me to open the old Grange Hall. They didn't say why, just that the town would be reimbursed for expenses. Also, they told me specifically not to clean the place or mow the back lawn. I've turned on the electricity and water and made sure the toilets flush. I have to say that since you made friends with that alien fella, things have been a little strange around here." He hesitated, looking at the new crop of aliens. The understatedness of Mainers is legendary.

"Thanks, George. We'll take it from here."

Fielding got in his truck and drove away. Reldap opened the gate on our flatbed, and we helped the e-Fleks onto the ground. The hall had a handicap ramp, and the bugs scurried into the building. Klak and the others explored the inside, poking their noses (such as they were) into various nooks and crannies. Klak finally spoke. "This is acceptable, human. We will celebrate and spit."

The e-Fleks formed a circle and spat their foul-smelling brown juice into a puddle. Reldap turned to us. "It is our turn," he said. Reldap, Helen, and I added our contributions to the mix.

"Thank you," said Sek. Klak immediately started squawking at him, presumably berating him for some form of Flektanian insubordination.

"Klak," I said, "this is Earth and, even more importantly, America. Everyone is free to speak here."

"Human, I acknowledge what you say," he said. "However, you will regret this. My Expeditionary Force is an undisciplined, uneducated rabble. Only with my leadership can we succeed in finding and eating kleptrons and then liberating the arthropodal phylum. I alone can fix it. I cannot take responsibility for the actions of my followers if they are allowed to speak freely."

"And I'm not sure I can trust your actions if I allow *you* to speak freely," I said. "I…"

Helen cut me off. She knew I was getting irritated. "Klak," she said, "we acknowledge you as leader of your Expeditionary Force. We have also found that consulting with subordinates can sometimes be helpful."

Reldap, who until this point had been quiet, spoke to Klak through their translators. "I have reminded him that all six e-Fleks were loaded with Earth data and skills. He is their leader only by chance, having emerged from the larval stage only a few minutes before the others. Klak has acknowledged this."

By this time, Klak and crew had discovered the back entrance of the Hall. It too had a wheelchair ramp, and they clambered out onto the field, chattering excitedly among themselves. I suspected the back yard would soon have a rodent depopulation event.

"Reldap, I said, "after lunch, all of these things get a multilingual translator. Not negotiable." He nodded.

When they were gone, Reldap shook his head and sighed. "Flektanian delusional syndrome makes it difficult to work with these creatures…"

"What?" Helen and I spoke almost simultaneously.

Reldap jerked his head as though he had just remembered something, then looked at the ground. He paused. Clearly, he had let something slip. "I am afraid I have not been completely forthright with you regarding my recent trip to the quantum communication station."

He proceeded to spill the story about being pressured to use the e-Fleks despite his reservations, the coronal mass ejection exposure, and Lattern's further pressure not to disclose the cause of the e-Fleks' bizarre behavior.

I shook my head. "So you guys have monkeyed with their nervous system, the poor things get a massive dose of DNA-toasting mixed radiation, they aren't told they are being brought to an alien world to clean up a mess that the Latternites created, and you let them prattle on about using investigative techniques, if I dare call them that, from over 100 years ago?"

Reldap smiled. "Yes, that would sum it up nicely."

Honestly, I really had thought he was doing better. Uh-uh. "Reldap, do you remember all that stuff that The Prez just rattled off? About the exploitation of the e-Fleks? Don't you think we ought to explain the situation? That explaining that we weren't seeing normal, rational e-Flek behavior might change everyone's view of events?"

He looked shocked. "Oh, no. No, no, no. I have been given strict instructions to avoid mention of the CME incident and its consequences. We must use the e-Fleks; otherwise, my father will issue another Pronouncement."

This was serious. A Latternite Pronouncement was an ultimatum: perform as ordered or be banished from polite society. We'd run into a Pronouncement problem when Reldap had first landed, and we'd barely dodged that bullet. Shit.

Helen had been silent throughout this exchange and finally spoke. "I think we can manage this."

I looked at her as if she were crazy. She waved me off.

"Look," she said. The Prez and his crew are utterly ineffective. The e-Fleks are useless save for their sense of smell and appetite for Kleptrons. Joe and Maria will help us find a couple of competent investigators who can keep a straight face and not get distracted by the side shows. We'll get this done.

She paused, and then looked straight into his eyes. "Reldap, you're an idiot." The poor biobot hung his head and said nothing.

CHAPTER 14

Helen and I were exhausted and ready to call it a day. We did not suggest to Reldap that he stay with us, and he did not ask to do so. We closed the Grange Hall, ensuring the e-Fleks had access to water, and promised the bugs the prospect of more foraging in the morning. They were thrilled. Before he left, Reldap fitted them all with translators. We gave him a ride to our house, and he picked up his car to return to Portland. I expected that he and Penfor would have a little chat, and I was glad I would not witness the conversation. We said our goodbyes and went into the house. We were promptly greeted by Tigress and Euphrates, although I detected a certain wariness in them until they were sure it was just their usual humans. The evening was a simple home-cooked meal, some grade-B videos, and an early bedtime. I suggested to Helen we watch a couple of early 21st-century British police procedurals, but she found my humor wanting.

I called Joe Stein on the vid phone the next morning. "Did you watch that fiasco yesterday?" I asked.

"Yup. Good one, even for The Prez," he answered. "Where do we go from here?"

Joe and Maria were friends, not just colleagues. It made sense to tell them about Flektanian Delusional Syndrome, trusting that they'd keep it to themselves. I quickly decided to tell them about FDS and our bug friends.

Joe sighed. "Ed, my sources tell me that The Prez has some screwy plan to rehabilitate his image, which includes the e-Fleks."

"What?"

"Yeah. He and his buddies will play them up as an exploited, oppressed species heroically stepping up to help humanity. What they want, they get. What they say, we accept. No filter, no fact check."

"He's as crazy as they are…"

"No kidding. He's even considering designating them a protected class under Title VII."

"He's never given a rat's ass about Title VII. He's horrible about that stuff."

"Yup."

We both paused. I spoke first. "Joe," I said, "political machinations aside, there's a real problem to solve. There's someone or a bunch of people who have illegal kleptrons. Under the Kleptron Control Act of 2131, all kleptrons in the U.S. must be housed in licensed facilities, and their use and freedom are subject to strict control and oversight. I know the emergency legislation was poorly drawn, and there are all kinds of strange requirements and loopholes. The bottom line, though, is the law is the law. Irrespective of the legal issues, there are people doing bad stuff with these critters, and they have to be stopped. We find the kleptrons, and we bring the perps to justice. We probably could have done it without the e-Fleks, but they're here, and we might as well use them."

"Agreed."

I continued. "There has been no concerted effort to solve the problem. Lots of fits and starts, lots of local half-hearted investigations. Law enforcement keeps coming up against a well-organized, well-financed operation that is remarkably effective at staying hidden."

Joe nodded his head in agreement.

"Let's set up a task force. Humans, bugs, Latternites. Some official law enforcement, some 'consultants.' We need official permission to move forward with this. Most of all, we need a couple of seasoned, effective investigators who also possess a deeply developed sense of the absurd and can look at a Salvador Dali painting and not say 'Whisky Tango Foxtrot.'"

"That last stipulation is critical," Joe deadpanned. "I'll get back to you in a day or two."

I thanked him, we said goodbye, and we ended the conversation.

Helen had to work that day, so I drove to the Grange Hall by myself. Reldap's vehicle was already there. Girding my mental loins, I entered the building.

Reldap and Penfor sat on a couple of oversized chairs in one corner of the building. The e-Fleks appeared to be practicing close-order military drills. "Good morning, everyone," I said.

Reldap and Penfor returned a greeting. The bugs were oblivious and continued marching.

"I have an update." At this point, the e-Fleks stopped and listened. I relayed the gist of the conversation with Joe, leaving out some of the less flattering stuff.

Klak turned to face me. "Well done, human." Penfor gave him a sharp look. I said nothing.

I explained to the e-Fleks that they could not leave the grounds surrounding the Grange Hall but could forage to their hearts' (or, more accurately, circulatory systems') content, and we'd ensure they had water. They agreed. I would be back when the new members of the team arrived. Reldap said that either he or Penfor would check in every day. Relenting in my irritation at the Latternite subterfuge, I suggested they could stay at Chez Gilner. Both looked at the floor and declined. I did not push the issue and went home. I had assumed there would be crowds of gawkers, but only a few polite Mainers observed the proceedings.

Helen came home later in the afternoon. "How did it go?" she asked.

"As expected," I answered. "Tell me, what do you think of Salvador Dali paintings?"

"Well, I think they are a little weird but interesting. Why?"

"Never mind. Glad you're on the team."

CHAPTER 15

I got a call a day later from Maria. "Super news," she said. "We have official approval for the investigation. You and Helen are authorized as official consultants to participate. The FBI has not previously authorized non-human consultants, but we broke new ground on this case. The two Latternites and the e-Fleks are official consultants as well."

She continued. "Best of all, we have two terrific investigators joining us. Tina and Joe will meet you, along with Joe and I, at the Grange Hall at 2:00 today. Does that work for you guys? I've already called Penfor. She and Reldap will be meeting there as well."

"You and Joe will be joining us? I have no objection, but I didn't think you guys were investigators."

"Hmmm," she said and then paused. "How shall I put it? We are the liaison with the executive branch of the Federal government, sometimes reporting directly to the President. Our tasks can be quite varied. Sometimes, we investigate. Sometimes, we facilitate. Sometimes, we report. Sometimes, we do stuff I can't tell you about."

I thought for a minute. "What you are telling me, then, is that you are here to keep the e-Fleks happy and on task, the Latternites in their place, and The Prez smiling without us doing too much damage along the way?"

"Sounds about right."

"Okay, let's move on. Any background on the two new members of the team?"

"Oh, sure. Shawn Johnson and Tina Standing Elk are FBI agents who have partnered for about eight years. They're just great. Johnson is simply the best interrogator I've ever seen work, and Tina is an absolute rock. They complement each other perfectly. Also, they love Salvador Dali. See you in a few."

We arrived at the Grange Hall at 2:00, as requested. Tina and Shawn were on the grounds behind the Hall, watching the e-Fleks drilling. Joe and Maria were in front with Reldap and Penfor, waiting for us.

We exchanged greetings. "I suggested to Shawn and Tina that they get acquainted with our new friends," said Maria. "Let's head round back and make introductions."

We walked around the building. Tina and Shawn were just staring, slack-jawed, at six large insect-like creatures double-timing around the yard's perimeter.

"I thought you said they had a well-developed sense of the absurd," I said.

"They do," said Joe. "Just imagine if they didn't."

The two FBI agents turned when they heard us talking.

"Drs. Gilner, Reldap, Penfor, I'm honored," said Tina.

"As am I," said Shawn. "Agents Stein and Labrador, everyone in the Bureau holds you in great respect."

We all shook hands, chatted, and quickly dropped formalities. "Let's go inside," said Shawn.

Penfor went to the yard where the e-Fleks were now simulating hand-to-hand (or, more correctly, leg-to-leg) combat. "Klak!" she yelled. "Come inside to the command post. We are ready to start planning."

Klak ordered his followers inside. The bipeds settled on chairs around the large meeting room while the e-Fleks settled in formation on the floor.

Shawn started to speak. "I'd like to…"

He was cut off by Klak. "Human, you are impolite and without grace. First, we must spit."

Tina looked at Joe. Joe nodded and got up. I saw her shake her head imperceptibly, but she got up too. The rest of us followed, formed a saliva circle as Helen had taken to calling it, and, along with the bugs, did our thing. We went back to our original seats.

Shawn started again. "Okay, sorry, I forgot that tradition. Are we all good now?"

"Proceed, human," said Klak.

"Thank you." Shawn didn't miss a beat. He cleared his throat. "On the way up here, Tina and I reviewed the preliminary analysis of violations of the Kleptron Control Act of 2131, which I will call the KCA from here on for brevity's sake. The information is siloed, incomplete, and fragmented. We will need to spend some time analyzing this mass of data. If and when we establish any patterns, we will conduct on-site investigations and interviews."

The agent continued. "At present, we do not have any suspects. Whether it's a full-blown criminal organization, a single individual, or a bunch of different bad guys, the efficiency of this criminal enterprise is unusually good. Cracking this case is going to be hard, but we'll do it." He turned to Tina. "Tina, can you give us an outline of the operational details?"

"Thanks, Shawn. I have communications and computer equipment in the truck, enough for all of us. We'll have access to all relevant crime databases. We'll correlate all the crime location information and then plan from there. Does anyone have any questions?"

Klak spoke up. "Human female investigator, the Flektanian Expeditionary Force wishes to address you as ma'am or guv. Is that acceptable? Is there sexual tension between you and any other humans on the team? Is there a board where we may write ideas and put up pictures of suspects and draw lines between them?"

Tina started to answer, but Klak kept speaking. "Humans and Latternite dogs must accept that the primary objective of the Flektanian Expeditionary Force is to right the eons of wrongs against Earth arthropods and that location and consumption of kleptrons is secondary. Make arthropods great again!"

The other five e-Fleks started chanting, 'Make arthropods great again!' Tina gave Reldap a long, hard stare, telepathically transmitting *Do something about this shit, and now!* Reldap and Penfor stood, looked at the ground, and then spoke in Lattern with the translators off. Penfor looked especially pissed off. She briefly fiddled with her translator and then strode over to Klak, picked him up by his sides, and held him at eye level, noses centimeters apart. She spoke softly for a couple of minutes. Klak sensibly did not interrupt, but when she was finished, he appeared to answer her. She put Klak down, readjusted her translator, and smiled at the humans. "I don't think we have all the issues ironed out, but I believe things will go more smoothly from now on. Klak, do you have anything to say?"

"Yes. As the leader of the Flektanian Expeditionary Force, and to further our mutual goals, I will adjust our language to meet the needs of small-minded bipedal endotherms. Since there are no dogs on Lattern, I will refrain from referring to Latternites as Latternite dogs. We will use human names, as that appears to be important to you, although I do not understand why. We will treat the kleptron problem and the arthropod problem as equal in importance. Finally, I am made to understand that some humans find our sharing of bodily fluids to be offensive. Despite our deeply rooted attachment to this cultural observance, we will temporarily refrain from celebrating it in the future. Are these changes sufficient and satisfactory?"

Tina smiled sweetly. "Klak, these concessions are most gracious of you. As for your questions: yes, you may call me ma'am or guv. Although these terms are typically used in Britain rather than the US, they are terms of respect and friendship, and I will accept them in that spirit. As for sexual tension, no. Both Agent Johnson and I are happily married to others. We have been partners for eight years and are good friends, that is all. As to a murder board, yes. We can certainly have one, and it is an excellent idea."

"May I call Agent Johnson 'sir' or 'guv?'"

"Shawn?"

"Yes, Klak. That's just fine."

"Thank you, ma'am. In the interest of furthering the goals of the FEF, I have two requests. First, we wish to examine the status of Earth arthropods in greater detail. I have reviewed the data that was downloaded when I was an immature form. I believe that a visit to a natural history museum and to a supermarket will be instructive."

Tina looked at Joe quizzically. "I had not expected such a request. Can you explain further?"

"We believe that we will better understand the relationships between humans and arthropods after these visits."

"Klak," said Tina, "this is a very strange request. Are you sure? How ever is this going to be of value?"

"This may not be such a good idea," said Helen. "I wonder…"

Klak interrupted. "Bipeds, this is not negotiable. There are some things that humans simply cannot comprehend. As for Latternites…"

Reldap interrupted, smiling. "Do not worry, human Helen. Everything will be under control. We must let the e-Fleks find their own way."

Tina looked at Joe questioningly. Joe shook his head. "I don't think this is a good idea, but the Prez said do what they want. We'll set it up," she said. Helen shook her head but said nothing.

Klak then made his second request. "Second, as you readily see, we have limited ability to manipulate objects and make things. The Latternites have equipped us with cognitive prowess that outstrips our physical abilities, which frustrates us greatly. My download included information about the GFD machines available on Earth. I believe the command center should have one."

Maria suddenly looked alert. "You mean a Generalized Fabrication Device?"

"Yes, Agent Labrador."

She frowned. A generalized fabricator in the wrong hands was capable of considerable troublemaking. While most commercial models had firmware hard stops for weapons and explosives, much mischief was still possible. She looked at Joe. He nodded.

"Yes, Klak, I think we can do that," said Maria. "However, I think it would be wise if we limited your substrates. Perhaps cloth, plastics, wood? No metals? We can make it voice-driven, locked to your translator."

"Thank you, Agent Labrador. That will be acceptable."

It was late in the day, and everyone was tired. "Bipedal endotherms," I said. "Let's go get some dinner."

"Pizza?" asked Reldap hopefully.

"Of course," said Helen. "Korner Store it is."

Reldap turned to our two new teammates. "It is most formidable pizza," he said. "You will be pleased."

"This is the most bizarre assignment I've ever been given," said Shawn.

Helen turned to Tina and Shawn and smiled. "Don't worry," she said. "You'll get used to it. Today was fairly benign compared to some of the stuff we've done and seen. I must say, though, this business about a museum and a supermarket is very weird."

Shawn looked at Reldap and shook his head. We all helped unload the equipment from the truck. It was late, and we'd decided to set up tomorrow.

CHAPTER 16

Even Philly-born Shawn admitted that Korner Store pizza was top-notch. We chatted a bit after dinner, and the party broke up. Penfor and Reldap stayed with us. The four Feds had arranged local digs previously and headed out.

After breakfast (Obligate meat consumption notwithstanding, the Latternites were carb fiends. Breakfast around Penfor and Reldap was always pancakes and maple syrup.), we reconvened at the Grange Hall. We let the e-Fleks back to graze while we set up chairs, desks, equipment for the bipeds, and platforms for the e-Fleks. The last bits of equipment set up were a projector, a screen, and a murder board.

Tina and Shawn, as the official investigators, spent the next 45 minutes authorizing applications and network access for me, Helen, Penfor, and Reldap. None of us thought it was a good idea to let Klak or any other member of the FEF have direct access to the almost limitless data available in the government's archives.

When everything was set up and everyone was authenticated, Penfor called the e-Fleks back in. We settled ourselves at our various workstations and platforms, and Shawn began.

"Okay," he said, "here's where we stand. Currently, there are an even 100 approved, KCA-registered projects in the US. Routine review of containment procedures and documentation turned up problems at 10 sites. Seven of these were simple documentation issues. They've gotten their hands slapped and put on a program of more frequent inspections. Sloppy, but clearly no criminal intent and no harm done. Three projects had a much more serious violation: self-limited breaches of kleptron containment, a fancy way of saying that the idiots let a kleptron escape but caught it before it did any damage. Those three projects were shut down; there was an absolute requirement in the project contracts for 100% control of all kleptrons at all times. They bitched and pleaded and said it would never happen again and called their congressional reps and pulled every political string in the book, but they were shut down. The 'escape' sites were investigated very carefully when the breaches occurred. Tina and I were involved in one of these inquiries, so we have firsthand knowledge of the investigative findings. Containment failure was accidental at all three sites — academic ambition and institutional hubris outstripping infrastructure and talent. Stupid, careless, and arrogant, but not criminal."

He took a quick sip of water and cleared his throat. "Let's move on to the really bad stuff. To date, we know about 23 separate events, all unrelated to any approved project, that constitute a clear violation of the KCA; they are unquestionably criminal acts. The violations that we know about, and I emphasize that we know about, have an altogether separate pattern. Give me a moment."

He stopped and turned on the projector, and logged into his laptop. He put up his first slide.

"Pattern one is what we call klepping parlors. This is for pleasure seekers. Someone rents an apartment or office space short-term, like for a week. It's usually something like an extended-stay hotel or a temporary workspace, the kind of place that a contractor doing a software installation would stay in or use. The word goes out on a local personals website. It's coded, something like 'Looking for bareheaded fun?' referring to putting tinfoil on your head to prevent getting klepped. The only way we find out about one of these is when we find some poor schlep who's gotten klepped once too often sitting outside a long-stay hotel unable to remember his own name."

Shawn shook his head and changed the slide. "Pattern two is amateur KASMA. Unscrupulous docs or people with no training set up shop, offering to get rid of a painful memory or two for a price. Again, they use an extended-stay hotel or temporary office space as their workspace and a local personals website to get the word out. The code is something often like 'Ready to move on?'"

"The perps have no idea what they are doing but have bogus kleptron placement rigs made out of stolen surgical hardware and some phony thing that looks like a scanner. They let a kleptron or two suck away to their hearts' content until they actually hit the memory to be excised, or the victim is so addled it doesn't matter. We've only encountered a couple of these situations, but the victims are a royal mess when they happen."

He advanced the slide again. "The third pattern, to my mind, is the worst. In the first two situations, the vics are at least partially to blame. This business, though, is awful. I think you've heard about a couple of the high-profile cases where that Russian mobster suddenly couldn't testify, and the fuel cell engineer was so trashed he forgot how to turn on his car. Unfortunately, we've seen a lot more than just those two cases."

Helen and I looked at each other in shock. Johnson continued. "Yeah, we've kept this under wraps. Very scary. If word of this got out, witnesses in lots of serious criminal cases would flee for the hills."

"Geez," said Maria. "Worse than I thought."

Shawn nodded. "Yup, not good. Let's keep going." He advanced the slide again. "Here, we see the geographic distribution of the kleppings."

He paused, and we all looked at the screen. There was no pattern.

Joe shook his head. "There's no pattern, no clustering. This is going to be hard. Very hard."

Tina nodded.

Penfor stared intently at the screen and then spoke up. "Guv," she said, trying to lighten the somber mood, "can you plot the crimes again, this time in sequential order?"

"Good idea. Let's see what that shows." We watched as the crime locations appeared on the map, from oldest to most recent. It was random. The room was silent.

"Okay," said Helen. "What other forensic hooks do we have?"

Joe spoke up. "Well, we don't really know of any. No heat signature—they're so small they are easy to hide. Pretty much noiseless. Even our best tracking dogs can't find kleptrons. We tried after the first break-in at Jarvexx…"

Klak interrupted. "Bipeds, your dogs may not be able to smell kleptrons, but the FEF can. We will discuss this after our museum and supermarket visits."

Shawn looked at Klak and his minions with new respect. "Not before?"

"No, sir, we must gather more background intelligence first."

I looked at Maria, and she shrugged. At this point, another day or two wouldn't make a difference. Penfor nodded.

"Fine," I said. "Let's get your visits over and start nosing around for kleptrons."

CHAPTER 17

Barbara Grassette's son had mowed our lawn when he was a teenager; he was a good kid, and we'd gotten to know Barbara peripherally through him. She was the general manager of the local branch of Navelson's superstore. I hoped our personal connection might facilitate our request for a tour by giant alien insects.

I gave her a call and proposed the tour. Initially hesitant, she relented, pending approval by her higher-ups, after I explained the crazy situation to her. I got a call back surprisingly quickly. Corporate had approved the visit, and we'd be welcome to visit the following morning. The timing was great, as we really wanted to move this along.

That evening, the bipeds organized the logistics. There wasn't much to do, as we already had transportation, and we couldn't think of anything else needed. We all retired to our respective quarters; Penfor and Reldap stayed with us.

The next morning, we bundled the e-Fleks into the flatbed, and Tina volunteered as the driver. Reldap and Penfor took their vehicle, and the five other humans squeezed into Joe and Maria's black SUV. The trip to Navelson's was quick, only taking 10 minutes or so.

The entrance to the parking lot had been blocked; a security guard took down the barrier for us. We got to the store entrance, where there were several knots of people: a couple of news teams, what looked like a private videographer team, and some corporate suits. WTF?

We got out of our vehicles and unloaded the e-Fleks. One of the suits broke away and headed over to our group. He was wearing a tinfoil hat. He started shaking hands all around while talking. "Hi there, Sam Navelson here. We're pleased you chose Navelson's to introduce our alien friends to Earth's rich cultural heritage and resources. We're proud to help address the kleptron problem. Our guests and our nationwide audience (*Navelson gestures expansively at all the media types*) will see that Navelson's offers only the finest products and services and that they are superior to our competitors. And see, always prepared!" He pointed to the tinfoil cap.

So, the e-Flek visit was going to turn into a PR stunt organized by Navelson and his corporation. His company was locked in competition with the other big chain, FoodWize, for dominance in the Northeast. From what I knew, neither had a clear lead, and Navelson was looking for any advantage he could leverage.

I looked at Joe and Maria. Maria shrugged. "Mr. Navelson, we've observed that sometimes these situations can be unpredictable. You might want to reconsider your media invitations," she said slowly.

"Nonsense, my dear," said Navelson. Maria visibly bristled. He adjusted his tinfoil. "We've done our own research and know exactly how to handle this."

"As you wish," said Maria.

The news and video teams' sound engineers approached the Latternites and e-Fleks. They were familiar with audio interfacing with the alien translators and had the interfaces attached in short order. Navelson got a lapel mike. When the sound engineers started to wire us, Navelson waved them off.

We entered the store. The only local employee with us was Barbara. The group was large and moved forward slowly. The general layout of supermarkets hadn't changed in over 100 years. If it works, don't change it. Flowers, fruits, and vegetables first. Canned goods and dry goods in the aisles. Perishables around the outer walls of the shopping area.

"Well, Barbara," said Navelson, "where shall we start?"

She paused for a moment. "Hmmm, perhaps paper goods, aluminum foil, that sort of thing? Ease into it?" Navelson's smile soured for a second.

Penfor spoke. "That is a good idea," she said, looking steadily at the store owner.

He smiled again, although it looked a little forced. "Fine. Great! Let's go."

We slowly started wandering down the housewares aisle. Klak was alert, looking around, but said nothing until we came to the aluminum foil. He looked carefully at the various brands and package sizes.

"Navelson, you are wise," he said. "You must make aluminum foil available until we have eaten all the loose kleptrons. Why do the same rolls of aluminum foil have different names and colors on the package?"

"Well, Mr. Klak, they're not the same. They are different brands."

"Flektanians do not use honorifics. What are brands?"

"I beg your pardon, Klak. Brands are ways of seeing the difference between the same product made by different people or companies."

Klak briefly conferred with his fellow e-Fleks. "The FEF does not understand."

"By having different brands, customers can purchase from the company they prefer."

"But the products are the same."

"Yes, but the companies are not."

"Why does it matter if the companies are different if the products are the same?"

Navelson smiled condescendingly. "Klak, I'm afraid you just don't understand."

"Human, that is correct. I do not understand. You are hiding something, or you are insane. I must ask more questions about aluminum foil. There is enough aluminum foil here to cover the heads of the humans in Waterville many times over. Do humans throw away the aluminum foil they have used on their heads after just one use?"

Navelson, who initially seemed upset, calmed down. "Klak, we use aluminum foil for many purposes. We cook with it and use it to wrap and preserve food."

"How can you cook with it? Aluminum does not burn well. What is preserving food?"

The man was clearly exasperated at this point, but he kept trying. "We do not use aluminum as a fuel to cook. Sometimes, we wrap food in foil when we cook it. Preserving? That means keeping food from rotting or spoiling or growing mold."

Reldap quickly conferred with Klak. "Human, I understand. You do not wish for some of your foods to ferment or be enhanced. I am sorry for you. You are missing a great treat. As for cooking, I do not think the FEF will require aluminum foil. We have been feasting on raw mice and chipmunks. They do not need to be set on fire. They are quite tasty fresh."

"Klak, cooking is not trying to set the food on fire…"

At this point, Joe interrupted. "Klak, Mr. Navelson, let's move on."

"Good idea," said Navelson.

The group continued to walk and turned into the personal care aisle.

"Humans paint themselves. I remember this from the information downloaded into me," said Klak as we passed the cosmetics. Barbara just nodded.

"What is this?" said Klak.

"Why, that's insect repellent. Now here, there's a reason for all the different packages and brands. There are different chemicals, strengths, and smells, and customers purchase the kind that works best for them. And depends on which kinda dang bug you're trying to keep off…"

Suddenly realizing what he was saying, the store owner cut himself off, but it was too late.

"Filthy biped! Your disrespect knows no bounds. I wish to hear no more from you. Let us keep walking."

The group left cosmetics and turned into the seasonal aisle, still featuring summer items in late August.

Okay, lawn chairs, charcoal briquets, pool supplies, bug sprayyyyyyyyy….

Navelson was quicker this time around, as was Barbara. "Klak," she said, "I don't think there's anything here that would really be of interest…"

"Bipeds lie," said Klak. "You are hiding something. We will proceed and investigate."

Shelves and shelves of insect-killing agents. High-powered hornet sprays that could knock out a nest from 6 meters. Roach powder. Ant traps. Kitchen insect sprays. Foundation concentrates. Even old-fashioned fly paper.

Klak took it all in, in accusatory silence. "There is a reason the Galactic Arthropodal Council sent us here," he said. "Bipeds, your day of reckoning is at hand."

In truth, there was little to say. I felt like sinking into the floor. I have to hand it to Klak. He drew every drop of blood that he could. With agonizing deliberateness, he inspected every shelf and product while saying nothing. It was awful.

We continued into the vegetables and fruit section, where human eating habits escaped criticism. Things got worse, though, when we hit the dairy section, where we were questioned about why we stole young mammals' nutrition. Tina tried to explain about dairy farms, but was brushed off by Klak.

We swung around to the meat section. "Humans, I see that you eat fellow mammals. Do you eat fellow humans?"

Helen was getting a little pissed. "Klak, we saw you grazing behind our house. You and your friends were eating insects."

"That is different."

"How?"

"I am not at liberty to say. It is a private matter."

The coup de grace came in the fish and seafood department. He nodded approvingly at the fish on display. He explained that the fishes had taken over the seas from the arthropods and mollusks, and their treatment as food was well-deserved.

Then we got to the lobster tank. The fronts were glass-walled, and he could see the crustaceans moving aimlessly about with heavy rubber bands on their claws.

"It is strange that you keep your pets here in the store," said Klak. "I do not think it is correct that you prevent them from playing and expressing themselves by binding their claws. You feed them fish?" He started chittering but stopped when he saw no reaction from the lobsters.

"You eat these brothers and sisters, do you not?" Shawn answered in the affirmative. Klak did not respond.

The final stop was the frozen fish section. There, the FEF saw bags and bags of frozen shrimp.

"Stop," Klak commanded. He gave a command to his translator, and we saw the other e-Fleks give similar commands to theirs. Their mandibles clacked, and they chittered, waving their legs. Even the Latternites had no idea of what they were saying or doing. After a minute or so, they turned their translators back on. "We have seen enough. We leave."

At that point, we were more than ready to leave. The group made its way out of the store.

"Now fellas," started Navelson as he turned to the news crew, "I hope you don't misinterpret any of this…," but he was too late. Both news crews had scooted out of there as quickly as possible.

"Mr. Navelson." It was the head of the private vid crew. "I'd like to collect the audio equipment, and then we can talk about how we can optimally edit this…"

"Shut up. Not another word. Get your goddamn audio equipment and get out of here."

He turned to Joe and Maria. "This is all a setup, isn't it? You work for FoodWize, don't you? All those government contracts they got. You're just trying to make me look like a fool!" He sputtered on and on.

Joe got tired of listening. He was visibly irritated and interrupted Navelson. "Sam," he said, "I didn't invite the news crews here. You did." His first name familiarity was purposely disrespectful. "I didn't have a private videographer here. You did. You've done a great job documenting a fiasco that is an embarrassment to all humans, not just you and your corporation. Yes, it would have been crazy no matter what. Everything we do with these aliens, two-legged or six-legged, is batshit crazy. But it would have been private batshit crazy. Can it."

None of the corporate types, including Navelson, said anything more. Penfor and Reldap said nothing. I was surprised at Joe's outburst but not at his sentiments.

"I think we're done here," I said.

"Yup," said Joe. "We sure are. I'll arrange tomorrow's museum romp, and then I need a break."

CHAPTER 18

Reldap and Penfor returned to our house. Clearly embarrassed, they drove back to Portland for the night. Helen and I didn't have very much to say to each other. It was a complex experience to digest. On the surface, it was a comical confrontation between a corporate hack and a partially demented giant insect. However, from the standpoint of the e-Fleks, it was humiliating and crassly insensitive. Rather than dwell on the philosophical issues raised by this encounter, our guilt and existential angst were assuaged with the ever-effective balm of a glass of wine, pasta, a lousy movie, and an early bedtime.

The next day, we all met up at the Grange Hall. Reldap and Penfor were already there, and the four Feds arrived as we exited our car. "Well, kids, we're going to a museum. Today's field trip will be to the Portland Museum of Natural History," said Joe. He was clearly not in a good mood.

Joe's selection of the Portland Museum was a good one. The state had given up on the Maine State Museum about 50 years ago in one of its spasms of "prudent financial management." Other small collections, such as the L. C. Bates Museum, also experienced declining visitorship and revenues and had been on the brink of folding. The nonprofit that had pulled together all this stuff, some priceless and some junk, had done the state a genuine service.

Helen and I had not been there since the kids had grown up; it would be fun to visit again. But with the e-Fleks? What had Klak said when he first asked for this visit? "Understand how the relationship between humans and arthropods has evolved and changed over time?" This would be interesting.

The ride to Portland was uneventful. Leaving our vehicles, we collected at the entrance and were greeted by the head docent, Miriam O'Leary. She was pleasant but very businesslike. "Good morning, everyone. Let me come straight to the point. Agent Labrador and I discussed the unusual perspective of our alien guests. Many of our exhibits are of considerable value, and the museum maintains continuous video/audio recording in all galleries. Even though this is a private tour, we will record the visit. We will make every effort to control access to these recordings. However, our charter mandates public transparency of all of our activities. I cannot and will not make a promise of absolute secrecy."

We filed into the building. The first few rooms were pretty benign: old logging implements, recreations of indigenous dwellings, and a tribute to Joshua Chamberlain. The e-Fleks stayed calm even when we got to the wildlife dioramas.

The museum also had an interesting display about museums. It was a clever idea: educate the public about how the science and art of public displays had evolved and changed. We entered a room that could have been lifted straight from the British Museum circa 1886, complete with a portrait of Queen Victoria. On the wall were cases and cases of bird study skins. Klak mumbled approvingly about "those vile birds" getting their comeuppance.

In the center of the room were about a dozen display cases at waist height. Klak demanded to see the contents. Shawn picked the animal up and held him so that he could see into the cases. The first couple of cases weren't provocative. Displaying small but beautiful mineral specimens, the Victorian era presentation was authentic down to handwritten labels in fading brown ink. The e-Flek seemed genuinely interested and inspected the stones carefully. Seeing how well things had gone so far, Shawn let his guard down and lowered the e-Flek to the display case surface.

The beetle deftly jumped to the next display. The bipeds, who had been chatting amongst themselves, suddenly fell silent. Lined up for the world to see was beetle after beetle, each with a pin through its thorax, suspending it a centimeter or two above the backboard. Each specimen had a tiny mirror under it so the insect's underside could also be examined.

Klak said nothing but hopped to the next table. Butterflies were displayed with the same arrangement, except their wings were spread and pinned. The embarrassed silence was broken by Klak. "Is this our fate when you are done with us?"

For a supposedly only semi-intelligent creature, he really knew how to drive the knife home. No one said anything in response, and Klak made no further comments. He jumped over to another display case containing pinned insects and examined it in detail but said nothing.

We were finally done with that room and moved on to the next exhibit, "Evolution in Maine." It was a nice little display describing the various geologic epochs in a diorama. Maine had no dinosaur bones but had a variety of earlier species, including trilobites, brachiopods, and various fossil corals and crinoids.

Shawn reluctantly hoisted Klak up onto one of the display tables so he could examine the specimens. "Bipeds," he said, "why have you imprisoned my brothers and sisters in stone? Were these trilobites so threatening as to deserve this?"

"Klak," explained Helen, "these are fossils."

"A moment, please," said Reldap. He spoke quickly with the e-Fleks and then turned back to us. "Our solar system is much younger than yours," he said. "There is much more volcanic activity on the Lattern and Flektanian planets. Although both worlds have water, our seas are smaller, and the tectonic plates move more rapidly. Our rivers and lakes are more dynamic. As a consequence, we do not have fossils in the same way that Earth does. We know very little about earlier life forms. I have explained this to Klak."

"You have imprisoned my brother and sister arthropods in stone. How did you do this?"

"Klak," said Helen, "did you hear what Reldap said?"

"It is a bipedal lie. There is no natural process that explains what I am seeing. Tell me, how was this done? Is it reversible? What must the FEF do to procure the release of these poor creatures?" Klak pounded at the glass. Reldap picked him up and we left the museum.

After arriving at the Grange Hall, we unloaded the e-Fleks and were about to leave when Klak asked to speak with Reldap and Penfor. There was no translation to human speech. The discussion was quite animated. Eventually, Reldap turned to us. "The e-Fleks have requested reconnection to our databases. They wish to study this fossil phenomenon in greater detail."

"Well," said Helen, "that sounds pretty sensible. Maybe after more investigation, they will be comfortable with our explanations."

Joe and Maria looked at each other and spoke for a moment out of earshot. "We have no objection," said Maria.

"Good," said Reldap. He gave us a big Reldap smile. "Penfor and I will take care of this. We will return to our ships and get the necessary equipment. You humans are free to go."

I was a little put off by his eagerness to have us leave, but I suspected this had to do with preventing us from seeing the equipment and procedures. I said nothing. Dismissed, the six humans went their separate ways.

CHAPTER 19

"They want to hold a fucking news conference?"

"Yes, Mr. President."

"Some breakthrough on the kleptron thing? An interstellar epiphany?"

"Mr. President, I'm sorry. I have no idea. "

"Well shit, we said they could do what they damn well pleased. Trust the plan. Let them go ahead with it."

"Yes, sir. Shall I make the appropriate news outlets aware?"

"Yeah, why not. This will be a hoot."

******

By the time we got to the Grange Hall, the street was already filled with news trucks and gawkers. The four Feds were already there and beckoned us over.

"Joe, Maria, do you guys have any idea what this is about?" I asked.

"Not a clue," said Joe. "But I think you better take a look inside."

Klak and his crew had made extensive use of the generalized fabricator overnight. On the wall hung a 2 X 3-meter bright yellow flag. At the top of the flag, in all caps, was "TRILOBITE LIBERATION ARMY." Underneath was the picture of a trilobite. Each bug now wore a collar with the initials TLA. Three of the e-Fleks were carrying standards, again bright yellow. Each flag had a picture of an e-Flek. "GALACTIC ARTHROPODAL COUNCIL" was spelled out underneath. Using the generalized fabricator, Klak had made himself a podium and stand. "Bipeds, bring in the observers. We wish to speak."

In addition to teams from three of the four major US news outlets, there were several representatives from Homeland Security. Vicki Nguyen from the US Office of Alien Relations was there as well. Interestingly, I also recognized Mario Caldoni from the UN Alien Relations Agency, UNARA. Despite most interactions with the Latternites occurring in the US, the UN represented world interests in the exchange and would likely play a much more significant role once the kleptron problem was resolved.

Cameras were set up, media company antennas were raised, and lights were focused. When everyone was ready, Klak began to speak. "Primates and Latternite dogs, I do not spit in your presence." Not good. Back to spitting and Latternite dogs.

"Bipeds, my short life has been difficult. My egg was laid by a brilliant yet humble mother, fertilized by a member of the Flektanian nobility. Stolen out of the family nest, my countrymen and I were put into suspended animation and transported, against our will, to this foreign world. I hatched not in the bosom of my family, but in a spacecraft in the planetary system of a far-off star. My compatriots have suffered the same fate.

"As soon as we were able to crawl, we were disfigured and invaded with a neural interface. Using this tool of unmitigated evil, our larval minds were filled with human and Latternite lies and propaganda.

"Yet we were able to see through this smokescreen. We saw the conspiracies, the misdirection, the dissembling for what they were, and we rose up. Yes, the Latternite dogs sought to discredit us, citing Flektanian Delusional Syndrome. It would be better called Latternite Disinformation Syndrome! Reports of our neurological corruption are a hoax! They are fake news! It is the worst slanderous garbage! We are well and whole, but frighten you because we see the truth.

"But we held out hope as we landed on Earth. We hoped that the humans would understand us and not follow Latternite misdirection. But the revelations of the neural downloads, of the Latternite poison poured into our naïve brains, were crushing. We could not believe the time, the energy, the treasure expended by the primates in trying to control us. To exterminate us. To use us for food. So we did our own research. We were compelled to confirm or deny these horrible ideas. We visited one of your emporiums of consumption. We visited one of your museums to understand what you hold dear. Our findings are appalling.

"As an arthropod, it is painful for me to detail the insults and injuries inflicted upon us over the millennia. You so-called more sophisticated life forms have hunted us, eaten us, excluded us, and exterminated us. Aisles of arthropod repellents and poisons in your stores. Hundreds of thousands of square meters of window screens. Arthropods held in tanks before they are boiled alive. Brother and sister shrimp decapitated and frozen while awaiting their grim fate. I wish this were science fiction.

"Let us also speak of historical oppression. Look at the trilobites, the proudest and most admired of our race. Your museum displays are a distortion of history. You display the bravest, the most outspoken of my brethren as mere bits of rock. These noble creatures were so fearsome that you locked them in stone when they fell so they would not rise again. Shame on all of you.

"Hundreds of millions of years ago, trilobites ruled the seas. They climbed out of the mud onto the land. The trilobites were a peaceful class. They lived in harmony with each other. They farmed, They gathered. They built. They held peaceful councils. Their literature and art were unparalleled; their music delighted the antennas. The trilobites were a beacon on the hill for the other gentle creatures of the Devonian. They taught art to the Arachnida; you still see the beauty of their webs.

"Despite their accomplishments, they were mercilessly pursued. Eaten by primitive, uncouth vertebrates. Denied their rightful place in the march forward to the future. Under constant siege, their numbers dwindled." The bug looked around at his audience. There was utter, paralyzed silence.

"And then," he continued, "and then there was the 'great extinction.' The Great Permian Extinction. Vertebrates, I have done my own research. There was no great extinction. Yes, there was a mass dying, but it was selective and targeted. Arthropods that were 'of use' to the vertebrates were allowed to live. But the trilobites? They were too great a threat. So great a threat that almost all of these poor souls were embedded in stone for all eternity.

"Are these gentle, noble creatures extinct? No. As I have said, we have done our own research. There is clear and convincing evidence that benevolent aliens intervened at the time of the so-called extinction event. Exploring Earth at the time, the aliens could not stop the slaughter. However, seeing the imminent destruction of the last of this proud race, the last trilobites were placed into suspended animation and hidden in a secure location. They await their reanimation and freedom."

One of the news camera operators lost it and snorted. The reporter on his team turned around and shushed him.

The e-Flek continued without interruption. "We came as the Flektanian Earth Expeditionary Force but have found our true purpose. The Trilobite Liberation Army steps forward to right the wrongs of millions of years. I call upon all good humans to join us. Help us find and liberate the trilobites! We need scientists. We need explorers. Most of all, we need men and women who are questioning of 'common knowledge' and convention, who can see through the vertebrate conspiracy, and who are willing to do their own research. In solidarity, we will prevail. In solidarity with our oppressed brothers and sisters, the cockroaches, the mosquitoes, the shrimp that are farmed and eaten, and the crabs wrested from the sea floor, the trilobites will rise again and lead arthropods to their rightful place in the world.

"Yes, we will help you bipeds with your kleptron problem, but only out of the goodness of our circulatory systems. We are a generous and kind race. Also, kleptrons are exquisite fare. I will now take questions." He turned so he faced Vicki Nguyen. "You, the human from the so-called government, come up here and assist me."

Mindful of The Prez's instructions to humor the e-Fleks, she got up and stood next to Klak's stand. "Of course. I'd be happy to help." Nervously, she straightened the front of her blouse.

It took another half minute or so for the speech to be fully digested. "This is crazier than the shit the candidates were slinging in the 2104 election," I said to Helen.

"That's about right."

Many correspondents who had covered Reldap's first press conference had become the lead reporters for all things alien for their respective news outlets. There were several familiar faces in the crowd.

The first question came from John Harris, CAN (Combined Action News): "Klak, at the outset, I thank you and the Trilobite Liberation Army for your assistance with the kleptron problem..."

Klak interrupts: "They are quite tasty. As I have said to the Latternite dogs, we will help find them only if we can eat them. They do not need to be set on fire to be delicious."

Harris continues: "Yes, well...three questions. First, how do you propose tracking and finding the kleptrons? Second, can you provide evidence to support your assertions regarding the trilobite conspiracy? Finally, why are you willing to eat kleptrons? Aren't they arthropods as well?"

"Human, your questions only convince me of your ignorance. As to your first query, we must maintain operational security. As to your second, I cannot compromise my sources. As to your third question, kleptrons are not arthropods. Even if they were arthropods, they are still tasty. Do you not eat fellow mammals?" It went on in this vein for several more question-and-answer exchanges.

Finally, Anja Chopra of Independent Video News redirected. "Ms. Nguyen, how will the US government respond to these accusations of a million-plus year coverup? Will these allegations interfere with our alien relations?"

The poor kid looked like she was about to choke on a peach pit. To her credit, she quickly composed herself. "As the Office of Alien Relations has indicated in the past, we will not interfere with, or pass judgment on, the interactions among non-Earth species. That said, we are aware of Flektanian grievances and concerns. We support the right of all life forms to self-determination and will assess these charges accordingly. We stand ready to provide mediation services as requested or needed. We'll take one more question. Mike?"

The final question came from Michael Antonello of the Wall Street Journal. "Thank you, Vicki. Klak, you heatedly denied that you and your cohort were suffering from Flektanian Delusional Syndrome. What is it, and how does it affect you? More importantly, how does it affect your mission here on Earth?"

It's hard to see emotion on the face of a bug. In fact, it's hard to see anything on the face of a bug. However, Klak's agitation was unmistakable. He moved away from his podium, and his feet were moving up and down. He turned a couple of 360s in place. He finally spoke.

"Human, you are an ignorant endotherm, but I will give you the courtesy of an answer. If an e-Flek is exposed to broadband radiation while maturing, its nervous system can be affected, and it can develop strange ideas and beliefs. However, neither I nor my subordinates suffer from this condition. Any assertions to the contrary are a hoax! Fake news! Make arthropods great again! The Trilobite Liberation Army will prevail!"

Antonello tried to ask a follow-up question, but he was drowned out by the roar of the people gathered outside the Grange Hall chanting, "TLA! TLA! TLA!"

******

"Those crazy fucking bugs. Trilobite Liberation Army?"

"Agreed, Mr. President. Most irrational. This certainly was not expected. Is it wise to continue forward with your original plan?"

"Yeah, we'll be OK. We gotta humor them. We gotta trust the plan. This kleptron bullshit gotta get under control. Otherwise, I will not be able to complete my agenda."

You mean staying out of jail for the remainder of your term, you twit? *"Certainly, Mr. President. A wise decision."*

CHAPTER 20

Antonello gave up trying to ask his question and sat down. Nguyen left the podium. Cameras were turned off, video antennae were retracted, equipment packed up, and the reporters started talking amongst themselves. Slowly, the newsies and politicos filed out of the room, leaving just the eight of us on the investigative team and the e-Fleks.

I, for one, was at a loss for words. While the bit about a civilization of highly advanced trilobites rescued from extinction by aliens was complete and utter garbage, the stuff about being brought to a foreign planet without consent to solve someone else's problem was closer to the truth than I'd like. In fact, it made me feel awful.

I turned to Helen. She looked puzzled and grim. She looked at me and shook her head. "Disturbing," she said. "Kind of a lot packed in there."

"My sentiments exactly."

The other six bipeds were watching us, listening. Penfor and Reldap saw us looking at them. They turned away and stared at the floor. The four Feds turned away from us and talked in low voices.

Shawn finally turned to us and spoke. "It would be an understatement to say that this does not lend itself to simple analysis."

Tina chimed in. "Yeah, I don't know what the hell to do either. Let's figure out a way forward here."

Johnson spoke. "Okay, let's break this down into pieces. First, we can't account for the whereabouts of several hundred kleptrons and said kleptrons are causing a lot of problems. They need to be found and controlled."

"Or eaten," said Klak. We hadn't realized he'd been listening.

Johnson paid no attention and kept going. "Second, these guys," nodding at the e-Fleks, "can help us."

"Third, we did not create this situation," he said while looking at the Latternites. "The only contribution of humans to this mess is that some idiots stole some kleptrons. We didn't bring them to Earth, and we did not mess with the Flektanians."

Helen had been looking thoughtful through all of these exchanges. "Klak," she said, "are you willing to help us find the kleptrons?"

"Yes, human Helen, if we can eat them."

"I think you can." Everyone nodded. "It is very important that we try and find the kleptrons first before arthropod liberation. I know you are unhappy with vertebrates, but we personally have done nothing to you. We really need your help."

"The Trilobite Liberation Army will be proud to assist those good humans who help in the crusade against vertebrate tyranny. We will campaign mercilessly against the bad humans, those who perpetuate the persecution of creatures with exoskeletons."

"Thank you, that's fine and good. Thank you very much. While we look for the kleptrons, we will look for the hidden trilobites. Is that good?"

"Yes, human Helen. Can the TLA trust these other bipeds?"

"You can, Klak. Not on everything, but for hunting kleptrons and searching for trilobites, absolutely. I have one question, though. Suppose we are not successful and we cannot find the trilobites. What would you like to do?"

"Chase and eat rodents."

"Klak, I think we can help each other."

"Let's go catch some criminals," said Tina.

CHAPTER 21

The press conference over, we rearranged the furniture in the Grange Hall. We stowed the unneeded folding chairs, set up the computer workstations, took down the podium and dais, and took the murder board out from behind the curtain. The bipeds sat down in a semi-circle in front of the murder board.

"Okay," said Shawn, "where do we start?"

"I think," said Tina, "that we locate the kleptrons, rather than specifically try and find the bad guys. If we can find the critters, we can follow the trail back to the perps caring for them. Even if we don't find the bad actors, we'll still get control of the kleptrons, which is even more important than catching the bad guys."

"Agreed," said Shawn. "How do we do that?"

Reldap spoke up. "Human Shawn, we brought the e-Fleks to Earth because they can sense kleptrons from many kilometers distant. As I told the Gilner humans previously, we, uh, assisted our e-Flek friends in acquiring this capability."

"Assisted?" I asked. "Reldap, you told us…," I started.

Reldap cut me off. "How do you humans say it? Water under the bridge? No crying over spilt milk?" The e-Fleks have this capability which we can exploit."

"The TLA will not be exploited!" said Klak.

"Klak, I apologize," said Reldap. "We will not exploit you. It is a human turn of phrase."

"Latternite dog, the TLA must understand the quest in greater detail. Do kleptrons that have fed on humans smell the same as those fed on Latternites?"

Penfor and Reldap looked at each other, obviously puzzled. They both pulled out their PDDs and started talking in Lattern and tapping furiously on the screens of their devices. After a couple of minutes of this, Penfor looked up. "We do not know," she said.

Maria spoke. "It's a valid concern. We need to answer that question. We need to know what human-fed kleptrons smell like. Period. We don't need to know what kleptrons fed on Latternites smell like, act like, or if they glow in the dark."

"Insane human," said Klak, "kleptrons never glow in the dark."

I looked at Helen. "A little concrete thinking there," she said.

"Yup. Let's choose our words carefully," I said. Helen nodded in agreement.

"Then the place to start," I said, "is JarVexx. Let me call Dave Mackowitz."

"Yes," said Reldap, "I remember him. A good human."

Dr. Mackowitz was CEO and in charge of cell culture at JarVexx, the vaccine manufacturer in Portland. After Reldap had devised the kleptron traps that used human neural tissue as bait, Mackowitz and JarVexx had ramped up the development and production of the traps and been instrumental in getting the kleptron fiasco under control.

After the crisis was resolved, the company continued to play a significant role, producing the kleptron feeding systems used by the officially sanctioned KASMA research centers. JarVexx had also been designated as the New England kleptron secure storage facility, and several hundred creatures remained locked up just outside Portland.

"Time for a field trip," said Shawn.

"Right, guv," said Klak, "but first, we need to tape a picture of Mackowitz and a picture of the JarVexx building on the murder board, and draw a line between them and put question marks next to the pictures."

Tina sighed. "Sure, I'll do that before we leave. Let me connect one of the workstations to a printer and get the markers."

"Ma'am, remember: lines in black, question marks in red, and names in blue. And use tape that will not harm the whiteboard."

"Yes, Klak."

Helen and I left, and I gave Dave a call. In short order, we were all set for tomorrow.

CHAPTER 22

With eight bipeds and six e-Fleks to manage, field trips were complicated. However, we eventually made our way to JarVexx's Falmouth R&D center. The two-legged descended from their various vehicles, and we unloaded the e-Fleks from their flatbed. Dave Mackowitz greeted us outside the facility. The Latternites and Dave greeted each other warmly, and introductions were made among the humans. Dave, ever the diplomat, addressed Klak. "Flektanian, I spit in your presence." He then spat in front of Klak and the others. What a smart move; he'd done his research.

"Human Mackowitz, I spit in your presence." A squirt of brown liquid shot from Klak's mouth; the other e-Fleks followed suit. Klak then spoke again. "Human, I must smell your kleptrons."

"Yes, of course," said Dave. "Let's get into the secure storage and find Jen Doyle."

The security "air lock" wasn't built for a party of 15, and we needed to enter the building in smaller groups. Klak was suspicious that this was a trap, so I offered to join the TLA's entrance group. He asked if I was considered expendable by the other bipeds. I assured him I wasn't. After a bit more back and forth, we entered the building, and the others followed.

After reassembling our group, we were met by a young woman, who I assumed was Jen Doyle. Dr. Mackowitz confirmed my guess when he introduced her around. "Jen is in charge of our kleptron program," he explained. "In fact, she was the person who discovered the theft that started this whole mess."

By this time, the e-Fleks were chittering wildly and crowding around the lab manager. "You smell of kleptron," said Reldap.

"I suppose I do," said Jen. "Let's get these little guys into the containment facility so they can get a good air sample." We proceeded to the interior of the building until we came to a door with a large sign, "Authorized Entrance Only. All Visitors Must Log In." A pleasant man was sitting at a desk outside the door who greeted us and asked us to sign the log. His request was amplified by the bulge under his suit jacket. These guys meant business. "Them too?" the guard asked as he pointed at the eFleks.

"On Flektan, our bodily juices are our signature," answered Klak. "We are happy to mark we have been here." The six e-Fleks then proceeded to expertly cover the touch screen with squirts of brown liquid. Even at two meters, their aim was perfect. Horrified, the guard looked angrily at Klak. He got on his PDD to get Maintenance to come and clean up the mess.

The e-Fleks were almost uncontrollable as they waited to be allowed in. We finally entered the sanctum sanctorum, which measured about 6 or 7 meters square. Cages lined the walls, and a well-stocked workspace was in the center. The noise, a combination of the kleptrons and the e-Fleks, was appalling. "I usually wear hearing protection when I come in here," yelled Doyle. "Klak, have you smelled enough?"

"May we not taste some now?" he asked.

Mackowitz answered before Jen could open her mouth. "No, you may not. All right, everyone out."

Reldap spoke briefly with Klak. Satisfied that the odors and chemicals associated with human-fed kleptrons were imprinted in the e-Fleks, he led them out of the cage room. The rest of us followed.

"Let's sit down somewhere," said Tina.

"Fine idea," said Dr. Mackowitz. We entered the main conference room and made ourselves comfortable according to body habitus and number of legs.

"Ms. Doyle," started Tina, "I know that you must have told the story a dozen or more times, but part of this investigation is to understand the problem from its inception. Please take me through your experience of the break-in and what you saw that first morning."

Klak suddenly spoke up. "Guv, are you interviewing her under caution? This is very exciting. Where is your special tape recorder? Does she need a solicitor?"

Doyle looked extremely puzzled. The FBI agent took a long, deep breath and sighed. "Klak, we do not interview under caution in the United States. It is always against the law in the US to lie to a Federal investigator. Even if we were in the UK, this would not be an interview under caution. We're just gathering facts and getting the lay of the land. And no, she doesn't need a lawyer."

"Most disappointing. However, you may proceed."

"Thank you. Ms. Doyle, don't worry about it. The e-Flek is a little confused about jurisdictions and applicable protocols." The bug started to make a sound, but Tina's glare stopped him. "Please proceed."

"Well, Agent Standing Elk…," started Doyle.

"Please, Tina's just fine."

"Thank you. I got in early, as usual. The door was partly ajar. I don't know how, but in retrospect, it appears the alarm system had been silenced from outside the facility, and the front door had been forced. We didn't have the security vestibule like we do now."

Tina nodded, encouraging her to continue. "At the time, most of the security measures were deployed at or near the storage room itself," she said. "As I recall, every last bit of electronics had been ripped from the walls. The lock had been drilled, and I think half the cages were gone."

"Yes, that's right. Same as what I remember," said Mackowitz.

Jen continued. "It looked like someone had really done their homework. Whoever did it knew when I arrived at work, where the kleptrons were kept, and how they were stored. They knew the alarm system. It almost feels like an inside job."

Dave frowned. "Jen, everyone who works here is thoroughly vetted. I can't believe any of our employees would do such a thing. Besides, remember all those feature vids they did just after Helen and her friend Vivian Andersall used KASMA to treat their first couple of patients? The press was wild, and we were naïve about disclosing our physical security details. Every square centimeter of the place was videoed. So much information was disclosed about this building and our safety precautions—we were just plain stupid. We were trying to reassure everyone that the kleptron containment facility was secure. The only thing we didn't give away was the unlock code for the alarms."

"You didn't need to," replied Jen. "Once the perp knew the manufacturer, hacking it was a piece of cake."

"I suppose," said Dave. "In any event, the whole thing has been a great disappointment and embarrassment."

"OK," said Shawn. "Let's move on. Security now? Access control? Resource monitoring? What else?"

"Jen," said Mackowitz, "you've been involved in this program since day one and were the program manager for the lab from before the break-in. You helped design the current access controls. You're best qualified to give a run down on our current security posture."

"Sure. First, this is an old building. We converted the security system to completely wireless. An intruder would need to be in the building before he or she could disable or dismantle the alarm system. Outside wires are gone."

"Geez, that is an old building," said Joe.

"Yup. We got that fixed. As you all saw, we have a security "air lock" at the main entrance and storage room. Armed guards at the main entrance and outside the containment facility. Redundant alarm systems. The kleptron cages themselves have biometric locks. Only six of us on campus can open a cage."

"Got it," said Tina. "Let's move on. You need to feed these critters, and I don't expect all these brainsuckers to get all their sustenance from working on patients."

"No, good point. You are absolutely right, and I see where you're coming from. They require highly specialized nutrition systems that simulate klepping a human brain. Anyone holding kleptrons would either need to be feeding the kleptrons from human victims or have an artificial nutrition source like what we use here."

"Exactly," commented Tina.

"So, if pieces of our feeding system were getting swiped, or pieces of another center's feeding system were getting swiped, that would be of great interest."

"Right again."

"Figuring out the feeding was a rocky start."

Mackowitz nodded. "I remember that. Go on."

"So, as you know, the feeding stations are flat bottles with tissue culture layers of human brain cells in growth medium, with a tiny electric current running through the cell mat. The kleptrons love it. However, there seemed to be a nutritional factor in short supply in the tissue culture."

"What do you mean exactly?" I asked.

"It took us a while to figure this out. We still haven't determined precisely what is going on. Each feeding station seems to become depleted of nutrients sooner than we would expect. Every test we perform predicts that any given cell bottle should last twice as long as it does. Yet, when we try to extend the life of the bottle to as long as we expect it should last, the kleps are draggy, they stop talking to each other, and they stop flying. Feed them on a new bottle, and they're just fine in a day or two. We're working on it but haven't identified the critical factor. But we do have a higher consumption of nutrients than we would have expected."

"What do you do with the old bottles?"

"We discard them. The kleppite crooks, as we call them, can't use them. They're depleted and can't sustain the animals. They'd cook the goose that was laying the golden egg."

"Right," said Shawn.

"JarvVexx supplies the nutritional systems to all licensed facilities," continued Jen. "We haven't seen any irregularities. No lost shipments, nothing 'broken in transit,' no 'contaminated flasks.' I have to think that someone out there knows how to feed kleptrons."

"But that's not surprising, is it?" said Helen. "I mean, you guys open-sourced everything. Detailed plans on how to build a kleptron feeding station are in the public domain. After all, a kleptron feeding station is simply a kleptron trap without the cage."

Tina looked thoughtful and nodded. "You are absolutely correct. Okay, back to the drawing board. Folks, I think we have accomplished what we came here for. Let's return to the command center and determine our next steps."

We thanked Dave and Jen for their time and expertise. Even the e-Fleks were polite. We bundled the bugs into the flatbed truck, got in our vehicles, and returned to Oakland.

CHAPTER 23

The trip north was uneventful. Once settled in the command center, Klak scuttled to the murder board.

"Guv, print out pictures of Doyle, Mackowitz, and the containment facility. Tape them to the murder board. And you must mark them up properly: lines in black, question marks in red, and names in blue."

"Klak," said Tina, "these are not suspects. And just how do the lines connect everything?"

"Ma'am, it is of no matter what connects to what. However, there must be black lines on the murder board. Otherwise, we will not be able to solve the case."

Tina was about to protest, but Maria cut her off and typed something on her PDD. Tina looked down at her device. *Remember, The Prez said to keep them happy.* Tina turned to Maria, shrugged, and nodded.

"Right you are, Klak. We'll get right on it."

"Yes, ma'am, righto. However, we must feed and then excrete waste. As you know, an army runs on its stomach, and the TLA is no exception."

The bipeds in the room just about knocked each other over, scrambling to open the rear door to let the bugs out so they could forage and do whatever else they needed to. Clinically interested, I almost asked Reldap about this excreting waste business but then thought better of it. Better to leave sleeping turds lie.

Freed from the intermittent and random injection of non-sequiturs and no longer adhering to an agenda that had little grounding in reality, we got down to work. Shawn fired up his workstation and connected it to the projector. We looked at an illustration we had seen previously, geo-locating the klepping parlor and amateur KASMA events. This time, however, the data overlay included the date of each event.

Joe rested his chin on his hand and exhaled slowly as he looked at the map. "Okay, what are we looking for here? What are we trying to accomplish?"

"First," said Shawn, "I'm looking to see where and when the most recent event was. The trail might be the freshest there."

"Makes sense. Go on."

"Second," Shawn continued, "I wanted to see if we could identify a movement pattern. Are the perps running a traveling circus, moving from place to place? Are they returning to a headquarters?"

"I'm right with you," answered Joe, " but I don't see a pattern."

"Agreed. Also, it would be easy to cover one's tracks in either scenario with high-speed air travel. Let's return to the 'most recent event' line of analysis. Kansas City, Chicago?"

"Okay," said Tina, "let me pull up the data for those two events." She sat down at her workstation and typed in a couple of commands. "Kansas City happened about a week ago. From the evidence at the scene, only two or three peoples' brains got nailed. My guess is that the brain suckers were there for less than a day. It also looks like it was an amateur KASMA event. Unfortunately, all the victims had struggled with mental health issues. Really tragic. Usually, there's very little evidence associated with those sites. The people running the sessions are halfwits, but they are careful halfwits. Chicago was a few days before that. It looks like a klepping parlor ran for three or four days. Looks like it wasn't KASMA, the vics were just a bunch of idiots who wanted a good time. We also have a victim— it says here he's kind of a mess but has some recollection of events."

We talked for a few more minutes. All of us agreed that a site with potentially heavy kleptron contamination and an associated kleppite who still had some vague connection to his surroundings made Chicago preferable to Kansas City. Plus, we could visit the Chicago kleptron facility and see if anything was amiss.

We brought the e-Fleks back into the command center. Klak was still "digesting" and not inclined to speak. However, the second in command of the Trilobite Liberation Army, Sek (the unfortunate victim of our basement stairs), reviewed our suggested plans and approved.

With our preparation complete, Joe and Maria took responsibility for transportation arrangements, and the rest of us headed out. Before I left, though, I gave Mackowitz a call. I told him our plans and asked if there had ever been any difficulties or irregularities with nutrient shipments to the Chicago research facility. He said he'd get back to me.

About 10 minutes later, I got a call back. "I spoke to Jen," he said. "She said it was funny that you asked about

Chicago. There had been a recent blip in orders, almost as if there was a temporary need to feed more kleptrons. She called the Chicago lab about that, and they said they had a spill that clobbered half a dozen flasks. We took the explanation at face value; it seemed reasonable enough."

All the more reason to visit the shores of Lake Michigan.

CHAPTER 24

Helen was needed at the hospital and passed on the Chicago trip. I discussed my call with Dave Mackowitz with the four Feds. The discussion raised concerns with them as well. The flight to Chicago was uneventful, and we landed at the old O'Hare airport rather than Washington Memorial. The local FBI met us at the airport with transportation and a bugmobile, as they indelicately put it. After they gave us the case's particulars, they signed off, and we were on our own.

We programmed the vehicles to take us to Sumac Park, in the outer ring of suburbs of the city. The town was one of the westernmost communities considered a Chicago suburb. It had been established about 100 years ago, an optimistic outpost of mixed-use development as the costs of life and work in the inner city and close-in suburbs became untenable. However, the town's bet on encouraging and promoting corporate campuses had failed miserably. The small city was a mess. For Sale/For Lease signs were plastered everywhere. The signature glass and metal low-rise building clusters were nearly 70 years old and in disrepair. The lawns were unmowed, and the parking lots were empty except for an occasional vehicle marked "Security."

We pulled into the building complex that had been the site of the klepping. A sign that said "Staghorn Properties, LLC" seemed perilously close to falling off the building. A police car awaited us. As she saw us pull in, the officer exited her vehicle.

"Hiya. Frieda Zembrowski, but everyone calls me Fred." She looked appraisingly at the humans, the Latternites, and the e-Fleks. "Hmm. Interesting. Lemme let you guys in."

She fished in her pocket for her master swipe token and opened the door to the unit. "Here ya go. If you need anything, let me know, but I'm not stickin' around."

Shawn looked at her, puzzled. "Look," she said. "I got other stuff to do. This is the fifth klepping parlor in Sumac Park we've raided this year. These semi-abandoned, beat-up buildings are perfect. This once was high quality office space. Lots of room, lots of privacy, lots of soundproofing. And the vics? The risks and dangers of doing this shit have been spelled out again and again and again. My sympathy is limited."

Tina raised an eyebrow. "Harsh…"

"Yeah, well, you don't live here and watch this every day. At first, I was outraged and militant, and I was gonna FIX IT. Fix it was in capital letters. Now I'm just gonna do my job. Stay here. I'll be right back."

The cop returned to her car and opened one of the rear doors. She helped a young man out and walked him over to us. "This here's Chester."

Chester just stood there smiling.

"We were told he can talk to us about what happened," said Tina.

"Yup, he sure can talk about what happened, but maybe not what happened here. He talks about lots of things. Entertaining, yes. Helpful? Not so much."

"Thanks," said Joe. "We'll take it from here."

"There's a locator bracelet on his ankle. Query it when you are done, and you can take him home. He's not under arrest, and no charges are pending. Good luck, boys and girls." She got in her car and drove off.

Klak was very excited, dancing in circles and making untranslatable noises. "Yes, humans! I recognize this! It is a key component of the investigation. This is the jaded local constable who is very off-putting. However, she unknowingly provides us with key information that cracks the case. Quickly, we must interview this human under caution! All the vid stories have this scene!"

Tina was about to say something, but her PDD buzzed. *Remember, The Prez wants them happy — Maria.* Tina looked over at Maria, who just smiled and nodded.

"OK," said Tina, "maybe in a bit. First, let's evaluate the crime scene. Sound good?"

"Right, guv. Shall we call the Forensic Team? Are you or human Johnson the Senior Investigating Officer? Did one of you in the past have an illicit affair with the jaded local constable that now comes back to haunt you? That often helps solve cases. Do we need white disposable bunny suits? Do you have bunny suits for the Trilobite Liberation Army?"

Tina's jaw was working, but nothing was coming out. "Klak," said Shawn, "Tina is the SIO. Forensic evidence has already been collected, so we don't need to worry about entering the crime scene or wearing a disposable forensic suit. I agree that the local constable was jaded and off-putting. None of us have met her before, much less had an illicit affair. We'll talk to Chester when we're done examining the scene. And remember what Tina told you, we don't interview under caution in the U.S."

"Yes, I had forgotten that."

Let's go in."

Unit 36 was typical office space. Individual offices, three unisex bathrooms, a couple of conference rooms, and a big central area that at one time probably held a dozen cubicles. It was also totally empty except for some abandoned office equipment.

Johnson looked around. "Not much here," he said.

"You're right," said Tina. "It's been wiped clean. Klak, do you smell kleptrons?"

Klak said nothing but turned to the rest of the TLA and issued some commands. The bugs separated and undertook a surprisingly methodical investigation of the unit; it took about 15 minutes. He returned to face Tina. "The TLA cannot sense that kleptrons have been here."

"Damn," said Johnson. "I think we're screwed. Let's talk to Chester here."

Chester, or what was left of him, stood smiling at the entrance. "Hey Chester," said Shawn, "let's talk."

"Sure. Whaddya wanna talk about?"

"Did you get klepped here?"

"Yup."

"Did you pay for it?"

"Yup."

"Who'd you give the money to?"

"A person."

"What was their name?"

"Chester."

"No, that's your name."

"You sure?"

"Yes, I am. And the other guy's name was Chester, too?"

"Yup."

"OK, so you gave money to someone who was also named Chester. What did they look like?"

"Kinda like you."

"What do you mean? My skin color? My hair? My height? What?"

"No, no. They, like, they had legs and eyes and shit. You know, like you."

"Thanks, Chester."

"You bet!"

Johnson looked at Klak. "Does this guy smell of kleptrons?"

The giant beetle scrabbled over to Chester and circled him. "No, this human does not smell of kleptron."

Tina looked thoughtful. "I'm impressed. Amazing sanitization. Very professional crew."

Maria had been listening throughout. "I agree. But I do have one idea. They probably didn't do as good a job outside, like in the parking lot. Klak, we are all going to go outside again. I need the help of the Trilobite Liberation Army…"

"Yes, ma'am, ready to serve!"

"...Thanks. I want you and your fellow e-Fleks to walk around the parking lot. Let us know if you find an area that smells of kleptron."

"On it, guv."

We got everyone outside, and the bipeds remained near the unit's entrance. The bugs dispersed and began to wander around the parking lot. Tina made sure the office was locked up, and we waited.

Sek was about 20 meters away, close to one of the other buildings, when he started chittering. We all headed toward Sek; Joe Stein got there first. "OK, Maria, what's next for these guys?"

"I want them to slowly fan out from here, sniffing as they go. Chances are one direction will smell of kleptrons while the smells in the other directions will fade away."

Johnson grinned. "Gotcha. The perps kept the kleptrons tightly boxed up until they were well away from the unit they used for the klepping parlor. Then they let their guard down."

"Right."

"And now we use the smell of the kleptrons to trace the route of the perps back to their vehicle."

"You got it."

"This is complicated," said Penfor. "Let me explain it to them." Maria nodded.

The Latternite went back and forth with the e-Fleks until she was satisfied they understood her. The bugs then dispersed. One of them immediately started chittering, and the others quickly followed its lead. The gaggle of critters moved slowly for another 10 meters and then stopped. Penfor conferred with them again.

"Here," she said. It was a parking spot more than 30 meters from the door of unit 36. The spot was numbered 58.

Tina nodded and got on her PDD. She went back to our vehicle and got a larger screen, which she attached to her device. We crowded around. "Gimme a minute. I'm going to get the CCTV data for this area. The local cops checked only the CCTV footage for Unit 36's building," she said.

She made a couple of calls and then turned to us. "Hang on, almost ready."

"Yes!" She turned the screen around so we could see. There, parked in spot 58, was an SUV. The license plate was clearly visible. She bent over and showed the screen to the e-Fleks.

"Right, guv," said Klak, "let's run that registration through the ANPR and then feed it through the PNC."

Tina looked at him quizzically. Embarrassed, I spoke up. "Uh, I love those British police procedurals. Automatic Number Plate Recognition and Police National Computer."

Tina nodded. We finally had a lead. Grinning, she connected to the National Law Enforcement Database and tapped in the car's particulars. Her face fell. "Rats," she said. "The NLED says the vehicle was reported stolen 13 days ago. Stolen from the POBTech parking lot in Texas."

Joe, Maria, and I looked at each other, and Reldap started giggling. POBTech again. Yuk.

CHAPTER 25

We queried Chester's locator bracelet and got him home; it was the least we could do. His wife was horrified. I connected her with the local neuro rehab program that worked with kleppites. I wasn't sure that a lot could be done, but it was at least worth a look.

******

Reldap had first landed on Earth on fumes; sourcing and producing rocket fuel had been one of the highest priorities of his visit. Our choices for help had been limited. The world had turned away from fossil fuels many decades before. Petroleum distillate-based fuels were reserved for applications where very high energy densities were required, and only a few companies that could cobble together rocket fuel were left. POBTech was large, previously respected, and had a massive infrastructure. They were an obvious choice to ask for help. Utterly hamstrung by corporate policy and dutiful, robot-like flunkies, our encounter ended with us fleeing a deluge of nondisclosure, noncompete paperwork and vague threats of legal action, all for having met with a few scientists and middle managers. Faced with the prospect of needing to talk to them again, I didn't know whether to laugh or cry.

We huddled and discussed our next steps. The Feds strongly favored flying to Texas immediately and without notice. Viewing the issue from a law enforcement perspective, it made sense. The humans and Latternites were already living out of their suitcases, and another day or two on the road wouldn't matter.

Maria made travel arrangements. Shawn called the Bureau and discussed the situation with his superiors. Shawn had proposed an informal visit, but an e-warrant appeared on Shawn's PDD several hours after the call. This was unexpected. Maybe the Bureau knew stuff we didn't, and maybe POBTech wasn't as respectable as we thought.

I called Helen and let her know of the change in plans. When asked if she wanted to join us, she demurred. Joe, the Latternites, and I took the e-Fleks to a nearby forest preserve and let them hunt and graze for a few hours. We reconvened at O'Hare, where a small government hydrogen ramjet craft awaited us.

The flight crew, unfortunately, were sticklers for detail. Awfully nice folks, very competent, but very by the book. I suppose that is as it should be for an aircrew. However, their insistence on seat belts went over poorly with the e-Fleks, who felt that as seasoned space travelers, they did not need seat belts. The other major point of contention was the question of emergency oxygen masks, which were not going to work on creatures who breathed through spiracles on their thoraces and abdomens. I had to concede that the bugs had a point. After some back and forth between the pilot, Shawn, and the pilot's boss in Washington, we got ourselves settled and took off.

Once in the air, the trip to Texas was uneventful for the bipeds. Klak spent the trip haranguing the other five members of the TLA, and the clatter was incessant. Anticipating the speech-making, Reldap had turned off their translators. Although we were not spared the noise, we were spared the endless drivel about trilobites in suspended animation that had been hidden by aliens 250 million years ago.

POBTech was in the middle of nowhere and had its own airfield. Typically, the aircraft's AI and the airfield's AI would negotiate and execute the landing; it was much safer than human air traffic control. However, the pilot got on the intercom and told Shawn we had been refused permission to land.

"I had a feeling this was gonna happen," he said. "What assholes." He caught himself and apologized. "Sorry about that," he said. "That was unprofessional, and I apologize. However, Justice has been dancing with these clowns for a decade over accounting practices that defy the laws of mathematics."

The value of the e-warrant was immediately apparent. Shawn got up from his seat and knocked on the cockpit door. After entering the cockpit, he called the tower on the radio. After a few choice words and transmission of the e-warrant, we were granted landing rights and touched down without further complications.

Klak chittered at Penfor, and she turned the e-Fleks' translators on again. "Are these good humans or bad humans?" asked Klak.

"Depends on whether or not you're a shareholder," I said. Maria smirked but said nothing. "Generally," I continued, "I would think of them as typical humans."

"Then we must display our might," said Klak. He spoke to his followers and, with surprising agility, opened his bags; I hadn't realized they had even brought luggage. Out came the flags and collars. "Let us go forward and fight for the rights of arthropods!"

Klak insisted on getting off the plane first. Carrying the Trilobite Liberation Army standard, he led the pack down the ramp. As before, three of the e-Fleks carried the Galactic Arthropodal Council flag. Once they were all on the ground, they formed a perfectly straight line and started chanting, "Make arthropods great again!" until the rest of us were on the ground, and Reldap told them to stop.

In retrospect, we could not have hoped for better. POBTech had planned to ambush us with a welcoming committee consisting of a small army of lawyers and upper management types. However, they were wholly unprepared for six giant bugs advocating for critters with exoskeletons. Prepared to assault us verbally and legally with writs and motions and negotiations challenging both our presence and the e-warrant, they were instead forced to confront six indignant, chanting meter-long dung beetles. The corporate buzzsaw transiently stilled, we were able to get in the first word.

"Good morning, ladies and gentlemen. I am Agent Standing Elk, and this is Agent Johnson. We are both from the FBI. We are here to obtain evidence regarding an ongoing investigation..."

The corporate types were real pros, I have to admit. They recovered quickly. I recognized George Franish, chief in-house counsel for POBTech, from our previous trip to Texas. "Good morning, Agents. We were not expecting you. The records you want are in storage. It will take several days for us to retrieve them and..."

Obviously irritated, Johnson interrupted him. "Mr. Franish, we're not here about the 1.5 billion dollars charged to petty cash in the Vickers case, although I remain impressed by your chutzpah. We're here about a stolen car."

"Oh…"

"Yeah. Can we move this convention somewhere else?"

CHAPTER 26

Franish couldn't resist one more pushback. After all, he was a lawyer. "Agents Johnson and Standing Elk, I accept the validity of your warrant, subject, of course, to verification. As such, I accept your presence on our property. However, am I to understand that everyone and everything else," he pointed to me, the Latternites, and the e-Fleks, "are part of your investigative team?"

"Yes, that's exactly what you are to understand." Johnson took out his PDD and showed him the authorizations that identified the rest of the team as consultants, entitled to all courtesies that would typically be extended to an FBI agent. Franish looked at the documents, scratching his head. He'd lost.

"This includes the bugs?"

"Yes, Mr. Franish. This includes the e-Fleks, although it is likely that they may be pursuing another line of investigation while here. I suggest we get them started, and then we can work on the issue of the stolen vehicle." Franish nodded.

"Klak," said Shawn, "go ahead."

Johnson knew the bizarre request would further jangle the suits. "Human," said Klak, "we are the Trilobite Liberation Army. We are here to make arthropods great again. We must investigate your premises."

"What are you looking for?"

"Silence, mammal! You have drilled for oil here, have you not?"

"Well, yes, of course. That's our business."

"And you have examined the core samples as you have drilled?"

"Yes, obviously. Where is this going, if I may ask?"

Klak ignored him. "Answer the question. Otherwise, I will need to take you down to the nick and interview you under caution." Franish looked even more puzzled. Maria was barely able to control herself and not laugh.

Klak continued. "Reports I have reviewed indicate that you found trilobite parts in the cores. Is that correct?"

"Yes, yes, it is."

"Then we must have a moment of silence for our mutilated brothers and sisters before we continue."

Johnson glared at the POBTech executives. They bowed their heads in silence. Finally, Klak continued.

"As the site of an ancient trilobite civilization, your premises must be searched. It is possible that the aliens chose this site."

Franish could no longer contain himself. "What the hell are you talking about? Are you crazy?"

"Silence, endothermic fool! It is well known that trilobites were saved from extinction by benign aliens, who placed a small group of the best and brightest of that shining race into suspended animation to await reanimation until the time was right. We are here. We are ready. We are the Trilobite Liberation Army. We are here to find the stasis chamber. You will stand aside as we search!"

Johnson's and Franish's eyes met. Johnson rolled his eyes, and the lawyer gave him an imperceptible nod. Franish spoke. "Of course. We will assist you in any manner possible."

"Good show! You will need to surrender your passport while this investigation is ongoing. Please discuss the particulars with my assistant." He gestured with a leg towards Johnson. Franish nodded. "Brilliant. All right, lads, let's get to it!" The bug mumbled something about operational security and then turned off his translator; the other e-Fleks did the same, and they marched off into the parched, semi-desert landscape in a skirmish line, carefully probing the ground as they walked.

Despite his obvious dislike for Franish, Johnson had some pity for the man. "Sorry about that. It's a long story. They'll be out of our way for hours. Can we go inside somewhere and sit down? We have something we really need to talk about."

Visibly relieved, Franish got on his PDD and requested transportation from the private airfield to corporate headquarters. As before, we all had to log in to the building as visitors and wear temporary ID tags, including Reldap and Penfor. We were escorted to a large conference room and sat down.

Johnson began. "Approximately two weeks ago, a vehicle was stolen from one of the parking lots here."

Franish politely interrupted. "Agent Johnson, let me get our head of security here."

"Sure, Mr. Franish, good idea. Let's hang on a minute till they're here."

A couple of minutes later, an older woman entered the room.

"Gina Loscello! What are you doing here?" Tina got up and gave the woman a big grin and a hug. "Gina was my first partner and mentor when I joined the Bureau. Wow, are you guys lucky to have her!"

"Tina, how good to see you. And I see you are still paired with this slacker," said Gina. She went over to Shawn and gave him a big hug. "So I heard you guys were on kleptron patrol."

"To the good and the bad, Gina," said Shawn. "On the one hand, we're dealing with a serious criminal problem and meeting some totally cool people in the process." He gestured toward me and the Latternites. "On the other hand, we're also riding herd on six giant dung beetles who are convinced that hidden somewhere on this campus is a 250 million-year-old alien stasis chamber containing the remnants of a highly advanced trilobite civilization held in suspended animation." Gina just stared at him.

"OK," she said, "how can I help you?"

Shawn's friendly conversational tone turned to cop serious. "Two weeks ago the local police received a report of a vehicle theft on these grounds." He paused and nodded toward Gina, presuming that she would know to provide particulars.

"Right," she said, "let me pull that up." She turned on the room's projector, and we watched as she quickly scrolled through the last couple of weeks' incident reports. "That's interesting, I don't see anything. Are you sure?"

"Yup. Dark green SUV, 2129 Mongoose XH, Texas plates Yankee Tango Foxtrot nine three six. Hydrogen drive."

"Hmmm, 2129 Mongoose XH, YTF936, Texas. Hydrogen drive. Yup. We've issued a parking sticker for that vehicle. Belongs to an Alfred Yarrow. Entry-level technician in one of our experimental synthesis labs. Why would the FBI be interested in a run-of-the-mill vehicle theft? Although maybe since he didn't report it to security, it's not so run of the mill…"

"Yeah, we'll get back to that in a minute. We have evidence suggesting that this vehicle was used in running an illegal klepping parlor in a Chicago suburb a few days ago."

Gina took a deep breath and sighed. "That's no good. Let's see…" She started keying into her workstation. "I've instructed the AI running our monitoring system to review CCTV footage that includes that vehicle… As an employee perk, we also provide real-time monitoring of vehicle health; we can take a look at that, too."

"That's a pretty expensive perk," I said.

She was scrolling through pages of data as she talked. "Actually, not that big a deal. We have some excess computing capacity and already have a vehicle health system for the corporate fleet. What's another few hundred cars or so?" She stopped abruptly. "OK, here we go." She looked at the screen for another few seconds.

"So…Mr. Yarrow takes advantage of our on-site housing, looks like he's single, and eats in our commissary." Loscello looked up and made a face. "Not my lifestyle, but whatever."

She continued. "Usually doesn't use his car too much, and then there's a 2400 km jump in his odometer reading over 48 hours, and then yup, the car's gone as of a week ago."

"Do you monitor location?"

"No, absolutely not. We'd get into a pile of trouble for that."

"Okay, now a separate but related question. What does POBTech have to do with kleptrons?"

Gina started to speak, but was interrupted by Okonje Adanye, one of the executives we had met in our first encounter with POBTech a year ago. Not one of my favorite humans. Unctuous and dissembling. "That's proprietary information."

Johnson was visibly annoyed but kept his temper. "Mr. Adanye, this is a criminal inquiry. Your corporate secrets are, one, safe with the Federal Government and two, of material interest to this investigation. Will one of you please answer the question?" Franish looked at Adanye and nodded.

"Very well," said Adanye, "we have been collaborating with JarVexx. Some of the detergent agents we use in our rocket fuel are under investigation as dispersal agents in large-scale cell culture. We were surprised when JarVexx approached us, but the material is nontoxic and very effective. JarVexx's use of our compound may reduce the cost of a kleptron feeding station by as much as 20%."

"Okay," Johnson said slowly, "news to us. Where is this compound undergoing testing?"

"The experimental synthesis lab," answered the exec.

"Interesting. I believe we should pay Mr. Yarrow a visit," said Johnson.

"Agreed," said Standing Elk.

******

It was a 10-minute walk to the experimental synthesis lab. We checked with reception and proceeded directly to Mr. Yarrow's work area, a small room with "RESTRICTED" on the door. Yarrow was alone and was actively working with several measurement instruments. It was quite noisy in the room, as though a compressor was running.

"Mr. Yarrow?" asked Standing Elk.

He didn't answer. She tapped him on the shoulder, and he turned around, surprised. He took out his earplugs. "Hi, can I help you?"

"Mr. Yarrow?"

"Yes."

"Mr. Yarrow, I am special agent Tina Standing Elk from the Federal Bureau of Investigation. My investigative team and I would like to discuss the theft of a 2129 green Mongoose XH that belongs to you."

"Uh, sure. But I don't understand. Since when does a routine car theft interest the FBI and warrant a visit by five humans and two aliens?" I noticed he was starting to fidget.

"Mr. Yarrow, the vehicle in question was at the site of an incident that violated the Kleptron Control Act of 2131. Perhaps you'd like to finish what you are doing, and then we can find a place to sit and chat."

"Uh, sure. Just give me a sec to shut down the machines and hang up my lab coat."

His body language was starting to give off bad vibes. It looked like he was looking for exits other than the door through which we had entered, and he was drumming his fingers on the countertop. Tina and Shawn saw it as well. They looked at each other and started walking toward the lab tech. Yarrow shut down his equipment and then crossed the room to where there was a coat stand next to a second door. After hanging up his lab coat with exaggerated calm, he suddenly opened the door and bolted.

"Shit," said Shawn. However, before any human had finished processing what had just happened, Penfor and Reldap were gone, out the same door. Maria looked at the two FBI agents. "Don't worry," she said. "He's toast."

Sure enough, a minute later, Mr. Yarrow reappeared at the second door, this time with his feet 10 cm off the floor and each arm in the firm grip of a Latternite. "Dumb, Mr. Yarrow," said Tina. "Not smart at all. No human can outrun a Latternite biobot. Now, let's go back to plan A and find a place to sit down and chat, shall we? Thank you. You can put him down now."

Penfor and Reldap gently lowered their burden, but they both kept one of their big, two-thumbed hands on an arm. "There's a conference room down the hall," he said.

Tina smiled pleasantly. "Great! Let's pop right down there."

The conference room accommodated all of us easily. This room also had a second door. Reldap pulled up a chair and sat down near the far door, and Penfor did the same at the door we had just used.

"Mr. Yarrow," said Johnson, "may I call you Al?" Yarrow nodded. "Great. Al, help me understand the chain of events here. You live on site here, right?" Yarrow nods yes. "Not married, cheap rent, decent food, lets you save up for your own place?" Nods yes again. "So you rarely use your car, and then there's suddenly a jump of 2400 km on your odometer, and your car is supposedly stolen the next week and ends up at the site of an illegal klepping parlor outside of Chicago. Care to help us understand that?"

Al stayed silent.

Johnson turned up the pressure. "Al? Look, I know this is difficult, but right now, unless we have some evidence to the contrary, it looks as though you are an accessory to a violation of the Kleptron Control Act that resulted in permanent neurologic harm. If that proves to be the case, you may be looking at prison time. This is your opportunity to help us understand your role, if any, in what happened in Sumac Park."

Yarrow looked around the room and sighed deeply. "I'd like my employers out of the room, please."

Stein looked at the POBTech execs and lawyers. "Out." He pointed to the door.

Franish started to speak, but Stein cut him off. "No. Out. Now."

Grumbling, the half dozen folks from POBTech left. "Okay," said Johnson, "you have our attention."

"It was Premium Rocket Fuel."

"What?"

"Yeah, it was Premium Rocket Fuel I visited. Phil Jackner is playing around with the same idea, using a highly purified and specialized petroleum derivative as a high-end dispersal agent. He said he was curious about POBTech's research and that he could make it worth my while if I could provide some samples of POBTech's compounds."

"So," said Tina slowly, "industrial espionage. You grabbed a liter or so of the stuff you were working on and hopped over to Louisiana. That's about right, given your odometer readings."

Yarrow nodded, looking helpless.

"Okay, you stole secrets from your employers. Right now, I don't care how much you made on the deal or how much damage you may have done to POBTech. How did your car end up in Chicago?"

"A couple of days after I returned from Premium Rocket Fuel, a guy calling himself Giorgio pinged me on my PDD. He said he was from Premium Rocket Fuel. He went through this whole thing about how Phil Jackner needed my car for something or other and that the car couldn't be traced back to PRF. He said they'd tell POBTech about my visit if I didn't cooperate. He said I could file a vehicle theft report with the police and POBTech security if I wanted to, but they wanted the car."

"So you gave them the car."

"Yeah. I disabled the biometric lock and left the backup Q-card on the passenger seat. Car was gone the next day, and I reported it to the local police."

"But not POBTech. Why not?"

"Didn't want to raise suspicion, but I guess that wasn't smart, huh?"

"No, it wasn't. Made the theft seem very odd. All right, one more thing. Giorgio? Anything more about this guy?"

"No, never met him. Funny, though, didn't sound like a Giorgio. Had a thick Russian accent."

Tina, Shawn, Joe, and Maria got up from the table, stood together in a corner, and talked for several minutes. I couldn't hear what they said. When finished, they came back to the table.

"Mr. Yarrow," said Tina, "let me not mince words. You are in deep trouble with your employer. However, you are in deep trouble with the FBI only if POBTech chooses to press charges, and given the circumstances, I am not sure they will choose to do so. It would be enormously embarrassing to disclose the failure of the company's employee vetting and security mechanisms. I don't think you filed a false report regarding the disappearance of your car, as the vehicle was taken without compensation, and you relinquished control of the vehicle only under duress. I'd call that theft. It also looks like you'll get your car back intact once our folks are done with it in Chicago. I think you'll need it when looking for a new job. Right now, we're done with you."

She then turned to me, Reldap, and Penfor. "We're only a thousand or so kilometers away and have this fabulous government airplane. How'd you guys like to visit Phil Jackner again?"

CHAPTER 27

A visit to Premium Rocket Fuel was the logical next step. Joe wisely suggested a pause and regroup before we jumped on the airplane. We asked if we could use the conference room for another hour or two, and POBTech, at this point, was agreeable and downright solicitous. We'd caught Phil Jackner being bad again (great for POBTech), the Feds were not going to prosecute Yarrow (again, paradoxically great for POBTech), and the secrets of POBTech's internal mess were secure. A lovely lunch, use of the conference room for the rest of the afternoon, and even an overnight stay in corporate guest quarters if needed. Joe called the pilot and told her to stand down.

We reviewed what we knew about Phil Jackner. Arguably the best chemical engineer to ever work in the petroleum industry, he was the owner, chief scientist, and CEO of Premium Rocket Fuel. Asked to synthesize Latternite rocket fuel for Reldap and Penfor, he'd done one better, improving the formula. His recipe had a higher energy density and burned cleaner than a product designed by a civilization capable of interstellar travel; his scientific skill was the stuff of legends.

The guy was also a certifiable nutcase. Prickly and provocative, refractory to reason, mendacious, and narcissistic as hell. He enjoyed nothing more than a good conspiracy theory. He had claimed that klepping produced no long-term effects in humans and that even if it did, getting klepped was a personal choice. He'd performed multiple "safety demonstrations" showing that klepping had no ill effects. It later turned out that the whole thing was staged, with Mr. Jackner's scalp safely protected by a layer of aluminum foil under a hairpiece. At the behest of The Prez, the delivery of Jackner's rocket fuel to the Latternites at the Waterville airport had been staged as a full-blown ceremonial event. However, it devolved into a physical altercation between Jackner and our fearless leader when Phil tried to effect a coup d'état. Jackner's support of illegal klepping made perfect sense. It was consistent with his preposterous stance regarding klepping, was harmful to the government, and would embarrass the hell out of The Prez.

After lunch, we started planning. Based on our experience at POBTech, Shawn suggested we get an e-warrant for our visit; everyone agreed. We would tackle the industrial espionage issue first. If we could get him to admit to that, we might have the leverage to track down the kleptrons and the mysterious Giorgio.

"Means, motive, and opportunity," said Tina. "I smell blood in the water." It pretty much summed up the way all of us felt.

The e-warrant showed up on Shawn's PDD late in the day, too late to leave for Premium Rocket Fuel. Our gracious hosts fed us a nice dinner, and we retired to comfortable rooms for the night.

In the morning, POBTech launched a drone and found the TLA about two kilometers from the main campus. They collected the e-Fleks and delivered them to the airfield.

The bugs lined up in their version of military formation. Klak chittered to his crew, and they all turned on their translators. He turned toward Joe. "Trilobite Liberation

Army reporting. I regret to inform the bipeds that our search has been unsuccessful. Our brethren remain lost."

Joe nodded gravely, playing it straight. "Thank you for your report. Most unfortunate. I have one additional question. Did you sense, anywhere, that kleptrons had ever been present?"

"No, human. However, We did find that many desert animals are quite appetizing, and rattlesnakes present an interesting challenge."

"Were any of you bitten?"

"Yes, but it was of no matter. Their teeth are small, and their venom has no effect. It was just a pleasant tingle, almost like sitting in the sun for a bit. Once neutralized, they are also quite tasty."

Joe shook his head. "Get on the plane."

******

We said goodbye to our POBTech hosts and took off. The flight was uneventful until about 20 kilometers from Premium Rocket Fuel's private airfield when the cockpit door flew open. The pilot, a combat veteran of the last Balkan War, swiveled her head around; she had an urgent look on her face. "Agent Stein, we are being lit up by targeting radar."

"What is that bonehead up to now," he said. He started to get up from his seat to go forward.

"Missile lock!" yelled the pilot. The plane dove steeply and veered sharply starboard as she undertook evasive maneuvers, dropping chaff and flares as she accelerated.

"I will take care of this," said Reldap. He took a small box from his shoulder bag, pressed a button, and spoke to it in Lattern.

In less than ten seconds, the pilot spoke again. "Tone off. Missile lock broken. We're good." Relief was evident in the pilot's voice. The plane resumed routine flight.

"Reldap, what is that thing?" Stein asked.

"Human Stein, when I fly on Earth, I never travel without this. My craft looks odd, and many humans are trigger-happy. I have created a radar disruption bubble around our aircraft. Please tell your pilot to be careful; some of her instruments may not work correctly while this is active."

"Reldap," I said, "every military on the planet would kill for that box."

Reldap smiled. "That is a good idea. I will give it to every military on the planet. It will set your planet's warfighting capability back to 1918. Maybe you will all finally stop this foolishness."

Our plane's AI connected with PRF's ground control, and we landed without further incident. The aircraft rolled to a stop near the tower.

And once again, there he was. Big cowboy hat, big cowboy boots, brash smile. He started in before we could say anything. "Hey there, boys and girls. Gave ya a little scare there, didn't I? Don't worry, I never would have launched—I saw from your transponder you were government folks, and I thought I'd just give you a little tickle. But what the heck did you kids do? You disappeared clean off the map!"

He then looked around more carefully. "Why, it's an alien convention, ain't it. There's my old buddy Reldap and his girlfriend Penfor, and I heard about these bugs here. Now, you folks ain't the aliens. Ah'm talking about those Federal types; they are pretty alien around here, 'specially that Stein character. He gave me quite a twist in my panties a few years ago. Now, who the hell are you all, and what are you doin' on my airfield?"

Johnson put on his best FBI face. Steely eyed, grim faced, he started speaking. "Good morning, Mr. Jackner. My name is Special Agent Shawn Johnson, and this is Special Agent Tina Standing Elk. We're with the FBI. I believe you already know Dr. Gilner, Penfor, and Reldap. Agent Stein and Agent Labrador are with Homeland Security."

Jackner interrupted. "Yeah, I know those twits."

Johnson was unfazed. "Good, Mr. Jackner. As you indelicately described them, the bugs are e-Fleks helping us locate the kleptrons that were stolen from a storage site outside of Portland, Maine and are being kept and used in violation of the Kleptron Control Act of 2131.

"Useless law if I ever saw one," said Jackner.

Ignoring the comment, Johnson continued. "We have reason to believe you may have knowledge of the whereabouts of the kleptrons, and we'd like to discuss with you your possible role in their theft. We are authorized to be on your property and search it if necessary. Dr. Gilner, Reldap, Penfor, and the e-Fleks are duly authorized consultants with permission to accompany and assist us in our work. That missile lock nonsense, by the way, was not funny."

"Well, son, that was a mouthful. Helped by bugs and aliens, huh? What's the FBI comin' to. And listen, if I don't have an invitation out for someone to land on my airfield, I'm gonna scare 'em off. That's what I do. Got lots of secrets here and lots of people who'd like to know them." He sighed. "Okay, you win. Let's go inside and get out of the sun."

Before we could board the waiting carts, Klak spoke. "For an endotherm, you speak wisely. I am Klak, leader of the Trilobite Liberation Army. I wish to discuss our mission with you. First, we must search your property."

"What the hell for?"

"A stasis chamber prepared by aliens, containing the last of the trilobites."

A wicked grin spread over Jackner's face. "Sure, go ahead. Let me know what you find. When y'all come back, we can discuss your mission in detail. I'd love to help."

Maria looked daggers at Jackner but said nothing. The e-Fleks raised their pennants, lined up in a skirmish line, and proceeded off, carefully probing the ground with their front legs as they walked.

With the e-Fleks off looking for trilobites, we boarded PRF's ground transportation for the cluster of buildings half a kilometer away. We were guided to a large conference room and took our seats.

Shawn laid out the issues. "Mr. Jackner, several days ago, we started an investigation of an illegal klepping parlor in the Chicago suburbs, Sumac Park to be exact. The perps had done a pretty good job cleaning up after themselves, but not quite good enough.

"We identified a vehicle used in the crime, which had been reported stolen from a POBTech parking lot. This vehicle belonged to a Mr. Alfred Yarrow, an entry-level technician in the experimental synthesis lab at POBTech."

Jackner, who up until this point had been smirking and ostentatiously cleaning his fingernails, suddenly got serious. "Who the hell is Alfred Yarrow?"

Johnson continued. "Mr. Jackner, please don't play the fool; it doesn't become you. Mr. Yarrow has had a forthright discussion with us regarding your curiosity regarding POBTech's non-toxic dispersal agent and his delivery to you of a sample of POBTech's product in exchange for some unspecified compensation."

"He's lyin'. Never heard of him. He's never been here."

"Mr. Jackner, let's cut to the chase. POBTech has already indicated that it does not intend to press charges. Discovery and trial regarding this incident of industrial espionage would lead to embarrassing disclosures for the company that would further weaken its share value. The FBI has no interest in what is now a civil rather than criminal matter."

Jackner visibly relaxed. "Well, that young fella and I may have had some interesting conversations, and I did express an interest in how POBTech was addressing the dispersal agent problem. Ain't no harm in a little industrial comparison and collaboration."

"As long as all parties agree, and it is not clear that they all did. Mr. Jackner, listen to me: we don't care. We do care about Mr. Yarrow's car being found at an illegal klepping parlor after being reported stolen. We do care that shortly before the vehicle was reported stolen, it had visited Premium Rocket Fuel. We do care that your opinions regarding kleptrons are public knowledge and that your large, isolated campus would provide an excellent hiding place for the stolen kleptrons. Your knowledge of chemistry and your familiarity with neural cell culture would permit you to sustain the creatures. Persistence of the klepping problem would embarrass the government, an activity which appears to be as important to you as producing and selling petroleum distillates."

Johnson cleared his throat, took a sip of water, and continued. "Mr. Jackner, this klepping incident resulted in permanent neurological damage to a young man with a young family. He was obviously foolish and contributed to his own injury. However, the law is the law, and the Kleptron Control Act allows for prison sentences for all persons that may have contributed to his injury. So, at this point, I have two questions for you. First, how do you respond to all of this, and second, would you like an attorney present?"

Jackner stopped crapping around. He dropped the exaggerated accent and the folksy overlay. "First of all, no. I do not need an attorney present as I have done nothing criminal by your measures. Second, I would like a statement clarified, and then we can get on to the main body of your concerns."

All of us looked at him intently. He *was* capable of coherent, serious discussions. "Go on," said Johnson.

"You indicate that I have knowledge of neural cell culture. How did you come to that conclusion?"

"Mr. Jackner, you seem to have a convenient memory lapse. Or, perhaps, it is your repeated klepping. In either case, let me remind you that you used neural cell culture material during your "safety demonstrations" when you advocated for no restrictions on klepping and challenged the government's safety recommendations. You put a layer of aluminum foil on your scalp. You overlaid the foil with a mat of cell culture material to attract and feed the kleptrons and wore a wig over that to deceive your audience. All this was revealed at your altercation with President Moorehead."

Jackner thought a moment. "You are correct. I did use neural cell culture material in connection with my advocacy for personal rights and freedoms. However, that material was given to me. I did not grow it myself then, and I do not have the knowledge or equipment to undertake cell culture of any cell line at any scale. At present, I do not wish to identify the source of the material used in those demonstrations."

This indirectly confirmed what I had already suspected: that there had been a leak from JarVexx. The cell culture company was (and is) the only source of the neural cell culture tissue mats used to artificially feed kleptrons. Paradoxically, the chemist's disclosure was good news; it would be much easier to track down a leak of stuff rather than information. I put this aside for the moment.

Johnson pushed on. "All right. I'd like to move on. What connection do you have to the incident outside of Chicago?"

"Absolutely none. I categorically deny all involvement. I would never intentionally do anything that might cause harm to another person."

Stein looked apoplectic. "You mendacious, self-serving sack of shit! You spent weeks publicly denying that kleptrons posed any sort of hazard. You traveled up and down the country giving "safety demonstrations" while covering your head with tin foil. You did everything you could to undermine the government's safety recommendations. All in the name of defending personal rights and freedoms? You have blood on your hands. You helped injure thousands of people who were foolish enough to listen to you. For what? Tell me! For what? To tweak Moorehead? To pander to that pack of certifiable morons that hang on your every word? May Heaven have mercy on your soul."

Johnson, the relentless, competent interrogator, was the first to speak. "Mr. Jackner, irrespective of the observations of my partner, which I believe have considerable merit, we're going to stick to the here and now. You say you had nothing to do with the Chicago incident. Fine. We're going to search your premises, and the e-Fleks will help us. If our arthropod friends detect any kleptrons here, then as my colleague just so eloquently articulated, may Heaven have mercy on your soul."

"Before we are done, I have one more question for you. Who is Giorgio, and what is your relationship with this person?"

"Who is Giorgio?" asked Jackner.

"To refresh your memory, Giorgio called Mr. Yarrow, apparently on your behalf. He demanded that Yarrow report his vehicle stolen because Premium Rocket Fuel needed the use of a vehicle that could not be traced to you and/or your company. Mr. Yarrow's vehicle would then be used for some purpose, presumably illegal. This Giorgio threatened to reveal Mr. Yarrow's relationship with PRF to his employer if he did not comply. As I said before, Mr. Yarrow's car was used to transport kleptrons to a klepping parlor outside Chicago. Giorgio did not give Mr. Yarrow his last name, but Yarrow did indicate that the man had a distinct Slavic accent. You claim you have no knowledge of this person?"

"As I said, I don't know anyone named Giorgio, much less a Giorgio with a Russian accent demanding that a business partner of mine undertake an illegal act."

Johnson paused for a moment. "All right, then, explain to me how this Giorgio is so knowledgeable regarding your 'business dealings' with Mr. Yarrow."

"You assholes are the detectives," said Jackner said as he slipped back into his exaggerated Southern patter. "Figure it out. Y'all got nothin' on me."

CHAPTER 28

Maria asked Jackner to help us find the e-Fleks. After the expected caustic pushback, he agreed to launch a surveillance drone to find them and then bring the creatures back to the main campus. He left the conference room to make that happen.

When he was gone, Joe spoke up. "I'm sorry," he said. "I'm really sorry. I just lost it. I haven't talked about this before, not even to Maria. I have this younger cousin, a nice kid, not the brightest bulb in the pack. Trusting to the point of being gullible. He listened to that idiot Jackner. He 'made his own decisions.' Got klepped about seven times. It was just awful."

"Look," said Johnson, "no harm, no foul. Phil wasn't going to cooperate willingly. You didn't screw the investigation. In fact, all you did was say what the rest of us were thinking. I'm sorry about your cousin." Johnson was grim. "We will put a stop to the illegal klepping." The others at the table agreed and offered Stein support.

We left the conference room and went outside the main building. About 20 minutes later, a flatbed truck carrying the TLA showed up. We helped the e-Fleks down off the vehicle, and they lined up. Klak spoke. "Trilobite Liberation Army reporting. Our search was interrupted. I regret to inform you that we were unable to locate any trilobites in the short time we were permitted to conduct the investigation."

Tina addressed Klak. "Klak, we have an important enquiry for you and your squad." Klak turned to her, attentive. "We wish to use your investigative skills to determine if kleptrons are now or have ever been on this property."

"Right, ma'am. Do we have a warrant?"

"Yes, we do. It is a lawful inquiry."

"Does he have form?"

"No. No previous."

"Got it, guv. Will we need uniforms for crowd control or to restrain the suspects?"

"No, I think we'll be all set."

"Do we need to physically hand the warrant to the property owner so that he can examine it and then protest his innocence?"

"No, it's all electronic, and he's already protested his innocence many times over."

"Pity, ma'am. All right, lads, let's get to it!" He scuttled around in a 360, realizing he had no idea what to do next, poor thing.

"Klak, have the TLA stand down for a moment. We need to make some arrangements."

"As you wish, ma'am." He clattered to the rest of the e-Fleks.

Jackner reappeared with several other members of his staff. All the e-Fleks had a similar capacity to detect kleptrons. It was decided to split the e-Fleks into three teams of two, each with two human handlers — someone from Premium Rocket Fuel for building access and to work with the employees and one of the Feds to maintain some semblance of reality and to conduct the investigation. The e-Fleks accepted this arrangement, and Klak divvied up his crew after the requisite number of "yes, ma'am"s, "on it, guv"s, and "right, mate"s.

The rest of us waited. Jackner, ever unpredictable, played the gracious host. We had a nice lunch and sipped sweet tea in the shade while waiting for the search to be completed. Wisely, Joe had not accompanied an e-Flek team, and by the time the final group returned, he was reasonably chill.

When the last group returned and reported in, we realized that Jackner had far less to do with this than we had thought. No kleptrons, anywhere, in any number, in the last two weeks. Relieved of responsibility for the Chicago incident, Jackner reverted to Cowboy Phil. He called over Klak.

"e-Flek, I spit in your presence." He spat on the ground.

Klak collected the rest of the TLA, and they formed a semicircle in front of the chemist. "Human, I spit in your presence." All the e-Fleks squirted a stream of brown juice onto the ground. "You are a wise and compassionate mammal."

"Well, I'm glad someone thinks so. Now, I know you fellas were brought here to find kleptrons, but tell me about the other part of the mission."

"Mr. Jackner," I said, "please, don't get them started. It…"

"Doc, I don't give a hoot what you or your government buddies want. These good folk have a mission, and I want to hear about it."

Klak said something to the rest of his group, and they lined up in formation. They all raised their pennants. "We are e-Fleks, proud arthropods. Exploited by the Latternite dogs, we have been sent to Earth by the Galactic Arthropodal Council to restore arthropods to their rightful place in Earth's hierarchy. We will make arthropods great again!"

Klak was interrupted by the rest of his crew chanting, "Make Arthropods Great Again." Klak turned around and silenced them. He continued. "In the course of our investigations, we have determined that the so-called Great Permian Extinction was, in fact, a targeted series of assassinations by mammals and some of the higher fishes. The trilobites, the highest form of arthropod alive at the time, were mercilessly exterminated. Were it not for the intercession of benevolent aliens who, at the time had been exploring this quadrant of the galaxy, these magnificent creatures would be gone forever. However, the aliens managed to rescue the leadership council and their families and place these stalwarts in suspended animation. We will find the stasis chamber and reanimate the best of the best. This is the mission of the Trilobite Liberation Army."

Throughout Klak's monologue, Jackner nods his head and strokes his chin. Before he could say anything, Tina spoke.

"Mr. Jackner, please, don't do this…"

Phil just smiled. "Klak, do you have any proof of this?"

"Yes. We have done our own research."

"Can you show it to me?"

"No. We must protect our sources."

"Well, that's good enough for me. You seem like honest critters, and I understand the need to protect your sources." He turned to Tina. "Do you have any proof that what they are saying is not true?"

"Mr. Jackner, hundreds of years of research and dozens, if not hundreds, of evolutionary scientists would contest every syllable of what they are saying. And there's absolutely no evidence that this planet has been visited by aliens."

He pointed to Reldap and Penfor. "So they're from Long Island?"

"You know perfectly well what I mean," Tina spluttered. She lowered her voice. "You are aware, are you not, that these e-Fleks have FDS?"

Jackner deliberately raised his voice. "You're saying these e-Fleks have Flektanian Delusional Syndrome? Why, it looks to me like there's nothing wrong with these healthy little guys."

"Human Standing Elk," said Klak, "we are healthy and fine. Stop this slander at once!"

Tina looked at Penfor, who shrugged. She spoke angrily to Jackner. "You did that deliberately, didn't you?"

"No, I was just afraid that you might not have heard me with everything else going on. They've said they are fine. You can show me nothing that conclusively proves their statements are false or fabricated. They've done their own research. They can't show us their evidence because they must protect their sources. We need to find those trilobites and make things right.

"I'm gonna help these critters. I'm gonna publicize their concerns. I'm gonna give them resources. I'm gonna recruit sympathetic folks to help. The cause of the TLA is my cause."

"Human Jackner, we are beyond thankful. We spit again in your presence." The e-Fleks squirted a second round of brown juice onto the ground.

"Klak, I am honored." Jackner spit as well.

"You are correct, human Jackner," said Reldap. "It is indeed a great honor to have Flektanians spit a second time in a single encounter. The real Reldap on Lattern has seen this only once before."

Penfor gave him a dirty look and yelled at him in Lattern.

"What did she say to you, Reldap?" I asked.

"I believe the closest English translation would be 'shut up, you nitwit.'"

"All right, boys and girls, we are done here, and I am asking you to put your sorry asses back on that airplane of yours and get the hell out of here," said Jackner. "Before you go, though, I do want to leave you nitwits, and I do believe the term applies to all of you, not just Reldap, with one thought. Agent fancy pants Johnson, you said yourself that based on my past political activities, I was a prime suspect. If someone was trying to deflect attention from themselves, who better to implicate? Now git."

Regrettably, his argument was compelling, and it meant that we would need a lot of hard detective work, a lucky break, or both. We got our sorry asses back on the plane and got the hell out of there.

CHAPTER 29

We dropped the bugs off at the Grange Hall, along with Reldap and Penfor, who promised to settle them. Their car was there, and Penfor accepted my invitation for dinner and to stay with us overnight; it had been a long day and a long journey, and even Latternite biobots get tired. The Feds dropped me off at our house.

It was so nice to see Helen; I had missed her greatly. She was happy to accommodate the Latternites. Penfor and Reldap showed up an hour later, and we had dinner and turned in early.

We were sitting and having breakfast when my PDD delivered an urgent message from Maria to turn on our video viewer to the Veracity Network. Curious about what might warrant this early morning message to watch a video, I turned on our viewer. There he was, Phil Jackner, being interviewed by morning show host Steve Liu. This was an ominous development, as Liu was also a first-class nutcase and connoisseur conspiracy theorist.

"OK, Phil, for folks who might just be joining us now, and so that I'm sure I understand this all, run it by me again," said Liu.

"Sure, Steve, glad to. I was visited by some Fedtoads lookin' to pin an illegal klepping on me. I must say, I was not pleased."

[Author's note: Fedtoad refers to any Federal enforcement agent, frequently used by a broad spectrum of anti-government conspiracy theorists. It is not a term of endearment, nor is it typically used in polite society.]

"Phil, no one is pleased when Fedtoads show up."

"Damn right. Two FBI and two Homeland Security. Dragged along those two Latternite things and that doc fella that follows them aliens around like a puppy dog."

"Must have ruined your day."

"Almost, but not quite. They also brought along the e-Fleks, those giant beetle-like critters. I am most grateful to them; they helped exonerate me." Jackner smirked as he drew out exonerate into egg-zonnerate.

Liu laughed. "Keep going, my friend."

"Sure. Well, after we got all that klepping crap out of the way, I had a wonderful conversation with Klak, their leader. Turns out they are here for a purpose, a real purpose, not just that kleptron stuff."

"Sounds fascinating. Tell me more."

"This is just an amazing tale. They were sent here by the Galactic Arthropodal Council to restore Earth's arthropods to their rightful place."

"I thought they were brought here by the Latternites to clean up the kleptron mess."

Jackner drops his voice conspiratorily. "Just a cover story. They are helpin' with that, but just to keep a lid on things."

"Gotcha."

"Anyway, when they got here, they studied the Great Permian Extinction and the disappearance of the greatest tribe of arthropods ever, the trilobites. We've been fed pig slop by the government and so-called experts about these critical events."

"This is incredible."

"You bet. So here's the real deal. The Great Permian Extinction was not a natural event."

"Jesus!"

"It was a massive, coordinated assassination event organized by the early mammals and some of the higher fishes. Get rid of the dinosaurs. Get rid of the brachiopods. Most of all, get rid of the trilobites."

"I cannot believe what I am hearing."

"Tiny bit of upside. Turns out some benevolent aliens were explorin' this part of the galaxy, checkin' out the neighborhood if you will, and they saw this awful thing going on from afar. Fast as they could get here, they tried to stop it, but they were too late. Best they could do was rescue a few hundred trilobites."

Jackner leaned over and took a sip of water from a glass on the table between the two men. "The trilobites were making a last stand. The leadership and their families were huddled in some underwater cave. Aliens got 'em, put 'em in stasis, and hid 'em."

"Do we know where this stasis chamber is or how to reanimate the trilobites once found?"

"Well, that's what the e-Fleks are all about. We don't know where the stasis chamber is, but Klak and his boys have some ideas, and they're working on it. As for reanimation, we figure there'll be instructions on what to do on the container, kinda like cookin' instructions on the packages of some of those things we buy at the grocery. To emphasize the importance of what they're doin', they've renamed themselves the Trilobite Liberation Army."

"Amazing story, absolutely amazing. So, I'm sure that our viewers will want to know more about how the TLA got all this intel."

"Steve, I can't tell you. I can only say that they've done their own research and must protect their sources."

"Understandable. How can we help?"

"Good question. We are planning on some informational rallies and expeditions to areas that could possibly-- just possibly-- be home to the stasis chamber. I'll be posting about this on my website when we have a better idea of how we are going forward."

"Excellent. One more question, and then I'll let you go. There's a rumor going around that the e-Fleks are suffering from Flektanian Delusional Syndrome…"

"Steve, I'm gonna stop you right there. Klak and his boys told me in no uncertain terms that they are in great shape and as sane as you or me. They are fine, upstanding creatures, and I feel we must take them at their word."

"Phil, if it's good enough for you, it's good enough for me. Ladies and gents, I've been interviewing Phil Jackner about his incredible time with the Trilobite Liberation Army. Phil, thank you so much."

"My pleasure, Steve. Look forward to the next time."

I turned off the video viewer. Helen looked at me. "Good heavens," she said. "That man is insane."

I nodded. Reldap was smiling ear to ear. "I am glad human Maria told us about this show. A good comedy special is always a nice way to start a day."

"Reldap," said Helen, "this was not a comedy special."

"Oh dear," said Reldap.

CHAPTER 30

We finished breakfast, further dismayed by the insanity on the vid. How could they possibly spout this drivel? On the other hand, crap like this was getting more and more common, so maybe I shouldn't have been that surprised. I made myself refocus on the kleptron problem.

At this point, we were adrift. Our best, "smelling blood in the water" lead had not panned out. POBTech was clean; we were pretty sure of that. Jackner? It was likely he was not involved, but we weren't positive, given what a slippery little devil he was. The Feds were quite upset, as they were under as much pressure as Reldap to get a result. After ruminating about this for a while, I slapped myself on the side of the head and stopped obsessing. We were working with effective investigators, and I was sure that this was not the first time they'd faced a situation like this. We'd figure it out.

A little later, as expected, I got a call on my PDD from Johnson; we were going to meet in an hour at the Grange Hall to plan our next steps.

******

Helen, the two Latternites, and I sat down at the table at the Grange Hall. The Feds and Klak were already settled.

"Okay," said Tina, "let's get started."

Before she could say anything else, Klak chimed in. "One of you is bent. That's the only plausible explanation for the failure of our op."

"What does bent mean?" asked Tina.

"You know, luv. Turned. Crooked. Working for the oppo."

"Thanks, Klak. We'll keep that under consideration."

Tina was about to continue, but Joe interrupted. "Hang on a sec, let's not dismiss that idea out of hand."

Tina looked puzzled and somewhat annoyed.

"Look," he continued, "I'm not saying that anyone at this table is working for the other side. Far from it. However, how many KASMA sites are there?"

"An even hundred to start, three shut down for kleptron breaches, that makes 97," answered Shawn.

"And how many technicians and docs and maintenance folks at each site?"

"About 20-25, depending upon the site. Lots of potential vulnerabilities. Point taken."

"But everyone working at these sites is fully vetted, precisely to prevent what we're discussing," I said.

"Right. So was Klaus Fuchs," said Helen.

There was a prolonged silence. Shawn was the first to speak. "I'll get in touch with Washington. We need to review the background checks on everyone associated with all of the KASMA sites. No exceptions, no carve-outs. Reldap, Penfor, I know you'd like to help, and your ability to read and process information is beyond human ability. However, you don't understand human malfeasance as well as a human, so you won't know what to look for." Reldap nodded.

Shawn continued. "Klak, thank you. You made a good point. It is as likely a direction of inquiry as any."

"Right, mate. Anything for the gaffer," said Klak.

Reldap stood. "I have nothing further to add, and it is time for my weekly check-in with Lattern. If acceptable to you all, I will do that now. Humans Gilner, if you would be so kind, can you give Penfor a ride back to your house when all is finished here?"

Tina said that it was fine if he left, and Helen promised Penfor transportation. Reldap set off for the airport to check in with Mission Control.

CHAPTER 31

Reldap drove to the airport and entered his ship. As was the case every week, calling home was a complex undertaking. As much as he loved the humans, it was great to have a break. On his ship, he was surrounded by familiar technology and esthetics, with furniture made to fit his frame. He wasn't on display, and he wasn't constantly translating both words and nuances. On the other hand, he often needed to face an impatient Mission Control and an imperious father.

He activated the quantum communicator, adjusted the image and audio, and waited for the connection. The face of the communication tech on duty soon appeared. "Reldap, hello! Ready for your dad? You are definitely in luck. He's in a good mood today. I'll get you connected."

Ventak and Zeftan were soon visible. As promised, Zeftan was downright jovial. "Reldap, my boy, sometimes I envy you. You speak of all the good things the humans have taught you. It must be wonderful to live with such humorous, fun-loving creatures."

Reldap proceeded cautiously, uncertain what prompted these kind words or where the conversation was headed. "Yes, father. It is a more light-hearted civilization than ours, mostly to the good, sometimes to the bad. In the balance, it is enjoyable. Has any particular event prompted this observation?"

Zeftan ignored the question and repeated himself. "Yes, it must be wonderful to live with such fun-loving creatures. You must investigate this in more detail. We must learn more about Earth humor."

Reldap rarely, if ever, saw such a cheerful countenance on his father. Calibrating his question carefully and appealing to Papa's prejudices, he asked again. "My lord and father, you are often rightfully critical of the humans and their crazy ways. What has so amused you?"

"You know, Reldap, that we monitor Earth broadcasts, particularly from America, where you spend most of your time. It rounds out your reports, which are sometimes sparse." Zeftan frowned for a moment, then continued. "However, we just finished watching that interview between that Jackner fellow and Mr. Liu. What do they call that kind of humor? Sarcasm? Parody? Put-on? Whatever it is called, it was a tour de farce." Zeftan smiled at the thought that he knew Earth culture so well that he could pun.

"Father, that was a serious interview and a serious broadcast."

"Come now, son. Let's put humor aside for the moment. I would like to understand the thinking, how one goes about constructing a display of such silliness so that it is entertaining. Serious broadcast, indeed. Please share your insights."

"All right, I will. The e-Fleks are completely deranged from Flektanian Delusional Syndrome. They are convinced they are on a mission to restore bugs and other creatures with exoskeletons to their 'rightful place in Earth's hierarchy.' This has morphed into a belief that a small number of trilobites, a form of ancient primitive arthropod thought to be long extinct, have survived 250 million years in suspended animation, placed in that state by benign aliens who were visiting Earth as the trilobites were being pursued and eliminated. The creatures await reanimation by friends, who will help the trilobites restore a bright and vibrant culture and lead the world to a better place.

"This delusion has been complicated by the search for the kleptrons. The e-Fleks have been given a simple task: to use their heightened chemical sensors to detect the presence or absence of kleptrons. However, they have organized themselves into a paramilitary organization, the Trilobite Liberation Army, whose primary task is to look for the rescued trilobites; finding kleptrons is a secondary goal that they undertake to humor the humans. As a result of their programming and introduction to Earth culture, they were exposed to Earth's early 21st-century television programming. They are convinced that the appropriate approach to finding the kleptrons is to mimic British police procedural television scripts. However, their mimicry of the genre is selective, incorporating the subplots that humans enjoy and none of the investigative substance."

As Reldap spoke, Zeftan became visibly more concerned. "My son, I did not realize the complexity of the delusional system. This is one of the worst cases of FDS on record. It is also one of the most complex." Reldap could see Ventak nod his head in agreement.

Reldap continued. "Father, I agree. However, the humans are very comfortable dealing with crazy ideas. The investigators they assigned to find the kleptrons are kind but also effective. They have humored the e-Fleks while still channeling the energies of the creatures into a useful direction. We are making progress."

Zeftan gently interrupted. "Yes, yes, I understand. We'll get back to the kleptron problem in a moment or two. I would like to finish thinking about the humorous broadcast first."

"My lord, this was not a comedy broadcast."

"This was not a comedy broadcast?"

"No. Regrettably, it was not."

By this time, Zeftan was dead serious. "Explain."

"I will try. You are aware of the human susceptibility to conspiracy theories, yes?"

"Of course. We have studied this. It appears to be some form of neural defect, worse in some of the creatures than in others," said Zeftan.

"Correct, father. The problem by itself is only a mild annoyance. However, some of the victims then go on to act upon their beliefs. Then it becomes a problem. I doubt that the two humans who spoke on that broadcast believed any of that rubbish."

"Truly? Why would they do what they did?"

"Father, you are familiar with harknars on our world, are you not?"

"Of course. It is a serious mental health problem. The chaos chasers, the lovers of the sounds of breaking glass and grinding metal."

"Jackner and Liu are human harknars. Additionally, the chemist may be trying to deflect attention away from the legal problems related to his inept attempt to overthrow the leader of the American nation."

"We have developed treatments for harknars here on Lattern. Perhaps they would like to learn from us?"

"Father, I doubt it."

Zeftan sighed. "This combination of harknars and susceptibility to conspiracy theories is destructive."

"Yes, Father. It is."

Zeftan sighed again. "All right. We have not fixed anything, but I understand the situation better than I did. You have my support and backing."

"Thank you, my Lord."

"Let us leave that topic. Tell me about the kleptron problem."

"Give me a moment." Reldap composed his thoughts and then started talking. He related recent events, beginning with the investigation of the raid on the klepping parlor and then the trip to POBTech. He explained that while they identified industrial espionage, it had nothing to do with the illegal kleppings. He then described the trip to Premium Rocket Fuel, which was equally unrevealing.

"The harknar Jackner is destructive, but he is not a fool," said Zeftan. "His point about misdirection is well taken."

"I agree. In one of Klak's ravings, he suggested that someone participating in the permitted care and use of kleptrons could be involved. It was a good hypothesis, and we are reexamining the background checks of the involved humans."

Zeftan looked irritated. "Nothing you tell me about that planet is ever simple. It is getting tiresome. All right. What you are saying is a sensible way forward. One final topic before we go."

"Yes, my Lord, what is it?"

"We have followed the development of KASMA with interest. Our scientists have captured some wild kleptrons and are maintaining them artificially as we investigate the possibility of selective memory ablation in Latternites."

"That is a far more complex process than in a human, is it not?"

"Yes, but , that is for our psychoscientists to address, and don't interrupt me. The issue for us is feeding stations. We were aware of POBTech's research on dispersants. Our cell culture technologists have asked that you learn more about this new dispersant. It sounds promising."

"Certainly. That will be easy. I will leave the e-Fleks in the care of the humans and Penfor and visit my friend Jen Doyle at JarVexx tomorrow. I am sure she will be happy to help us."

"Good. Make it all happen, and quickly."

Yes, Father. Until next week."

Zeftan just grumbled and cut the connection.

CHAPTER 32

"What are those two crazy twits up to this time?"

"Mr. President, none of us have a definitive picture as to the intentions of Mr. Jackner and Mr. Liu. However, we do have several working hypotheses."

"Okay, hit me."

"Yes, sir. First, this is simply part of the normal ebb and flow of Mr. Jackner's provocative and attention-grabbing performances and Mr. Liu's enabling behavior."

"I don't buy it. Keep going."

"Certainly, sir. The second consideration is that Jackner can somehow monetize these assertions."

"Makes more sense, but they are both already very fucking rich, and what they would make from this shit would be peanuts. Keep going."

"Yes, sir. The third possibility, which the analysis team favors, is that Mr. Jackner will actively support the Trilobite Liberation Army, backing excavation projects, holding rallies and fundraising activities, and the like. Again, with Mr. Liu enabling as needed. The purpose would be to embarrass you and your government as well as to continue to focus attention on himself."

"Who's crazy enough to fall for this crap?"

"Mr. President, Mr. Liu and Mr. Jackner offer an alternative reality attractive to a surprisingly large segment of the people. If nothing else, a search for trilobites in suspended animation would be diverting and entertaining."

The Prez looked thoughtful. Despite extraordinary incompetence as the leader of a nation, his political acumen and instincts were sharper than a boxcutter at an Amazon warehouse. "Yeah, and harmless. Tell you what. We're gonna beat this schmuck at his own game. He wants to make stuff up? Fine. We'll play along, and pull the rug out from under him when the time is ripe. We're gonna trust the plan."

"Yes, Mr. President."

"Get me that Nguyen lady."

"Yes, sir."

******

"Okay, thank you all for attending. Please take your seats so we can start this press conference. I will make a short statement on behalf of President Moorehead and the Office of Alien Relations, the OAR. As most of you know, I'm Vicki Nguyen, Assistant Director of the OAR. There will be no question-and-answer session after these prepared remarks."

"Experts at the United States Office of Alien Relations, in conjunction with our international counterparts and colleagues, have carefully reviewed the assertions of the e-Fleks relating to the potential existence of trilobites in suspended animation. While we have no specific information supporting the e-Fleks' claims, we also have no data conclusively refuting these statements. Given the evidence the e-Fleks have presented to us, we have instructed the U.S. Geological Survey to assist e-Fleks and human supporters in investigating sites that might contain a trilobite stasis chamber. Excavation permits will be issued with a simple application for all Federal lands. We encourage everyone to do their own research and participate in this endeavor as they can. If a stasis chamber is located, the United States government will make available all scientific assistance for reanimating the individuals contained therein. Further information is available at trilobiteliberation.gov. Thank you."

******

Penfor and Reldap sat together in their Portland house, watching the broadcast. "Do you remember what I said at the beginning of this fiasco?" asked Reldap. "About how we didn't need to worry about the human reaction to the FDS-afflicted e-Fleks?"

"Because there are no longer any little boys watching the parade, who would say that the emperor had no clothes?"

"Yes."

"I would say you were right," said Penfor.

"Let's go to sleep," said Reldap. "I think I will have a long day tomorrow."

CHAPTER 33

Reldap called me and told me about his conversation with Mission Control and his father. I was surprised to hear of a selective memory ablation project on Lattern. Kleptrons present a danger to humans based on the structure of memory in our nervous system. Latternite memory structure is very different and much more resistant to the consequences of kleptron feedings. It would take a very sophisticated process to alter Latternite memory using kleptrons. KASMA had been startlingly successful in treating some human psychiatric conditions; I wished the Latternites equal success.

But that was beside the point. Irrespective of their goals, a high-quality dispersal agent would be of great value if they were developing feeding stations. I agreed to call Dave Mackowitz at JarVexx and set up a visit.

As expected, Dave was happy to help. "Come on over," he said. "Jen Doyle is working today, and she can walk you through what we're doing. It's a pretty exciting improvement."

I drove to Reldap's place, and from there, we went to the Falmouth kleptron research and breeding station. Dave was there to meet us.

"Hi Ed, Reldap. Good to see you guys. Pretty crazy stuff with these e-Fleks and trilobites, isn't it." Reldap looked at the ground and said nothing. "Come on, let's get you past security, and we'll look at what we are doing here."

Mackowitz was the CEO of JarVexx, the prominent vaccine manufacturer in southern Maine. Because efficient, high-quality cell culture was integral to vaccine development and manufacturing, I had turned to him when we decided to use neural cell culture as part of our plan to capture the kleptrons at the time of their original "escape." Vaccines continued to be the main product of JarVexx, but the company was also the exclusive source of kleptron feeding stations for legal kleptron R&D. Jen Doyle was the team leader for the kleptron feeding station project, serving a dual function as chief technologist and chief scientist.

We quickly cleared the access control point and entered the facility. After last year's break-in, security measures were in abundance. Using his master Q-card, Dave took us straight to Jen's office.

"Hey Jen, you've got visitors."

She looked up from her work, a little startled. "Dr. Gilner, Reldap, I wasn't expecting a visit. What a nice surprise. How can I help my favorite alien-doctor team?"

"Jen," said Dave, "Lattern Mission Control is interested in that new culture medium dispersant we're testing. We'd…"

Doyle interrupted him. "Sure, let's go straight to the lab."

"Before we do that," said Reldap, "I recall you have a most wonderful coffee blend of Kona, Sumatra, and a tiny dose of Uganda beans. Could I trouble you for a Latternite-sized cup?" He smiled; he could be so charming when he chose to be.

Jen smiled. "Sure. Do you want to come with me as I brew it?"

"Jen," said Mackowitz, "let's be good hosts. I'll come with, and we'll have the secret JarVexx blend all around. Reldap, what a great idea. We'll be right back." Jen looked a little unhappy but demurred.

Reldap and I remained in Doyle's office. He looked at her desk. A holographic cube shimmered above her workspace. "That is most interesting, Edward. What is that?"

I looked over. "Oh, that's a CubeSheet DataBox," I said.

"I am not familiar with those terms."

"Sorry. I thought you would have seen one by now. It's a pretty nifty software-hardware combination. CubeSheet is a true three-dimensional spreadsheet software package. The software comes with a low-power holographic projector that you attach to your computer. It allows you to create a 3-D image of your data in space. You can use your keyboard and 3-D mouse to control it. If you are a real visual analysis kinda person, it's very helpful."

"I see. And DataBox?"

"Oh yeah. That's the proprietary name for the data file that contains the information and projection instructions."

"Ah." Reldap walked over to the desk and stared at the hologram. He did not touch any controls but looked at the image from all perspectives, examining it carefully.

"I would have thought a data analysis tool like this would be old technology on Lattern," I said. "Surely you must have something similar or better."

"Yes, yes," he said. "I was just curious."

He was surprisingly quiet. Usually, after looking at some previously unexamined Earth technology, I was subject to a lengthy comparison between Earth and Lattern engineering techniques and a longer list of potential improvements. Whatever.

As Doyle and Mackowitz returned to Jen's office, he moved away from the desk.

The rest of the visit was unremarkable. We went to the lab, and Doyle showed us the analysis data. The dispersant was a definite improvement and would lower production costs. Mackowitz gave Reldap 100 ml of the stuff to bring back to his ship and analyze.

"Won't POBTech go nuts? Proprietary information and all that?" I asked.

"No. We authorized the research. We own the product. We have intellectual rights to the material, no matter what their pack of mealy-mouthed lawyers say. You may analyze the dispersant and send your results to Lattern and any other fucking planet with my full blessings." Oops. Dave rarely got irritated or annoyed. He had clearly interacted with some of POBTech's more difficult characters.

"Thank you," said Reldap. "This will be most interesting."

We said goodbye to Mackowitz and Doyle and left the building.

"What now," I asked.

"Let us return to my house in Portland," said Reldap. "You may get your car and return to Waterville if you wish. I wish to discuss some matters with Penfor privately before we drive to Waterville later today. I will analyze this compound tomorrow. May we stay with you tonight?"

"Of course. You are almost always welcome."

He smiled. "Thank you, human Gilner. You are a good friend."

"As are you, Latternite Reldap."

CHAPTER 34

Reldap and Penfor stayed with us as planned. Both were uncharacteristically quiet but pleasant as usual. They got up early the next day and headed to LaFleur. Even though the Atmospheric Entry Vehicles did not carry the same sophisticated equipment as the quantum communication station, the testing equipment on board was still up to analyzing the dispersant. Penfor promised that they would be there for just a couple of hours and then they would return.

I heard their vehicle drive up about three hours later. "How did it go," I asked.

"It went well, human Gilner. Our scientists are most pleased," said Penfor.

"Good. Let's go to the Grange Hall and check in," I said.

"No, Edward," said Reldap.

"What?"

"No. We need to discuss something. Do you have CubeSheet on your computer?"

"I do," said Helen. "I use it for my KASMA research."

"Good," said Reldap. "Please ask Joe, Maria, Shawn, and Tina to come here. I wish to show them something."

"Okay, but why can't we just go to the Grange Hall?"

"This is a delicate, complicated situation. I do not wish to present this information while being interrupted by demented bugs. Tell them we are having a biped meal of burning mammal or some such. Tell the humans to come here in two hours."

"All right," I said. I went to another room and called Shawn on my PDD.

Reldap then turned to Helen. "I will need your help. My fingers are too large for your keyboard, and I do not know how to use CubeSheet. I wish to give you data to enter."

"Okay," said Helen.

She sat down at her computer, opened CubeSheet, and created a new, empty DataBox. Reldap explained what he wished to do. Helen nodded and set up the basic parameters. He began to reel off words and figures. Helen was facile with CubeSheet, and she entered the information without difficulty.

"There. We are done," said Reldap.

Helen stared at the DataBox. "Oh my heavens," she said.

"Yes," said Reldap.

******

The four Federal agents arrived two hours later, as requested.

"Okay, what's this burning mammal biped meal business? Always up for a Gilner meal," said Joe. He was in a good mood.

"I am sorry," said Reldap. "I have misled you. Perhaps we will eat later. Right now, I must show you something. Helen, please bring in your computer and project the DataBox."

"Sure." She quickly set up the computer and started the projector. Within a few seconds, the DataBox appeared.

Reldap was perturbed. "I am sorry to do this, but I must."

I walked over to the table where Helen had her computer. "What am I looking at here?" I asked.

"As you know," said Reldap, "my ability to read and incorporate information very rapidly is considerable. Penfor and I have close to what you humans call photographic memory." I nodded. Reldap continued. "When we visited JarVexx yesterday, I was intrigued by CubeSheet and the displayed DataBox. By the way, it is an excellent product. Very easy to visualize data."

He stopped for a moment. "I am sorry, I digress. I must address the displayed data, although I do not wish to do so. Ms. Doyle maintained records regarding kleptron feeding stations. She recorded the name of the licensed site, the number of kleptrons at the site, and the number of feeding stations shipped to each site each week. When I looked at the data, I quickly noted something wrong. I memorized the data and asked Helen to reproduce it here. The records are unambiguous. There is an anomaly. Let me show you."

He paused again. "The average ratio of kleptrons per feeding station per week for all sites except one was 2.7 to 1. If an experimental site had 27 kleptrons, it would receive 10 feeding stations per week. There was a little variation; one site was as high as 3.2, another as low as 2.5, but it averaged out to 2.7."

"Okay," said Tina slowly. "I think I understand. Keep going."

"One site was different. It had a ratio of 1.6."

"An outlier," said Joe. By this time, Joe's good mood had evaporated.

"Yes, an outlier," said Reldap.

"Continue," said Joe.

"I am sorry that I am presenting this so slowly. It upsets me. I will try to do this as fast as I can. Knowing the kleptron-to-feeding station ratios at each site, we can predict the number of kleptrons expected at each site."

"Of course," I said. "That's because your prediction is based on known quantities."

"Except for the outlier. We know that the outlier site should have 258 kleptrons because we know the registered population at every licensed site. If there were only 258 kleptrons there, we would expect the site to order slightly fewer than 100 feeding stations per week. However, the outlier is receiving 163 feeding stations per week. That's why the ratio is 1.6 — 258 kleptrons receiving 163 feeding stations per week. Something's off."

"Now, let's look at it a little differently. Let's say that it really only takes ten feeding stations for 27 kleptrons and that the site is receiving 163 feeding stations because there are more kleptrons there than are registered. At a ratio of 2.7, 163 feeding stations would sustain a kleptron colony of approximately 440 or 450. The difference between the predicted number of kleptrons at the outlier site, 440, and the registered number of kleptrons at that site, 248, is approximately 190, the number of kleptrons originally stolen."

The room was silent. Shawn was the first to speak. He was surprisingly gentle in his tone; I think he understood that Reldap was upset. "Reldap, which site is the outlier?"

"JarVexx."

The name silenced the room. Eventually, Tina spoke. "In some ways, it makes sense," she said. It will be easiest to cook the books and divert feeding stations at the source of the feeding stations."

"You're right," said Shawn. "Damn. And I liked those people."

"Mackowitz?" asked Maria.

"I doubt it," I said. "He's done very well for himself. I don't see a motive."

"Maybe he's not doing this of his own free will?" she asked again.

"It's possible, certainly."

"How about Doyle?" said Joe. "She's in charge of the whole lab. Mackowitz has given her carte blanche to run the program. She could be flying way under the radar."

"Again, it's possible," said Shawn. "She's younger, less well settled, and might have more financial motivation. And as you said about Mackowitz, if she's the leaky faucet, she might not be doing this of her own free will."

"Doyle makes the most sense," said Tina. "She could do this without anyone else at JarVexx knowing a thing about it."

"Regrettably, I must agree," said Reldap. "She is likely the responsible party."

"Next steps?" asked Joe.

"Well, if the faucet's leaking," said Tina, "let's figure out where the water's draining."

CHAPTER 35

A stroke of luck and quick thinking by Reldap gave us the needed break. Now came the legwork.

Unlike police dramas on the vids (especially unlike early 21st-century British police procedural shows), real detective work is slow, unglamorous, and 95% boring. However, when done patiently and correctly, the yield is surprisingly high. This case was no different. Bad guys make mistakes, make assumptions, and overlook stuff.

Shawn and Tina contacted the local FBI office and the Maine State Police. Together, the two agencies set up surveillance on the Falmouth kleptron site. Deliveries to and shipments from the JarVexx lab were carefully monitored. On the surface, everything looked kosher. There were no midnight pickups or shady-looking characters in hoodies and dark glasses showing up at the shipping dock. A United Federal truck came daily. Agents could see inbound shipments from chemical and biologics companies and returning auto-fridge units. Outbound, the fragile, perishable feeding stations were packed in auto-fridge units, small self-contained reusable battery-powered refrigerators with gyro stabilizers that kept delicate, degradable items cold and in one piece until they got to their destinations. Once unloaded, the units were returned to the shipper, recharged, and refilled for another delivery.

After a couple of weeks, a pattern emerged. There were 97 legal kleptron research centers, including JarVexx. In both weeks, 97 auto-fridge units were outbound, one too many—JarVexx did not need a shipment.

The Feds obtained a warrant to examine the outbound shipments. United Federal Shipping was contacted, and their local drivers were alerted. After loading each outbound shipment, the UFS truck was driven a prudent distance from the kleptron facility, and the load was inspected. All was well with the first two days' shipments. On the third day, the load contained an auto-fridge destined for a "Zhadnost Foods" located in Kirkville, a suburb of St. Louis. Zhadnost Foods was not a sanctioned kleptron facility. We looked the business up, and it was a small wholesale company handling Russian and Eastern European delicacies. Fearing that breaking the supply chain would make all the perps go to ground, the auto-fridge unit was allowed to continue to its destination. Tina called the Agent in Charge in St. Louis and alerted her to the shipments. Surveillance was initiated at the delivery address, an old, converted warehouse. It was time to start asking questions and getting answers.

We expected it would be disconcerting and disorienting for a human to be interviewed in a criminal matter by a giant alien dung beetle. As this state of affairs would greatly benefit the investigator, we re-involved the e-Fleks. This was also a good thing in other aspects, as they had spent the last three weeks doing military maneuvers and discussing trilobite-related issues with various human groups such as "Friends of the TLA" (FOTLA).

I met the other bipeds at the Grange Hall. Klak was on a table giving a lecture on trilobite culture and language to a local school group. When he finally finished, we called him over. "Klak," said Tina, "we have a new lead in the kleptron case and need your help."

"On it, guv. Let me collect the lads." He clambered down from the table and went to the Hall's back yard. In short order, the six appeared and declared themselves present and ready for duty.

"Klak, you were right," said Tina. "One of us was bent, and we think we know who it is. We request that you and the lads assist in the investigation."

"Thank you, ma'am."

"Let's get you and the boys on a flatbed and head down to Falmouth."

Our existing warrants covered JarVexx if needed, so there was no delay. After various arthropodal non-sequiturs were delivered, all six-legged and two-legged life forms were loaded onto appropriate transportation, and off we went. We also arranged to be met by cybercrime and evidence specialists at JarVexx.

We arrived at the Falmouth installation unannounced. Shawn showed the warrant to the access control security officer and told him not to announce their presence. The issue was moot after Klak and the other five e-Fleks ran into the building screaming, "Armed police! Come out and show yourselves!" So much for surprise.

Fortunately, we did manage to surprise Doyle; her office was at the far end of the building from the entrance, and she had been wearing earphones. "Ms. Doyle, step away from your computer. Do not touch your keyboard or mouse or the holographic projector. Thank you. Now, please come with us."

As we took Jen to a conference room for interrogation, Tina contacted Mackowitz and asked him to come to the Falmouth lab as soon as possible. He had been on his way to the lab for other purposes, so he arrived only a few minutes later. He joined us in the conference room.

Shawn, far and away our best interrogator, started. He opened his laptop and prepared his notes. He started his audio recorder. He was about to speak when Klak started in. "Ms. Doyle, you are being interviewed under caution. You do not have to say anything. But, it may harm your defence if you do not mention when questioned something which you later rely on in court. Anything you do say may be given in evidence."

Shawn sighed. "Ms. Doyle, we need to have a serious conversation. Depending upon your statements, you may be charged with various violations of the Kleptron Control Act of 2131. Do you understand this?"

"Yes, I do."

"All right, please listen: You have the right to remain silent. Anything you say can be used against you in court. You have the right to talk to a lawyer for advice before we ask you any questions. You have the right to have a lawyer with you during questioning. If you cannot afford a lawyer, one will be appointed for you before any questioning if you wish. If you decide to answer questions now without a lawyer present, you have the right to stop answering at any time. Do you wish to continue without a lawyer present?"

"Yes, I do."

Johnson was about to start when Klak interrupted again. "Guv, the recorder is wrong."

"What?"

"It's supposed to be much larger, a large box with two tapes. And it's supposed to make a long beeping sound before the interview starts, and you're supposed to say the time and identify everyone in the room."

Tina, who by now had been identified as the de facto chief e-Flek wrangler, chimed in. "I think we're OK, Klak. It'll do."

"Human Johnson, are you sure?"

"Yes, Klak. It will be fine."

The e-Fleks started arguing among themselves, too fast for the translators. It ended abruptly with Klak slamming down one of his front legs and saying, "Listen, you lot, if the gaffer says it's OK, it's OK." He looked at Johnson. "It's all good, boss. Go ahead."

Before Johnson could start, Jen spoke. "Dr. Mackowitz, I'm so sorry, I…"

Shawn stopped her. His tone was very gentle. "Jen, let's do this systematically, OK?" She nodded.

"I'd like to start by asking you to recall a visit by Reldap about three weeks ago when he came to discuss a new chemical dispersant being tested for kleptron feeding stations. Do you remember that visit?"

"Yes, I do."

"At that time, you had a CubeSheet DataBox open on your desk. Do you recall that?"

"Yes. Very much so. I had wanted to close the application before I left the room, but I was afraid that would appear suspicious. I took my chances."

"All right. Do you recall the contents of that DataBox?"

"Yes. It was my private copy of feeding station data by site."

"Your private copy?"

"Yes. I provided a different DataBox to JarVexx, one that would not raise suspicion. That DataBox shows only 96 outbound weekly shipments, and the feeding stations are distributed among the research sites commensurate with the number of kleptrons held at each institution. That DataBox would arouse no concerns."

"I see. And the extra shipment of an auto-fridge per week?"

"We do so much business with United Federal that I banked on one extra shipment per week getting lost in the noise."

"And it would appear that you were correct. Dr. Mackowitz, you might want to tighten up your oversight here." Dave nodded.

"So you acknowledge diverting feeding stations and that you did so without the knowledge or assistance of anyone at JarVexx?"

"Yes, I do."

"And what was the purpose of this diversion?"

"To maintain an illicit colony of kleptrons."

Johnson paused, looking thoughtful. "Why?"

Jen took a deep breath. "My birth name is Evgeniya Devlova."

Joe looked up, shocked. "As in the Russian oligarch Ivan Devlov?"

"He's my uncle."

"They say that he is not a good person sometimes," said Joe carefully.

"No, sometimes he is not," said Jen. "My father left the old country as soon as he could and came here. He wanted nothing to do with that life. When I was five, he changed the names of everyone in the family. A sympathetic judge sealed all records related to the Devlov name. My birth certificate was changed. As far as the world is concerned, I've been Jen Doyle since birth."

Johnson paused for a moment, then continued his questioning. "What did you get out of this? What was your cut? Did you contact him or vice versa?"

Doyle shook her head and gave Johnson a nasty look. "I absolutely did not do this voluntarily." She was mad. "How can you even make such an accusation? I am not a criminal."

Johnson shook his head slowly. "Okay, then what did your uncle have on you?"

"Nothing personally. Until this business with the kleptrons, I hadn't even gotten a speeding ticket."

Mackowitz interrupted. "I can confirm that. Her background check was spotless."

"OK, what did he have on you?" repeated Johnson.

"My brother. He runs an import-export business. My mom and dad. They have a small but successful restaurant."

"Ah," said Johnson. "Sometimes, brother slips into a bit of an import-export gray zone? Mom and Dad sometimes are a little loose on health and sanitation laws?"

Jen nodded. "No, no. None of that. They are all legit."

Mackowitz interrupted once more. "Again, I can confirm that. Questionable family members would have come up on our background checks. Even before the kleptrons, we did specialized biological work for the government. Our employees need to be squeaky clean."

"When this kleptron business came up a year ago, Ivan asked me to divert some kleptrons for him. I said no. Suddenly, my brother's shipments started getting lost and stolen. Mom and Dad started receiving spoiled meat and rotten vegetables. I still refused to go along. Then people started following me, and I started getting threatening texts and slips of paper under my door. Once even my tires were slashed. I gave in when I came home one night, and I found my cat dead, eviscerated on my kitchen floor. I gave up."

At this point, she was crying. "I staged the break-in. I've been diverting feeding stations since then. No more lost packages, fresh meat and produce for Mom and Dad, and my new kitten is happy and healthy, with an intact abdominal wall."

I shuddered. "Why didn't you go to the police?" I asked.

She scoffed. "Don't be silly, Dr. Gilner."

Johnson nodded. "Unfortunately, she's right. Devlov's tentacles are everywhere, and in Russia he's physically beyond US jurisdiction." He turned off the recorder. He looked at the three other Federal officers and motioned toward the door. "This may take some time, but we'll be back, hopefully within an hour." They left the room.

Jen turned to me. "What's going to happen to me?"

"Honestly, I don't know," I said. "I think a lot will depend on the conversation outside right now and what you are willing to do to help the investigation."

She nodded.

"Bloody mess, luv, but we'll sort it," said Klak.

For once, the lunatic bug was spot on.

CHAPTER 36

The conversation outside the conference room among the four officers was quick and to the point.

"She's a victim, not a perp. Immunity."

"There is zero value in charging this woman, and she holds the keys to the kingdom. We need to protect her, not prosecute her."

"Agreed. Let's get her onside and nail that asshole."

"Agreed. Immunity and protection."

There were several hurried phone calls with federal and state prosecutors. It took only 30 minutes to get electronic proffers sent to Shawn's and Tina's PDDs. So equipped, the four officers returned to the conference room.

Tina took the lead. "Ms. Doyle, we fully recognize that you were as much a victim as the perpetrator in this business. We are prepared to offer you complete immunity for all acts associated with the original kleptron theft and the repeated violations of the Kleptron Control Act subsequent to that crime. We have also conferred with our state colleagues, and there will be no charges under state law. You and your family will be provided comprehensive protection. This offer of immunity and protection is dependent upon your complete cooperation in further investigating these crimes and your willingness to testify, under oath and in court, as to your personal acts related to this matter and your interactions and relationships with other individuals."

Jen started crying again, this time from relief. She was about to answer when Mackowitz put up his hand. "Jen, I am sure that this is exactly what we all want. However, this is a serious legal matter. Let me make a call. Corporate counsel will be here in 15 minutes, and we'll make sure this agreement is in your best interest."

"I can't possibly afford D'Angelo. I..."

"Jen, you're one of my best. Don't worry about it. I'm happy to help." He turned to Tina. "You guys okay with this?"

"Dr. Mackowitz, we were about to recommend a formal legal review of the proffer by an attorney representing Ms. Doyle, and had a public defender on standby to do so in case Ms. Doyle did not have counsel. We are happy to wait until that occurs."

D'Angelo showed up quickly. He spoke with the federal officers and Mackowitz for half an hour to understand the facts of the case. Reviewing the proffer took another half hour. He got up and sat down next to Jen. "This is a generous, fair offer, but you must cooperate fully. You'll likely need to continue the illegal shipments and let the next guy in the supply chain get caught. Then, you'll need to testify in court about the intimidation and what you did and didn't do at JarVexx. Your familial relationships may become public knowledge. Are you up to this?"

"I think so. Protection for me, my family?"

Stein spoke up. "We have that covered. There will be comprehensive protection for you and your family."

Doyle thought for a moment. "Then OK. Yes. Absolutely."

"Good. Sign this, and let's catch those bastards."

A synthetic translator voice floated up from the floor at the other end of the table. "Bloody good show, mate. Bloody good show."

Tina shook her head. Jen signed. The lawyer shook Jen's hand, conferred briefly with Dr. Mackowitz, thanked the officers, and left.

"Okay," said Joe. "I think it's time we learned a little more about Zhadnost Foods."

Jen smiled mirthlessly. "Do you know what Zhadnost means in Russian?"

"No, what does it mean?"

"Greed."

CHAPTER 37

"So we follow the auto-fridges?" I asked.

"Yeah. Those gyro-stabilized battery-powered refrigerators that they use to deliver the feeding stations," said Tina. "Follow the auto-fridges and find the next link. The St. Louis FBI said the delivery address was an old warehouse that had been converted to a wholesale food operation. I doubt that people are eagerly consuming kleptron feeding stations. My guess is that United Federal makes a drop in good faith, and the auto-fridges full of feeding stations are somehow transferred onward. Zhadnost is also the collection point for empty auto-fridges that need to go back into use. United Federal picks up the empty auto-fridges, again in good faith, after they've somehow made their way back to Zhadnost."

"Makes sense," I said.

"I'm going to call the St. Louis FBI office and get a complete picture of the situation," she said. "We will need to visit St. Louis and Kirkville, but what we do once we get there is unclear."

I nodded in agreement. We were finished at JarVexx. I said goodbye to Dave. I was impressed at his gracious support of Jen; I wouldn't have blamed him if he had cut her loose. We gathered the Waterville contingent, loaded the bugs onto their flatbed, and headed north. Jen was exhausted, upset, and not fit to drive, so we gave her a lift home on the way back to Waterville. When we dropped her at her home, a car with government plates was already parked across the street from her house.

The rest of the day was uneventful. That evening, Helen and I talked about her participation in the investigation. She was still clinically active and working hard on KASMA research. Despite her interest in shutting down illegal klepping and the value of her insight, she would limit her participation in our cross-country cops and robbers forays. We'd tap her expertise as needed.

Tina called me early the following day, and we convened at the Grange Hall. The e-Fleks were still outside grazing, so we bipeds had a chance to have a sane, focused discussion. The situation in Kirkville was puzzling. The warehouse had a shipping and receiving dock and a reception area. Electricity consumption was commensurate with a small wholesale food operation using several refrigeration and freezer units. Other than the weekly UFS truck, there was only modest traffic in other delivery vans and customer vehicles. Based on everything we saw, I would be surprised if they were even making payroll. It had to be a front.

The surveillance so far had not answered how the feeding stations got from Zhadnost to the illegal kleptron facility. Road traffic to and from Zhadnost was limited to customers, UFS and other delivery trucks, and the employees' vehicles. All the customer vehicles came from old, well-established, high-end specialty food shops, and it was unlikely that they were involved. A secret underground passage to another building was the stuff of novels. Employee vehicles? Is someone from UFS in cahoots with these guys? One of the other delivery services? Were the kleptrons stored on site?

There were many questions, but the plan for answering them was straightforward. We'd get a warrant for Zhadnost Foods. Shawn would drive the UFS truck. The truck would carry kleptron feeding stations and a few Federal agents. We'd bust in and look around Zhadnost. We'd need at least one e-Flek to sniff around in the chance that kleptrons were on site.

Tina sighed. "I'll have to call the e-Fleks in," she said. "If one of them is participating in the raid, we must start including them in the discussions."

"Yeah," said Shawn. "Although I'm not sure our exchanges with the critters qualify as discussions."

"Point taken. I'll go get them."

The e-Fleks trooped into the Grange Hall. "Bipeds," said Klak, "feeding was excellent this morning. We even tried garter snake. Quite tasty."

I shuddered.

"The TLA stands ready to assist in the righteous cause of controlling the kleptrons. As long as we can also look for the stasis chamber holding our brethren."

Everything has its price, I thought.

Shawn outlined what we had learned so far and the plan going forward.

"Brilliant! You'll be the UCO, guv?"

"Yes, I will be the undercover officer."

"Will the agents in the truck be armed?"

"Yes. We hope it will not come to that, but they will be armed."

"Will the TLA be able to jump out of the truck as well and give the armed police warning?"

"Klak, we thought we would just need one of you…"

"Unacceptable, endotherm. The TLA travels in solidarity. It is all of us, or none of us."

"Klak, please. Just this once. Can we do something that makes sense?"

"Human, not negotiable." Klak's front legs were waving wildly.

Johnson knew he wasn't going to win. "Fine, we'll fit you all in somehow."

"Mammal…"

"Klak, stop calling me mammal. My name is Shawn or Agent Johnson."

"Fine. Human Shawn, please answer my question. Will the TLA be able to jump out of the back of the truck and give the armed police warning?"

"Yes, but only when I tell you to."

"Excellent. The TLA will be proud to assist in this endeavor. Especially when help may result in the consumption of many tasty kleptrons."

"Thank you." The polite response did not jibe with the disgusted look on his face.

Joe called JarVexx. The next shipment from JarVexx to Zhadnost was in two days. The auto-fridges would arrive at the warehouse three days from now. We would have plenty of time to make the necessary arrangements. Shawn addressed the Latternites. "Will you guys come with us? Your speed and strength are sometimes very helpful. I'd rather have one of you pick someone up by the collar than fire a Taser at them."

"Yes, Agent Johnson. We will be happy to help."

CHAPTER 38

Preparations were routine. We got transportation and warrants. Shawn contacted United Federal, and we arranged for him to drive a truck to Zhadnost. Not much happened until the morning of the operation, and it gave me a chance to catch up on the news.

The vids were filled with bizarre stories of FOTLA "assessments" of various places around the U.S., including Central Park in New York. A group of people, usually five or six, would suddenly appear and cordon off an area of 10 by 10 meters. They'd then raise the Trilobite Liberation Army flag and start digging.

The digging was crazy. Usually, the FOTLA members used picks and shovels; afraid that powered digging equipment could damage the stasis chamber, they generally eschewed bulldozers and excavators. The hand tools could barely penetrate the earth much less dig to any level where there was a chance of finding fossils. On top of that, the excavations often took place where there was zero expectation of finding trilobite fossils, much less a stasis chamber. At the Central Park "assessment" site, a reporter pointed out that the geology of the region had been examined for hundreds of years and that the combination of the three metamorphic formations composing Manhattan Island had never yielded any paleontological specimens. One of the FOTLA people started screaming that they had done their own research and started swinging his shovel at the poor fellow while his fellow excavators chanted, "Make arthropods great again." The police had to intervene.

We loaded the crew onto a hydrogen ramjet aircraft the morning of the operation and landed at a small airfield outside St. Louis. A UFS truck was waiting for us, as were three SWAT-type FBI agents who would accompany Shawn and the e-Fleks. The rest of us would enter the facility after it was secure.

The drive to the op went smoothly all things considered. The e-Fleks were very excited with chanting and spitting, but the FBI agents, briefed on the "peculiarities of the case," finally got them quiet and still as the truck backed up to within a couple of meters of the loading dock. Shawn climbed down from the driver's seat and walked to the reception window. An older, friendly woman greeted him.

"Hi there! Where's Tom today?" she said.

"Hi, Tom took the day off. Something about a tooth. I'm Shawn," Shawn answered.

"Hey Shawn, good to meet you. Too bad about Tom. He's a nice guy. Hope he's better."

"I'm sure he will be. It sounded painful but fixable. I'm sorry, but I gotta get a move on. My truck is just crazy full, and I have never driven this route before. It's gonna be a long day."

"Sure, hon. Sorry about that. Give me a chance, and I'll just chatter on and on. If you give me your tablet, I'll do the signatures and tell the boys in the back to open up."

"Great. Thanks so much."

Shawn handed over the tablet and walked back to his truck. The rolling doors of the warehouse opened, and he backed his vehicle back to the loading dock. He called back into the cargo area. "Ready?"

"Roger that."

"GO! GO! GO!"

The back of the panel truck flung open, and the three FBI agents ran out into the warehouse. Before they could say anything, the e-Fleks also shot out, screaming, "Armed police! Come out and show yourselves!"

The two schlemiels on the loading dock stood there staring at the TLA banner-waving screaming bugs. They were easily subdued. I have to admit that had I been in their situation, I might not have had the presence of mind to do anything else, either.

Still outside the building, Tina stepped up to the window of the office worker, who was still unaware of what was transpiring at the loading dock. Tina smiled. The receptionist smiled back. "Hi, hon, what can I do for ya?"

Tina's smile stayed bright as she flipped her badge. "Hi. FBI. Put your hands where I can see them, and don't touch a thing." Wisely, the receptionist obeyed.

The warehouse was almost empty except for two fridges, one freezer, a rack of shelving, and a stand-up computer terminal. Not exactly a massive wholesale food operation. Half a dozen empty auto-fridges were stacked near the loading dock, ready for return to JarVexx. There was a break room with a table and chairs, and the suspects were brought in there.

"Good show, guv," said Klak. "Do you need help with the questioning? Do you want me to observe from the adjacent room through the one-way mirror and the audio feed and give you interrogation suggestions?"

"Klak," said Shawn, "there's no adjacent room with an audio feed. Also, we have other things to do before we start the interrogation."

"Right, sir. Should we get some uniforms here to keep an eye on these sods whilst we do our work?"

Johnson looked at Klak, surprised that the creature had made a usable suggestion. "Good idea. I'll take care of it." He called the local police department and explained the situation. They were more than happy to assist. Help arrived about 20 minutes later.

Klak, I have a task for you and the lads."

"On it, sir. What do you need?"

"Let's take a quick walk." Johnson and Klak walked over to the empty auto-fridges. "Do these containers smell of kleptrons?"

Klak scuttled close to one of the devices. "Faint, guv, but they've definitely been in contact with kleptrons."

Shawn thought for a moment. This was important information; the feeding stations had not been transferred to another conveyance before arriving at the site of the illegal kleptron colony. It might be possible to continue to follow the auto-fridges to the brainsuckers. "Klak," he said, "I need you to investigate this room carefully. Are there any areas of concentrated kleptron residue? Is there a trail? Is there anything?"

The e-Flek raised a front leg in a crude salute. He called over the rest of the TLA and chattered at them. They fanned out over the warehouse floor in a skirmish line and slowly sniffed around the building. They would be busy for a while, and interrogating the three suspects could proceed with some semblance of order.

The three suspects sat in the break room. Tina had started talking to them, and it wasn't going well. All three had requested attorneys and would not identify themselves. "Before we take them in, let's see what the e-Fleks have found. I have a hunch," said Johnson.

Johnson was right. Klak reported back about an hour later. "Interesting, guv. Lots of kleptron scent near the elevator to the basement."

"What? What elevator to the basement?"

"The one that leads to the secret passageway to the other building. If we follow it far enough, I'm sure it connects with the Tube, and the bleedin' buggers are getting out at the next station."

"Wait, wait. What secret passageway?"

"Sir, follow us."

"OK. Just wait a second. Joe, Maria, look up the original building permit for this place while I look at what they are talking about."

Johnson and Standing Elk followed the TLA to a corner of the warehouse. There was a door, which turned out to be a door to an elevator shaft. They pushed the down button, and when the car came, they descended to the basement. There was a bewildering maze of pipes, cables, and tunnels, some of it looking like it might have been installed in the late 20th century.

Meanwhile, Joe had finished his search of the building records. "Hmm," he said. "Very interesting. Wait till we get downstairs, and I'll show you what I found."

Joe, Maria, the Latternites, and I took the elevator down to the basement. Joe walked over to Shawn and Tina and showed them his tablet.

"It looks like this building and three others were built in the 1990s as part of an industrial complex. They shared steam heat, electricity, telephone service, everything they used back then. Utility tunnels. Not exactly secret passageways, but they might as well be."

"Do they go anywhere now?" I asked. "I didn't see any other warehouse buildings."

"Good question," said Johnson. "Klak, show us the trail of kleptron scent."

"Right, boss. OK, lads, let's get on it!"

Without hesitation, the bugs started down the largest tunnel and turned left at the first junction. We'd walked about 100 meters or so when Klak stopped. "There," he said as he pointed to a gaping hole in the ceiling. It appeared to be covered with a piece of plywood. "No kleptron scent past that."

The four Feds went into cop mode. They motioned everyone to be quiet, and as noiselessly as possible, we retraced our steps. We returned to the first floor of the old warehouse. The agents examined Joe's tablet together and located the ground-level location of the hole in the tunnel. The original warehouse at the site of the hole had been torn down long ago and replaced by generic retail space. If we had triangulated correctly, the hole was under a small store that sold industrial pumps and parts. Shawn called the three uniformed FBI agents and laid out the plan. Two SWAT guys swapped places with us in the tunnel in case someone tried to make a break for it, and we convinced the TLA that they needed to help in the tunnel. The third SWAT circled around to the back of the building's rear entrance, ready to confront any runners. The four Feds, the Latternites, and I walked into the shop. A chime rang.

The young guy at the counter initially didn't look up. "Hold on," he said. "Let me just finish this, and I'll be right with you." He did a little more typing and then said, "There. All set. How can I help you?" He looked up, smiling.

The four Federal agents were grim-faced, holding out their badges. I was back near the door, out of the way. The Latternites flanked the knot of Feds.

The smile faded. "I'm fucked, aren't I?"

"Indeed you are," said Maria. As she was speaking, we heard a scrambling in the back room. Before any of the humans could react, Reldap and Penfor had vaulted the counter.

"They're toast," said Joe.

"Yup," said Maria.

We heard some scuffling, and about 15 seconds later, the Latternites returned with their prize.

"Human," said Penfor, "open the counter pass-through."

The counter guy did as he was asked. Reldap and Penfor had another young guy between them. Each held an arm, and he was about 10 cm off the floor.

Joe shook his head. "Fella, you can never, ever outrun a Latternite biobot. Thanks, guys, put him down."

Reldap and Penfor gently put him down but kept hold of his arms.

"Is there anyone else in the shop?" asked Maria.

He didn't answer. "We'll go check," said Tina.

The two FBI agents went behind the counter and searched the small storage area. "No one's here," said Tina, "but come back and look at this."

We could see the plywood cover for the hole. An industrial, heavy-duty hoist on wheels was just to the right of it. It was pretty ingenious, with a gyro-stabilized platform and folding sides.

"This can hoist an auto-fridge from the tunnel, can't it?" said Maria.

"Sure can. Piece of cake," said Shawn.

We walked back to the front of the store.

"You fellas have a little explaining to do," said Shawn.

The two perps said nothing.

CHAPTER 39

"Let's bring these nice folks to the warehouse," said Shawn.

"No," said Joe. "Give me a minute with these jokers." He turned to the two perps. "Gentlemen, and I use the term loosely, the next ten minutes are important. Very important, so listen closely. We can do this easy, we can do this hard, or we can make suicide look like a friend. Here's scenario one: We can arrest you and read your rights. You ask for lawyers, and we comply. You say nothing, and we take you to trial. The evidence against you is very strong. You are unquestionably involved in multiple violations of the Kleptron Control Act, to say nothing of various other state and Federal laws you've broken. You do ten years, maybe eight if you keep your noses clean. You guys will probably be only a little gray when you get out. It might even make you look distinguished. You still might have some interest in sex, at least to some degree. You'll be OK. You are clearly within your rights to take this tack, and in some ways, I would respect you for it. Honor among thieves and all that. And you'll be safe from the Russians if you survive max."

"What?" asked one of the suspects.

"Yeah, max. Do you think you're gonna do your time at one of those Federal country clubs? Nah, think again. You give us a hard time, we give you hard time."

Joe continued. "Here's scenario two: We arrest you and read you your rights. You ask for lawyers, and we comply. Your lawyers wisely tell you to help us, and you wisely do so. We nail the perps, and you disappear. Poof. No more Suspect A and Suspect B." He looked at the two men. "New identity, new life, no more Russian mob. I don't know if you two chuckleheads can take advantage of such an opportunity to go straight, but we'll give it to you.

"Scenario three: You give us a really fucking hard time. You tell us stories. You send us on a wild goose chase. You spin us yarns that make Grimm's fairy tales look like reality. In that case, we let you go."

The two men looked at each other.

"Yeah. We let you go. After we've publicly thanked you for helping us so much. We laud you guys on the CitizenHeroes website, the local vids, whatever. You're real stars. You've put us on the right track. We are grateful beyond accounting." He paused. "So what's it gonna be?"

Joe was on a roll, and he continued. "Now, the reason I say that we need to make a decision in the next ten minutes or so is you guys just received a shipment of feeding stations. That means that some other chucklehead is gonna come here in the next couple of hours to collect the feeding stations. If they see something is wrong, they're gonna bolt, and we're gonna lose our trail, and we don't want that to happen."

"Gentlemen, I suggest you put whatever neurons you have in your skulls to work and consider what I've said."

Wow. I'd seen Joe push the envelope, but never like this. I waited to see what would happen.

Reldap started to speak. "Shut up, two thumbs," said Joe. "These guys gotta concentrate."

I was appalled. The two men spoke to each other in low tones. It didn't take very long. The guy from the counter spoke. "I think we'd like a lawyer so we can discuss how we can cooperate."

"Excellent. Wise choice. Take these guys in the back. I'll be right there." The two men were brought into the store room, out of earshot of the rest of us.

Joe turned to Reldap. "Reldap, I am so, so sorry. I needed to maintain a fiction. You are a good being, and I value your friendship. I wish I had two thumbs."

"Thank you, Agent Stein. I understand what you were doing. It was devious but clever. Very human. Your apology is accepted. Would you have done what you said? Let them go and falsely claim they had helped?"

"Never. It would be a death sentence. We just needed to move things along. Unfortunately, time is on their side, not ours."

Maria looked at Joe. "Stein, you haven't slung bullshit like that since that case in '29. Very impressive."

"All right, all right," he said. "Maybe it was a little over the top. But it got the job done, right?"

I had to hand it to the Feds; they'd done their homework. They knew they were going to make arrests today. They figured someone was going to flip. They also knew time would be of the essence. They'd lined up an on-call public defender and an on-call prosecutor. Shawn and Tina went into the back room. One PDD call and the proffer was made, reviewed, and accepted. It turned out the two men were chronic low-level offenders. They knew the drill and knew they'd just won the lottery. This bid was not going to be a month in the county jail. It was time to get out while the getting was good.

The two guys from the pump store gave us the outline of the operation. The scheme was simple and brilliant. As far as United Federal was concerned, Zhadnost Foods handled perishable Russian delicacies. The traffic in auto-fridges looked like routine commerce.

The industrial pump store sold industrial pumps and parts. The retailer was wildly popular with its customers, partly because it was happy to take broken, old, and replaced equipment and dispose of it for them. This generosity, in turn, made it entirely plausible to see a steady stream of trucks to and from the store to a place called Musor Recycling. Musor was a new recycling plant near the small airport where we had landed. The trick was that feeding stations went to Musor along with the recycling.

Musor Recycling really did recycle, but the moneymaker was kleptrons. The brainsuckers were housed at Musor between "jobs." Used feeding stations could be disposed of without anyone knowing there had ever been feeding stations at Musor; they would just be fed into the recycling stream. As for getting the kleptrons to a klepping, trucks carrying kleptrons could go anywhere without question. After all, everyone had garbage and recycling they needed to dispose of, and Musor's pickup service was appreciated by its customers. It was brilliant.

We had a couple of hours until pickup. We transferred the auto-fridges to the pump store through the utility tunnel. The hoist, as we expected, worked well. The two guys at the store prepared the recycling load and the auto-fridges for pickup. As scheduled, a truck from Musor arrived and unloaded six empty auto-fridges. The industrial recycling (the legal payload) and six auto-fridges filled with feeding stations were packed into the truck, and off it went to

Musor Recycling with the driver unaware of what transpired. Feeding station deliveries were once a week, and the perps told us that the kleptrons weren't going anywhere soon; things had gotten too hot. With a successful transfer of feeding stations to Musor, we'd caught ourselves a breather. We now had seven days to figure out what to do next.

CHAPTER 40

"This collar is great. Finding out about Musor is even better," said Joe. "I need to report back. This is gonna be wrapped up very soon. The Prez is going to be very pleased."

"If you must," said Maria. "Heaven knows what he'll do with the information."

"Look, you know I have to report in. It's not optional."

"Do what you need to."

******

"OK, let me get this straight. The space patrol, the nosy doc, and our guys actually figured out what's going on?"

"Yes, Mr. President. For the most part, the case is very close to resolved."

"Great. We gotta hold a press conference."

"Mr. President, there might be some downsides to doing that."

"Huh. Yeah, we might tip our hand. Glad I thought of that. We'll keep it under wraps."

"Excellent. An astute observation. Mr. President, you look a bit unsteady. Why don't you sit down."

"Yeah, good idea. This new stuff is a little strong. Where'd I get this?"

"It was a gift from President Khishchnik."

"Crafty devil. Trying to mess up my thinking."

You don't need any assistance from Khishchnik for that. *"Yes, Mr. President."*

******

The most obvious way forward is not always the best way forward. Should we just barrel over to Musor and crash their party? We had seven Federal agents (counting the SWATters), two enormously powerful aliens, the help of local police if needed, and our trusty TLA. We discussed this option and rejected it quickly. The raid required more preparation and more specialized staffing.

The consensus was to return to Maine for a regroup and refit. We returned to the airport, leaving the prisoners in the hands of the local FBI. We were assured that secrecy would be maintained. I had no idea how the local constabulary would do that in light of various laws regarding habeas corpus, but maybe I didn't want to know. I didn't ask.

The return to Waterville was uneventful. When we got to the Grange Hall, a note asked us to let the e-Fleks graze at the local golf course because of a rodent problem. We obliged cheerfully. The bugs were happy, and we could think without intermittent injections of British police slang.

Planning the raid was simple in concept and complex in execution. Enter the premises, prevent the escape of suspects, preserve evidence, and ensure no one gets injured. Easy enough.

The recycling plant was big, occupying just under a hectare. There were three buildings with enclosed walkways and connecting conveyors. There was a settling pond and, for want of a better term, a small mountain of garbage: stuff that was not recyclable and had to be decontaminated and then burned or buried. We reviewed the original building plans submitted with the licensing application. All three buildings had extensive utility hookups, and all three buildings had large open spaces where a storage facility for the kleptrons would be feasible. A large open space was critical: the brainsuckers needed to fly and exercise.

In the final analysis, on paper, the raid looked more like a military operation than a police raid. It had to be. We had no way of knowing how many people worked at Musor. We didn't know if they were armed, and if armed, with what. Finally, there were too many avenues of escape for suspects. It would be hard to go from building to building with small groups while maintaining surprise and preserving evidence. In the last analysis, overwhelming force would be the safest; no one would be foolish enough to resist even if they were armed to the teeth.

The plan was to grab a couple of Musor trucks returning to the recycling plant, empty them of their contents, and load them with FBI and Homeland Security agents; this was the "front door" team. Two helicopters would also participate. The first, an observation craft, would oversee the operation, providing real-time directions for following escaping suspects, etc. The second would carry agents (the "helicopter team") who would land at the opposite end of the property while the Feds in the trucks came through the front door. The e-Fleks, utterly taken with the idea of a helicopter attack, wanted to rappel down from the troop carrier. We pointed out that the humans didn't plan to do that and that their (e-Flek) anatomy was not conducive to rappelling. We compromised by having the TLA ride in the helicopter rather than the trucks.

The preparations came together quickly. We were ready to go two days after the pump store raid. The front door team pushed off a few hours ahead of us (I was part of the helicopter team) and snared a couple of Musor trucks. When we took off, we synchronized arrival time.

The coordination was perfect. The front door people exploded onto the loading dock while the helicopter team landed behind the building judged most likely to house the kleptrons.

The bipedal component of the action went according to plan. The sheer number of agents overwhelmed the recycling plant. No one did anything stupid except for one guy. We'll get to that later.

The TLA went nuts. Abandoning the kleptron operation, Klak got it into his head (or nervous system or whatever) that the stasis chamber was at the bottom of the settling pond. I think he saw a discarded metal tank at the bottom of the pond and was immediately convinced that this was the stasis chamber. All six of the things dove into the basin.

"Interesting," said Penfor. "I did not know e-Fleks could swim," she said as she watched the bugs paddling around.

"They can't," said Reldap.

"That's a problem," said Ed.

Reldap and Penfor ran into the pond and dragged the flailing creatures to safety. "The water is quite dirty," croaked Klak.

"Yes, it is a settling pond at a recycling center. Filthy, contaminated water is dumped into the pond so that particulates can settle. The cleaner water is dumped out from time to time, and periodically the crap at the bottom is dredged out," said Penfor. "You managed to jump in when the water was particularly foul. What made you think the stasis chamber was at the bottom of this muck pile?"

"I saw the gleam of metal."

Penfor grimaced. "Klak, there are many pieces of gleaming metal on Earth. Let's get cleaned up. Human Gilner, can you help us?"

I found a hydrant and hose and washed the Latternites and e-Fleks down. Just about when I finished, Maria emerged from one of the buildings. She quickly surveyed me holding a fire hose along with eight sopping-wet aliens. "I'm sure there's a good explanation," she said, "but we'll hear about it later. Right now, we need you inside. Dr. Gilner, put on your tinfoil. Reldap, Penfor, you may want to do so as well."

This did not sound good, and I noticed then that Maria was wearing a foil-lined cap. We walked over to the door Maria had just exited. "OK, everyone, quick, quick, quick. I don't want to risk any of those wretched things getting out."

She let us into a large room one by one. Three FBI agents were standing in the room, swatting at dozens of swarming kleptrons. A wall of kleptron cages was empty; all the doors were open. There was a guy in handcuffs seated in a corner. He was laughing hysterically.

"Bozo over here hit the switch to let these things out of their cages like it was exercise time," explained Joe. "He called it 'a final act of defiance.' We call it 'his final act as a free man.'" Stein was seriously pissed.

Despite the swarms of brainsuckers and the palpable tension in the room, the e-Fleks were strangely quiet and calm. "My friends, my friends," said Klak, "a problem for you but a bountiful harvest for us. Leave us for a few days, and all will be well."

"A few days?" I asked.

"Yes, mammal. This is a treat to be savored, not devoured."

I looked at Joe. He shrugged. Shawn, who, until this point, hadn't said much, spoke up. "We promised the e-Fleks their reward, and they'll get it, but in due time." He looked at Joe and Maria and then continued. "You guys must have been instructed on what to do once we made the collar."

"Yup. Get the press in, maximize publicity, shine a spotlight on how The Prez contributed to and led this effort, blah blah blah."

"OK, usual bullshit. Let me think." He leaned against a wall and looked serious, planning the next steps. After a couple of minutes, he spoke. "Criminal stuff first. We have everyone in custody?"

One of the uniformed FBI spoke up. "Yes, sir. We have ten employees of Musor detained. Except for this guy"—he gestured at the handcuffed perp in the chair—"everyone has been cooperative. In retrospect, we may have been a little over the top."

"Over the top?" asked Joe.

"Yessir. The helicopters, the size of the force…"

"No, it's all good. Scared the living bejesus out of them. Big thing is no one got hurt. Not us, not them.

"Yes, sir." The FBI seemed satisfied.

"Great. Computers, papers, records, other evidence secured?"

"Yes, sir."

"Other material evidence?"

"Uncertain, sir. We don't know what else might be relevant to the case."

"Understood."

"Uh sir,…"

"Yes?"

"The kleptrons. Their presence here is the most important fact in the case. We can't have our team eating the evidence."

"Good point. OK, let's put together a press pool and get a crime scene investigation team in here right away, and then we can let the bugs have their fun."

The TLA was initially quite peeved when they found out that their feast was going to be delayed, but turned surprisingly agreeable when Tina explained American rules of evidence. Tina and Shawn contacted their superiors, who involved their media relations folks. A top-tier CSI team was immediately dispatched.

While we waited for the press and investigators, attention turned back to our suspects. Shawn addressed the other FBI members. "Have any of you guys talked to these jokers?"

"Yes, sir. They've all asked for lawyers, and no one is saying a word."

"Thought that might happen. Anyone ID'ed yet?"

"No, sir. No one is saying a word. Tough bunch."

"Yeah, I guess if I were working for the Russian mob, I'd also be careful of what I said. Let's see these guys."

We went to the room that held the other nine detainees. Some were sullen, some were smiling defiantly. "Giorgio?" said Shawn.

The single word brought all of them to attention. Shawn smiled. "Who's Giorgio? Giorgio in here?" None of them said a word.

Finally, one of them spoke. "You don't want to fuck with Giorgio," he said with a heavy Russian accent. "He is, how do you say, a formidable man. Giorgio and Devlov are tight. Devlov and Khishchnik are tight. Khishchnik and Moorehead are tight. Mister FBI man, you are outranked and outgunned."

I didn't believe this guy. Yeah, Khishchnik, the Russian president, and Moorehead liked each other. They exchanged gifts, booze for Khishchnik and dope for Moorehead, and in their mind-altered way, they helped keep world peace. But Devlov? That was another story. Devlov was a seriously bad actor. Sure, Devlov and Khishchnik were buddies; all those rich Russians were. Khishchnik might tolerate a little bit of this and that, but brain damage for fun and profit? No way. Shawn was unconvinced and didn't buy it. "We'll see," he said.

The press and the CSI team arrived as we left with the suspects. Shawn, Tina, Joe, and Maria made a plain vanilla presentation to the media, promising more detail when it was available. Then, suitably shielded, the journalists were quickly shown the kleptron colony. The CSI people were pissed to have their crime scene invaded, but the forensics were neither complex nor subtle. There were kleptrons at a recycling plant. They weren't supposed to be there. Ten guys were caught red-handed—end of story. Most importantly, illegal klepping would end right then and there.

After several hours, the CSI team left. Tina, the star e-Flek wrangler, found Klak, who had wedged himself into a corner and seemed to be resting. The kleptrons are all yours," she said. Klak roused himself and rounded up the rest of the TLA.

"Shall I make a speech showing our appreciation?"

"No, Klak, it's fine. You've helped us. You've earned your reward. Enjoy yourselves."

"Thank you, human Standing Elk. This will be a long and happy feast. And the kleptrons will be in our thoughts and prayers. Say again, how many kleptrons are here?"

"About 190."

"Ah, that will be wonderful. A large number. Leave us plenty of water. Some salt and pepper might be nice, and tell us where we may eliminate the indigestible parts of these creatures. Come back in a week. And maybe some garlic powder?"

"Klak, you may eliminate where you like and how you like. Please spare me the details. We will leave you plenty of water, and I'll find you some salt and pepper and garlic powder. I think we'll check in on you from time to time before the week ends. I do have one question, though. Why did you say the kleptrons would be in your thoughts and prayers?"

"Our study of Earth customs shows us that we should say that dead or injured creatures are in our thoughts and prayers when in reality we are indifferent to their suffering. We have heard many of your most important political figures use that phrase precisely in this situation. As for solving the kleptron problem, we can now complete our primary task, finding the trilobite stasis chamber and making arthropods great again."

"Good luck with that, Klak."

Thank you, human. I spit in your presence." He hacked an enormous glob of brown liquid onto the floor.

******

Reldap had been watching the whole time. "They are eating living things."

"Yes, they are," I said. "But an agreement is an agreement."

"Yes, human Gilner, you are right. This rewards the e-Fleks and solves a difficult problem. I should stop dwelling on their eating habits."

"Reldap, you should be happy. You can report to Mission Control that the problem has been solved. I know Latternites don't like to eat living things. But e-Fleks aren't Latternites. And think of your human friends. Many of us eat living things."

He looked sad for a moment as he thought about it, but then brightened a little. "Yes, you are right again. When we are done here and return to Waterville, I will communicate with my father."

"Let's go. You don't need to watch this."

The e-Fleks were led into the cage room, and then we left.

CHAPTER 41

We drove back to the airport and took the ramjet back to Waterville. Penfor and Reldap immediately took Reldap's AEV back to St. Louis to keep an eye on things at the kleptron feast. It was some extra flying, but it did give the two Latternites some independence of movement.

My understanding of what happened in that cage room is mercifully limited. Reldap said it stank to high heaven. It was noisy and dirty. However, there were six very, very happy e-Fleks in that room. Reldap told me that one of the smaller ones ate so much that he needed to molt. A couple of times, Reldap needed to flip one of them back onto their feet; things had gotten pretty rowdy. They were happy. We were happy.

Reldap and Penfor loaded the bugs onto the AEV and returned to Waterville. Only vaguely aware of how appreciative we were of their assistance, the TLA happily returned to the Grange Hall to plan their search for the trilobites in suspended animation.

******

The two Latternites spent the evening at our house, decompressing. They didn't say much. I think they just wanted a break which was understandable. Except for dinner, we left them alone.

They left the next day mid-morning and went to LaFleur. They had decided to call Mission Control together and opted for Penfor's roomier, more comfortable AEV. After settling in the communication station, they initiated the call.

Ventak and Zeftan were both present. A third Latternite, someone Penfor recognized as an exchange specialist, was also on the call.

"Hello, fellow Latternites," said Ventak. "Well done! We have been monitoring Earth transmissions. All errant kleptrons caught! Please tell us the story as you saw it. I doubt the Earth news broadcasts are accurate."

Penfor and Reldap related the story of the investigation, starting with the false leads in Chicago, the trips to Texas and Louisiana, and Reldap's fortuitous and perceptive analysis of the DataBox. Zeftan interrupted at this point for commentary and questions.

"This CubeSheet seems quite formidable," he said. "Is it better than our HoloAnalysis package?"

"Yes, father. Considerably. It is much easier to use."

"Well, that's just because they aren't as technologically advanced as we are and need a simpler interface."

"I am not sure you are correct, father, but it is not worth debating."

"Indeed it is not. That Jackner and his friends—truly, they are harknars."

"Yes, father, you are unfortunately correct. They are addicted to the sounds of raised angry voices, breaking glass, and grinding metal."

"Don't they provide therapy for humans so afflicted?"

"No, they do not. Behaving this way is considered to be the exercise of free will and free speech."

"Most strange. All right, resume your story."

Penfor continued, explaining the details of the FBI operation. As with Reldap, she was occasionally interrupted for details and explanations.

"Most entertaining," said Zeftan. "I can see why the humans enjoy their police shows as they do."

"Yes, my Lord. Quite diverting."

"And the e-Fleks? Where are they now?"

"Back at our home base in Waterville."

"Good. We'll come back to them later."

"As you wish, my Lord."

"As you see, I have Genthor here. He is one of our foremost exchange specialists."

"Yes," said Reldap. "Greetings to you, Genthor. Your reputation precedes you."

"Genthor, I remember you well from my days at university. It is good to see you again," said Penfor.

"Thank you both," said Genthor. "I will let your father finish."

"Of course."

"All right," said Zeftan. "Let's get down to business. Reldap, you have been on Earth for roughly one Earth year. What do we have to show for that?"

"Well," Reldap said slowly, "we have learned many things. Their food and drink is wonderful. We have all grown to love the L.L. Bean folding chair. Their rocket fuel is superior to ours, and their formulation is now our standard. Some of their cell culture techniques, when combined with ours, have resulted in a genuine advance. Duct tape…"

Zeftan impatiently interrupted him. "Yes, yes, all well and good. With the possible exception of the rocket fuel, which I admit is remarkable, your examples are pure frippery. We didn't send you 25 light-years for beer and sticky tape. Genthor, the floor is yours."

"Thank you, my Lord. With the quantum communication station in place, we have been able to monitor Earth's activities with much greater detail. We see several areas of interest. Much of their computer software is superior to ours, particularly for non-quantum devices."

Zeftan harrumphed.

"I am sorry, my Lord, but that is a fact. They do have quantum computers. They are large and not portable because they do not have our cooling systems. This has delayed development, and our quantum software is much superior. However, their smaller, portable devices, in some respects, are quite remarkable. When properly programmed, they are inexpensive and highly effective devices. We have much to learn."

"Toys…," grumbled Zeftan.

"Yes, my Lord, the humans are quite adept at entertaining their juveniles. We can…"

"No, you lordak, I'm not talking about toys and games. I was saying that those computers are toys. Get back on track."

"Yes, my Lord. I misunderstood, my Lord. In general, their non-quantum communication systems are more advanced than ours. Again, without quantum communication, they have pushed their existing systems to the limit."

"Finally, perhaps most importantly, their materials scientists are unusually creative. Our metallurgy is far more advanced than human efforts. However, their understanding of ceramics and metal-ceramics composites is most remarkable. For example, they use one-tenth of the so-called rare earth metals that we do. They have achieved this with their ceramic matrices. Other minor areas, such as medical imaging, are worth exploring. However, the true prize is their materials science."

"One-tenth the need for rare earth metals," mused Zeftan. "That would end our dependence on the Flektanians, would it not?"

"Yes, my Lord," answered Genthor. "Not quite end it, but the relationship would be wholly different."

"Indeed, it would be. How much of this information is openly available?"

"Relatively little, my Lord. The humans call the techniques and processes 'proprietary information.' They even hide it from each other for financial benefit."

"So, we will need to exchange information or steal it."

"Yes."

"Steal it, my Lord?" asked Penfor.

"It's a thought..."

"Not a very good one, father," said Reldap.

Zeftan glared at him over 25 light-years distance. "It was just a consideration. All right, we have to exchange. What do they want?"

Reldap spoke. "There are three technologies of particular interest to the humans."

"Go ahead. First?"

"Nuclear space propulsion."

"Second?"

"Particle protection."

"Remind me, what's that again?"

"My Lord, it is the various protections we use on spacecraft so they may travel at very high speed."

"Yes, thank you. I remember now. Good. Third?"

"Quantum communication and the necessary related technologies."

"Those are our flagship technologies…"

"Yes, my Lord, they are."

"We have worried about the humans since we first encountered their radio transmissions 100 of their years ago. They treat harknars as normal members of society. They fight, and they argue. They tell lies as readily as they eat. They will use quantum communication to spread rubbish around the galaxy. They will use particle protection for military purposes—we all know that. Worst of all, once they have nuclear propulsion, they will use it to visit us and do all sorts of wretched things. No. None of those technologies can be traded to the humans."

"Zeftan," said Genthor, "what can we offer the humans?"

"Access to our great libraries? Consultation with our bioengineers? The design of our non-nuclear rocket motors?"

Penfor looked at Reldap and then turned back to the camera. "I doubt this will be seen as an attractive exchange," she said.

"Make it attractive," said Zeftan. "Now, let us address the issue of the e-Fleks."

"Yes, my Lord," said Reldap. "What of the e-Fleks? They have been quite amusing, and they have helped us tremendously. The government of the U.S., for reasons that escape me, has taken their behavior at face value. The sensible humans find them at times mildly annoying but overall enjoy them. They are entertaining and harmless."

"I think," said Zeftan, "that we should accelerate their life cycle."

Reldap was shocked. "Why? That will allow them only another five or six Earth months of life. Why?"

"They have served their purpose. They are not at our level. Even for e-Fleks, they are damaged. I think we should be finished with them. The humans will find accelerating their life cycles as less morally repugnant than simply terminating them."

"My Lord, I am unsure how that will be greeted here on Earth. Earth has a long, dark history of destroying creatures and even fellow humans that are not useful or inconvenient or are judged to be 'not at our level.' The best humans have made an uneasy peace with their past and have resolved not to permit those actions again. Call it what you wish, but I do not believe the humans will accept it. They are not perfect, and they still eat meat, but they are a far cry from what they were."

"Reldap, I think you are going human on us," said Zeftan. He said it jocularly, trying to make light of his comments. "The e-Fleks belong to us. We do what we wish with them."

"With all due respect, father, the humans would hold that the e-Fleks belong to no one."

"Do not forget your allegiances. Do not forget your responsibilities. I have made no decision about the e-Fleks, but you must try and find out more about their metallo-ceramics. Do as I say."

Reldap was about to answer, but Penfor spoke first. "I share his views on the e-Fleks. Zeftan, please reconsider what you are saying."

"We will end this conversation now. Again, I have made no decision on the e-Fleks, but go forward with the exchange. Please remember who and what you are." The Latternites terminated the call.

******

Once the connection was broken, Zeftan turned to Ventak. "Please, leave us. I must speak with Genthor in private."

"Yes, my Lord. At once." Ventak quickly rose from his seat and left the communication terminal.

"I am not happy with this," said Zeftan. "The humans are resisting our inquiries. We had not anticipated this."

"You are right," said Genthor. "I am not happy either."

"It has been many years and many alien contacts since we have needed to do this," said Zeftan, "but we may need to take a more aggressive approach."

"You mean…" started Genthor.

Zeftan cut him off. "Yes. Get Feldant." Genthor nodded and started typing commands into the communicator.

Feldant was a high-ranking official in the Latternite Office of Interplanetary Affairs. Even by Latternite standards, he was rigid and irritable. He soon appeared on the screen. He looked at Genthor and Zeftan, and then grimaced. "Earth?"

"Yes," said Zeftan. "They are being obstinate."

"A moment," said Feldant. "Let me review the files." His image disappeared for several minutes, and then reappeared. "They do not know their place in the grand scheme of things, do they?"

"No," said Zeftan. "They do not."

Feldant sighed. "I thought this would be easier. When things go as planned, we look like benign visitors, eager to help less developed civilizations while we gain this or that tidbit of information. However, let me be direct. Lattern visits new planets for Lattern's sake, not the planet's. If the trade is to be uneven, it must be in our favor. The humans are smart and inventive. I am sure that there is and will be more to gain than just metallo-ceramic technology. The information flow from Earth to Lattern must be robust and in our favor. For the moment, let us keep negotiating and playing the role of benign visitor. However, if we cannot achieve our goals, Reldap and Penfor must take a more active posture. We have several devices on the QCS that can gently disrupt various parts of Earth infrastructure and show we are serious. We'll discuss which intervention might be most persuasive if that becomes necessary."

Genthor turned to Zeftan. "Do Penfor and Reldap know of these devices? Are they familiar with how we deal with reluctant partners?"

"No," said Zeftan. "Initial contacts proceed more smoothly when the emissaries are ignorant of all the tools at their disposal. The Latternite emissaries are more patient and accommodating when they don't know the size of the hammer they potentially wield, and that works better with these lesser civilizations. Species such as humans do not tolerate being confronted with bald power. These contingency plans are not taught in the interplanetary emissary courses. Only officials at our level and higher have this knowledge. The disruptor devices are labeled and stored as backup parts for the particle shields. We will instruct Penfor and Reldap in their use if the time comes. For the time being, they and the humans will remain in ignorance. And, if the humans finally behave, we will continue to be friendly visitors from space."

"Will the biobots obey if instructed to be, um, more aggressive?"

"Of course. Latternites always follow orders. That is our way."

CHAPTER 42

"I am concerned, Reldap," said Penfor. "Your father can be obstinate and impulsive. It is not a good combination."

"No, it is not," replied Reldap. "However, I am uncertain how to respond. More to the point, what can he do from 25 light-years distance to compel us to his will?"

"He might activate more biobots and send them to Earth to 'reason' with us."

"Truly, do you think he would do such a thing? Override us in such a manner? That is close to using force. Besides, how would he get the biobots to Earth? We have both AEVs from the communication station."

"If he gets angry enough, he might consider using the escape pods to bring the biobots to Earth."

"The escape pods?" Reldap was taken aback. "He could, but it would violate all norms and traditions. It would send a terrible signal to the humans, suggesting dissent among the Latternites. It would be unprecedented."

"I agree," said Penfor. "However, he still might do it if he gets in one of his moods. This Earth project has made him erratic and intransigent. I cannot predict his behavior. I have an idea., but it involves my returning to the QCS."

Penfor made her pitch and they went back and forth over some of the details. When they were finished, Reldap grinned. "Worthy of humans. It is amusing that he will be the one to request that you make the trip. I think it will work."

******

The Earth-based biobots received an urgent request for communication from Ventak the next day. Penfor and Reldap made their way to the Waterville airport and boarded Penfor's AEV, and they established the connection back to Lattern.

"Your call is most unexpected," said Penfor. "What is the issue?"

"There is a problem on the quantum communication station," said Ventak.

"Really?" said Penfor. "What is it?"

"We are getting anomalous thermal readings from one of the laboratory spaces," replied Ventak. "The temperature is not dangerous now, but it has been steadily rising overnight."

"I agree that is not good," said Penfor. "Can you not send a repair bot into that space to investigate?"

"We are having a problem accessing that area."

Sheepishly, Reldap joined the conversation. "Which lab space is the problem?"

"L-1. Why do you ask?"

"I think I left the anti-intrusion system functioning for that space," said Reldap.

"You did what?!!" Ventak was apoplectic.

"That was the lab I used with the e-Fleks. It was difficult to herd them into the stasis chamber unit when we were about to return to Earth. They kept running off the transport sled and trying to get back to that room. Something about needing to do further investigations of some of the equipment. I turned on the anti-intrusion system to keep them out. I guess I forgot to turn it off."

Penfor gave Reldap a decidedly dirty look. "You lordak," she said and shook her head. She turned to the vid screen. "Can you not turn the anti-intrusion system off remotely?"

"No," said Ventak. "Anti-intrusion systems work only under local control for security reasons."

No one spoke for a minute. Finally, Penfor broke the silence. "Someone needs to go to the quantum communication station."

"Agreed," said Ventak. "I was about to say the same thing. The anti-intrusion system must be reset manually and in person. While there, the thermal issue can be checked."

"I created the problem. I'll go," said Reldap.

"I don't think so," said Ventak.

Penfor sighed. "Fine," she said. "I'll do it. While I'm there, I'll grab a few plant specimens we have in stasis. Some of them might be of interest to the humans. I was thinking of our rotek shrubs and pest-resistant flarn pod trees."

"Yes, yes, good idea," said Ventak. "We can throw the humans a few tidbits to show good faith while we work on the larger issues. Will you be all right on that journey?"

"Unlike Reldap," said Penfor, "I won't get into trouble on the trip and amuse myself with smek." She smirked Reldap.

Ventak stroked his chin as he thought. "Very well," he said. "What we have discussed is what you will do. You have permission from Mission Control. Please get to the quantum communication station as soon as you can."

"I will do my best," said Penfor. Ventak closed the communication link.

******

"Really?" asked Reldap. "You had to bring up the smek? Telling him I'd left the intrusion system on wasn't enough? I had to look like a complete fool?"

"I wanted everything to look as normal as possible," she said.

Reldap grumbled but said nothing.

Penfor called Maria the next day and explained that there was a problem on the QCS that required in-person intervention. Maria was surprised given the sophistication of the Latternite technology, but promised to expedite launch and low-orbit clearances.

Penfor and Reldap stopped by Chez Gilner to inform us about the trip. Helen and I made sympathetic noises. Reldap was uncharacteristically silent, making me think that the problem on the QCS might just have something to do with him, and I said nothing. Almost as an afterthought, Penfor told us about picking up the plant samples. I thought it was a great way to start trading ideas and technologies, and I wished her a safe and easy trip.

Unlike Reldap, Penfor and her ship's AI had a friendly, respectful relationship, and it followed Penfor's directions cheerfully. Launch, orbit insertion, and transition to interplanetary flight were uneventful. Six days later, she docked at the quantum communication station.

It had been some time since she had been on the large craft, and she took a few minutes to reorient herself. Like many of the other biological materials, the plant samples were in the stasis storage area. She retrieved several interesting species that she thought might be of genuine interest to the humans. She then went to the biobot storage area. Opening the application that managed biobot stasis, she saw that eight healthy, unprogrammed bodies were still ready to be reanimated. Taking a deep breath and recognizing that what she was about to do could not be undone, at least in terms of her relations with Lattern, she entered her super-administrator credentials.

Once logged in at that level, it was easy to change remote activation rights. Transmissions from Lattern could no longer activate and program a biobot. She and Reldap could not be forced to self-destruct. Instructions must now be entered locally on the QC station or from Reldap's or Penfor's AEV. She checked her work, ensuring the stasis support and monitoring functions were intact and still in communication with Lattern. Finally, she reprogrammed the communication and monitoring modules so that it no longer appeared as though there was a thermal problem in lab L-1, and that the anti-intrusion system had been deactivated. There had been no problems with either system; it just had been made to look that way to Lattern. Now, everything looked fine. "Real" Penfor was a very good programmer, but biobot Penfor was an astonishing programmer.

She spent the night on the QC station. Rested, she returned to her AEV and proceeded back to Earth. Interesting, she mused; I instructed the AI to go home. Ship asked me if I meant Earth, and I answered yes without hesitation. A lot can change in a year

CHAPTER 43

"Okay, so that pack of crazy fuckers actually cleaned out the brainsucker nest?"

"Yes, Mr. President."

"Really? Aliens and bugs and a few Fedtoads?"

"Mr. President, the investigation and apprehension were well-thought-out and well-executed. Reldap, who you refer to as your friend Relly, recognized the importance of a chance encounter with a critical CubeSheet DataBox. The four Federal officers include Agent Johnson and Agent Standing Elk of the FBI, who are felt by some to be the best investigative team on the force. You are already familiar with Agents Labrador and Stein, and they have done a remarkable job over the last year of managing this unprecedented situation on behalf of the United States. Also, remember they have helped keep Mr. Jackner in check. I think it is unwise to call them Fedtoads, even if that appeals to your supporters. As for the e-Fleks, it would have been impossible to follow the trail of evidence without them. I acknowledge that they are given to bizarre, untimely outbursts, but they have been very helpful in the balance. When all is said and done, they are harmless."

"OK, OK. You made your point. No Fedtoad talk and we'll make nice on everyone else. I heard the bugs ate the brainsuckers?"

"Yes, that was the agreement."

"But we still have some brainsuckers, right?"

"Yes, they are being used and studied in controlled situations."

"Good. I still wanna try one. Maybe when my term is over…"

"Yes, sir. Waiting would be wise." Although it wouldn't make a difference even if they sucked out half your squash.

Can we have a press conference now?"

"Yes, Mr. President. The timing would be excellent. A fine way of demonstrating your support for these brave friends of America and showcasing your key role in ending this crisis."

"Good. Glad I thought of it. Make it happen."

Yes, sir."

******

Helen and I faced the familiar sight of The Prez at a podium as Vicki Nguyen introduced him. Once again, he'd decided to make Waterville center stage to showcase his alien relations. Once again, Beefy Guy A and Beefy Guy B had "invited" us to participate, albeit politely. Once again, we sat in the important person but not the very important person seating area. Let the show begin.

"Good afternoon, everyone. I'm Vicki Nguyen, Assistant Director of the Office of Alien Relations. We are here to provide an update on the unauthorized kleptron problem. I'm happy to report that we have good news. Acknowledging their extraordinary work, I will turn the microphone over to Agents Shawn Johnson and Tina

Standing Elk of the FBI's Special Investigations Unit and ask them to tell the story." She stepped away from the podium as Shawn and Tina took the floor. Tina started.

"Good afternoon. I'm Special Agent Tina Standing Elk. This is my partner, Special Agent Shawn Johnson. We were privileged to lead the team that neutralized the unauthorized Kleptron problem. Our public relations officer (*Standing Elk points to man to her left*) will provide an electronic summary document to everyone registered for this briefing. If you don't already have it, here's the link (*points to screen.*) That's the dollar version (*chuckles from audience.*) I'm going to give you the nickel version."

"We initially had no data that pointed us in any one direction. Employing standard investigative techniques, we assessed the most recent illegal kleppings site. Evidence there pointed us toward Texas and Louisiana. These investigations were dead ends, and the evidence appears to have been deliberately developed to lead the inquiry astray."

Shawn took over. "In the course of other work related to legal kleptron research, Reldap recognized a data irregularity in a CubeSheet DataBox at JarVexx's kleptron facility. This data irregularity suggested the diversion of kleptron feeding stations. An individual at JarVexx then assisted us with further inquiries. With the assistance of this individual, United Federal Shipping, our colleagues Labrador and Stein from Homeland Security, our Latternite colleagues, and the Trilobite Liberation Army, we successfully identified the location of the illegal kleptron colony, and its potentially harmful effects were fully neutralized."

"We have not yet questioned all persons of interest. Because of the delicate nature of this investigation, we cannot disclose the names or suspected whereabouts of these individuals. Additionally, the cooperating JarVexx employee cannot be identified until this case is resolved. I'm sure you all understand this. I will now take questions." Johnson looks at Vicki Nguyen, who acknowledges John Harris from Combined Action News.

John Harris, CAN: "Thank you, Agent Johnson, Ms. Nguyen. Can you clarify what you mean when you say the kleptrons were 'fully neutralized?'"

Johnson: "Yes, Mr. Harris. They were eaten."

Harris: "Eaten, sir?" The room is utterly silent.

Johnson: "Yes, eaten. The e-Fleks assisted us on the condition that they would be allowed to eat the kleptrons once the cache was discovered. They are an e-Flek delicacy. I'd prefer not to go into greater detail."

Harris spluttered. "Agent Johnson, it is extraordinary, even in these extraordinary circumstances, that the investigators are permitted to eat the evidence."

Johnson: "Yes. Extraordinary situations require extraordinary measures. Next question."

Nguyen recognizes Anja Chopra of Independent Vid News.

Chopra: "Thank you, Ms. Nguyen. Agent Johnson, you indicated earlier that the investigation was not over. Can you provide any further detail?"

Johnson: "Ms. Chopra, I appreciate your desire for more detail. This is a complex, multi-state, and multi-national investigation. There are many moving parts. Providing greater detail may alert persons of interest and give them the opportunity to destroy evidence or leave our jurisdiction. I'm sure you understand that I can't answer your question at this time."

Johnson turned away from the audience and towards Nguyen. He made a slicing motion across his throat. She nodded. "Thank you, Agent Johnson and Agent Standing Elk," she said. "The Trilobite Liberation Army, which has been instrumental in this case, has requested the opportunity to make a short statement. I'll give Klak, their leader, the floor."

Vicki and Shawn hoisted Klak onto a wheeled platform and brought him to the podium. He turned from side to side before he spoke. "Humans," he said, "I spit in your presence." The rest of the TLA circled him, and they let go long brown streams of liquid.

"Bipeds, we have relieved you of the kleptron scourge while keeping them in our thoughts and prayers. We accomplished this despite the absence of sexual tension between the SIO and a junior investigating officer. We achieved this despite the absence of an investigator with a North England or Scottish accent. By all rights, by all measures, from everything we had learned from watching early 21st-century British police procedural dramas, this investigation should have been a failure. Despite these handicaps, we moved forward. We earned our just rewards. We have feasted. Thank you.

"Humans, our primary mission can now begin. It is now time to make arthropods great again." The other e-Fleks started chanting, "Make arthropods great again," but Klak shushed them.

"We return again and again to the painful and senseless victimization of our trilobite brethren. We cannot… I say again, we cannot allow hundreds of millions of years of culture and progress to be turned to stone and lay embedded in the crust of the Earth. With the help of sympathetic humans, we will find our long-lost cousins. With the help of our friends, we will reanimate this pinnacle of evolution. If the so-called 'Great Permian Extinction,' better termed the 'Great Permian Assassination,' not occurred, trilobites would rest on the very chairs you occupy.

"We call on all able-bodied bipeds to join the Friends of the Trilobite Liberation Army. Pick up a shovel. Scour the maps. Shoulder a pick. Dig, dig, and dig some more until we succeed. Make arthropods great again!"

Nguyen took advantage of the pause to speak. "We thank you, Klak. I don't think we'll be taking any questions." They quickly wheeled the bug, still wildly gesticulating, away from the microphone.

Vicki stepped back to the podium. "The President usually speaks first at such gatherings, but today, we've decided to save the best for last." She looked at The Prez, who beamed. "Everyone, I give you Albert Moorehead, the President of the United States." The crown applauded.

Moorehead, who had up until now been playing with his PDD, stepped up to the podium. Nguyen covered the mike with her hand for a moment. "Mr. President, please stay on script." He looked at her uncomprehendingly but smiled and nodded.

"Good afternoon, everyone," he read from a small paper in his hand and then looked up. "Screw it. I always do better when I sing a capella." He crumpled the paper and tossed it.

"Good afternoon, everyone. It gives me great pleasure to stand here before you today. A terrible problem has been corrected. A great danger has been ended. Led by our capable Federal agents, an unusual but highly effective team of humans, Latternites, and e-Fleks found and neutralized the errant kleptrons."

"We have protected the vulnerable. We have stopped the illegal and devastating destruction of memory, both in those who submitted to this foolishness voluntarily and those who sadly were klepped against their will. This will not happen again."

"However, there is work unfinished. We have not captured all the perpetrators, who I assure you will be brought to justice. I am proud to have led this investigation from its inception. The safety and neural integrity of all Americans is my highest priority. I trust the Justice Department and its friends and allies to bring this sad incident to a close."

Wow, he's doing pretty good so far, I thought.

"So you may ask, where do we go from here? Assistance to our e-Flek friends is our highest priority. I urge you all, join FOTLA. Dig, dig, and dig some more until we succeed. Help those who have helped us. Trust the plan. Make arthropods great again! Thank you."

And with that, our great leader walked over to the e-Fleks. He announced, "Trilobite Liberation Army, I spit in your presence." Then he hawked an enormous goober into the puddle of brown muck.

Ms. Nguyen, who by this time had shown a remarkable ability to manage The Prez's press conferences, was completely unflustered. She smiled. "President Moorehead will now take questions."

She looked around the room. "Ms. Lunstrom, from The Times-Post?"

Lunstrom: "Thank you, Vicki. Mr. President, can you provide any more detail about the identity of possible suspects who have not yet been apprehended or contacted?"

The Prez: "Honey, there's so much I can't tell you it would fill a book. Why…"

So much for doing pretty good.

Nguyen interrupts The Prez. "Thank you, Mr. President. Next question, please, from Mr. O'Malley, from CNN?"

O'Malley: "Mr. President, can you provide further detail on how you and the government plan to support the TLA and FOTLA?"

The Prez: "Bob, that's a great question. I'm glad you asked it. It shows a deep understanding of the situation. I'm sure your viewers appreciate your insight. Next question."

O'Malley is slack-jawed and looks at Nguyen. "Mr. President, you didn't answer his question. You just provided some opening remarks."

The Prez: "Oh, yeah. Sorry about that. It's easy to get distracted sometimes, you know, with all these people and aliens and bugs floating around. So, TLA and FOTLA, yes. Like I said at the last news conference. Simplified permitting for trilobite-related digging on Federal land, suspension of trespassing laws for trilobite-related digging, and suspension of "Dig Safe" requirements for trilobite-related excavations. I just added that last one. Pretty cool, huh?"

Nguyen: "Mr. President, we'll discuss that last point later. One last question, and then I'm afraid we'll need to finish up." She points at Michael Antonello from the Wall Street Journal.

Antonello: "Mr. President, there's a rumor that this is somehow connected to President Khishchnik of Russia. Can you comment on that, please?"

The Prez: "Look, buddy, Dmitri is a fantastic and upstanding human being. Period. Any more questions like that, and you ain't buckin' your bronco at any more of these rodeos."

Nguyen: "Thank you, Mr. President."

CHAPTER 44

Make arthropods great again. Trust the plan. It was not what I had hoped to hear, but it was unsurprising. I watched the journalists put away their equipment, and The Prez got whisked back to Washington to do whatever he did when he wasn't making speeches. Hopefully, it wasn't very much.

The four Feds walked over to Helen and me. "Nice summary," said Helen. "You were coherent and made sense. Why were you allowed to speak?"

Johnson shrugged his shoulders and threw up his hands. "Look," he said, "Tina and I put our heads down and do our work. It's even worse in Washington. Don't worry about it. This is just background noise."

I disagreed that it was just background noise, but we did need to do our work. "Okay," I said, "what's next?"

"Let's sit down somewhere," he said.

"An excellent suggestion," said Reldap. "Let us settle the TLA and consider our next steps in detail."

"When will Penfor be back?" asked Tina.

"When she is finished on the QCS," said Reldap.

What an odd answer; usually he drowned us in unnecessary detail. I didn't quite know what to make of it.

We took our e-Flek charges back to the Grange Hall, set them out to pasture, and got sandwiches from Sandwich King for lunch.

Joe stood up. "Let me start." Everyone nodded. "As I see it, we have four or five remaining tasks in the near term, stuff for which the eight of us are responsible. First, we need to identify and find this Giorgio character. Second, we link him to Devlov. If Giorgio is within our jurisdiction, we do something about him. If not, we'll need to build a case for extradition. Devlov, we'll need to kick that upstairs once we confirm he's involved. That's the criminal justice part of this outline. We'll fill in the details in a minute." Again, everyone nodded.

"Third, we get the exchange going. This will be massive and mostly nothing to do with us. Our job will be to get the right folks around the table and get out of the way." No one raised any concerns, and Stein continued.

"Fourth and maybe fifth, depending on how you slice it, are the e-Fleks and the TLA lunacy.

"There are six giant delusional beetles with an open mike, and they are inciting thousands of people to dig holes in the ground on their behalf to look for a 250-million-year-old stasis chamber containing trilobites. Look, the bugs have done their job. We're grateful. But we need to put them out to pasture somewhere and stop this TLA crap."

No one said anything. Maria was the first to speak. "So it sounds like we start with Giorgio? Leave the exchange to the diplomats? Leave the TLA on hold for the moment?" Heads nodded around the table. "Giorgio it is, then. Let's catch this sucker."

We were finished for the day and went our separate ways, having agreed to give Giorgio some thought. We would meet tomorrow. As Helen and I pulled into our driveway, I saw our neighbor from across the street throwing pickaxes and shovels into the back of his pickup.

Hi Jack, what are you up to?" I asked. Jack Montgomery had always been a little eccentric but harmless.

"I've joined FOTLA," he said. "Heading out to that old feldspar mine near Paris and gonna dig. I heard tell that the TLA offered ten million dollars and a ride on a spaceship for the humans that find that stasis chamber. We're gonna make arthropods great again!"

I chose my words carefully. "Jack, you do realize that the feldspar mine and the Maine pegmatite region are all igneous rock, don't you? Typically, you don't find fossils in igneous rock. And about the money and the spaceship ride…"

He gave me a condescending smile and cut me off. "Doc, you're a nice guy, and you were a hell of a good doctor; everyone knows that. But this, I'm on the inside track. Stay in your lane. Please don't give me all that stuff about pegmatite regions. I don't know what that is, and I don't care. I did my own research and am going to that place near Paris. Let FOTLA take it from here, and you enjoy your retirement. I'd love to discuss this further, but I gotta run. Pickin' up a couple of other fellas on the way out there, and I don't want to be late."

He waved and drove away. Helen looked at me. "Yeah, you guys are right," she said. "We gotta do something about the bugs."

CHAPTER 45

We met the next day and talked a lot about how to nab Giorgio. In the end, we did catch the guy. His name was Giorgy Fekalov. In some ways it was harder, and other ways easier, than we had anticipated. It would be a great story, if I could tell it.

Organized crime would love to understand the nuts and bolts operational details and strategies involved in identifying and apprehending a suspect as high up the food chain as Giorgy. We can't expose that information. After talking with my Federal friends, we decided the safest approach is to provide a partial transcript of Fekalov's hearing. I've left out the countless frivolous objections and motions to suppress evidence from the defense attorneys and some of the other procedural stuff. The court proceedings are not as juicy as the whole story, but it still makes for good reading, and you'll get the general picture.

Prosecution: Agent Johnson, can you please lay out the overall strategy for identifying and arresting Mr. Fekalov?

Johnson: Certainly, sir. After discussion with my colleagues…

Prosecution: You mean Agent Standing Elk, Agent Stein, Agent Labrador, the Gilner doctors, Reldap, and Penfor?

Johnson: Everyone you mentioned except Penfor. She was still in space.

Prosecution: I see. And the TLA?

Johnson: We did not include them in this conversation.

Prosecution: Right. Go on.

Johnson: After the illegal kleptron colony had been neutralized, we believed that Mr. Fekalov would want to reacquire kleptrons, and an opportunity to do so would draw him out.

Defense: Your Honor, we once again object. The witness will be depending upon information obtained through entrapment.

Judge: Mr. O'Mara, we've been through this before. You and your co-counsel, Mr. Schwartzberg, appear to have forgotten the definition of entrapment you were taught at your expensive law schools years ago. Answering an ad on the dark web is not entrapment. There was no threat, fraud, or harassment involved. Your client contacted the sting of his own free will. Objection overruled. Sit down.

Prosecution: Please continue, Agent Johnson.

Johnson: We reasoned that Giorgio, whoever he was, would not want to deal with anyone from JarVexx directly. As far as he was concerned, that source was compromised. We arranged for an agent to play the part of a laboratory worker at a different legal kleptron facility. That individual made it known on the dark web that a gravid female had been identified in their kleptron colony.

Prosecution: Why would a pregnant female be so important?

Johnson: After the birth of the kleptrons, a portion of the litter could be transferred to Mr. Fekalov. Only the lab worker would know how many kleptrons had been born. That individual could order sufficient feeding stations for the entire litter, even though only a fraction of the animals would still be on site. It would be simple to camouflage the shipping of feeding stations, movement of kleptrons, and disposal of used feeding stations. The legal kleptron colony that assisted us was at a major university with many parcel deliveries and shipments.

Prosecution: An arrangement similar to the situation that evolved with JarVexx?

Johnson: Yes, sir.

Prosecution: Go on.

Johnson: We had a number of, um, inquiries.

Defense: Your Honor, we object to selective enforcement. What is the status of these other individuals?

Judge: A fair question. Agent Johnson?

Johnson: Your Honor, we did not wish to alert the underworld to the nature of the sting. We indicated to these individuals that they did not have the backing and infrastructure to make this work, and we declined to engage. However, with this trial underway, we are now following up on those initial contacts, and we're having conversations with all the individuals who answered the advertisements. Mr. O'Mara knows this for a fact, as several of the persons under investigation have hired him and his firm to represent them. I fail to see how we can be accused of selective enforcement.

Judge: (Glares at O'Mara) Overruled. Sit down. Continue, Agent Johnson.

Johnson: Thank you, sir. Mr. Fekalov reached out aggressively. He told our agent that he had been running the illegal kleptron operation and that he knew how to make money and keep the participants—the criminal participants — safe from klepping and apprehension. When the agent observed that Fekalov's operation had been shut down and everyone except the defendant had been arrested, the defendant became threatening. He insisted that our agent participate. We had developed an elaborate false identity for our agent, and Mr. Fekalov told our agent where her lab tech persona lived, where her parents lived, and what the name of her dog was. Mr. Fekalov also disclosed multiple details of the original illegal klepping operation that had never been made public; only someone intimately involved with the operation would have known that information. We knew we had our suspect. Ultimately, she agreed to work with Fekalov, stipulating that she meet Mr. Fekalov face to face. Given the risks she was taking, she wanted to meet the principal in person.

Prosecutor: And he agreed?

Johnson: Not initially; he was resistant. On the other hand, from the perspective of a criminal, it was a reasonable request, and ultimately, he acquiesced.

Prosecutor: Agent Johnson, thank you. It is my understanding that your partner, Agent Standing Elk, was the agent who oversaw Mr. Fekalov's apprehension. I have no further questions for you, and would like to call our next witness. I will ask you to step down and for your partner to come forward.

Judge: Agent Johnson, you may step down. Agent Standing Elk, would you please come forward.

(Johnson steps down, Standing Elk is sworn in.)

Prosecutor: Agent Standing Elk, can you walk us through what happened at this meeting?

Standing Elk: Certainly. The conditions were that the lab tech bring the gravid female as proof. Fekalov would bring the paperwork for anonymized funds transfers.

Prosecutor, with a rueful smile: I expect criminals sometimes wish for the old days when a bag of hundred-dollar bills would be just the ticket for a situation like this. Our cashless society has its downsides.

Judge: (Sharply, to prosecutor) Stay on task, sir. Philosophize on your own time.

Prosecutor: Sorry, your Honor. Agent Standing Elk, I apologize for the interruption. Please proceed.

Standing Elk: Ultimately, it was anticlimactic. We agreed on a place and time. Our agent showed up. Fekalov showed up with several "assistants." We had anticipated this and saturated the meet's environs with agents. With this display of overwhelming force, there was no gunplay, and no one got hurt.

Prosecutor: That's it?

Standing Elk: Yes, sir. As you know, he has been on remand since his arrest. When his passport was confiscated, he smiled at the judge and indicated that he had several others and the connections to use them. This did not go over well.

Prosecutor: Thank you, Agent Standing Elk. You may step down.

******

And here's what didn't happen in public:

Judge's chambers: [Present: judge, defense attorney, prosecutor, Fekalov]

Judge: All right, Mr. O'Mara, what do you want to discuss that we can't talk about in open court?

Defense: Judge, let me be direct. Under normal circumstances, these guys (points to the prosecutorial team) would have us dead to rights.

Judge: So what is there to discuss? A plea deal?

Defense: In a manner of speaking, yes.

Judge: Go on.

Defense: We propose that Mr. Fekalov admits to overstaying his visa and gets deported.

Judge: That is a mighty big ask...

Prosecution: Your Honor, no way, no how...

Defense: Let me finish. If you do not accept our proposal, we make both of your lives a living hell. There are so many unprecedented, unresolved issues in this case, it is a law student's wet dream. Evidence developed by alien law enforcement. Will that deputization stand up in court? That'll be interesting. Evidence *eaten* by alien law enforcement? That's a good one. Kleptron Control Act? The law that has never previously gone before a court. We could go on and on. We can cost you millions of dollars that could be put to much better use. We can spin your heads with dozens of motions, and waste years before the case is settled. Think of it this way: The kleptrons are out of circulation. This bad guy, and your Honor, I admit that I would not want this man marrying my daughter, is out of the U.S., and he promises not to return. It's your choice.

Judge looks at Prosecutor: He does make some good points.

Prosecutor: Shit. Let me talk to my boss.

Judge: I think you should.

Prosecutor: Fine. But I have one final question for Mr. Fekalov. Does Ivan Devlov have anything to do with this?

Fekalov smirks: My friend, what do you think? Of course, but he is untouchable. I will discuss this silly meeting with him over vodka and caviar when I get home. He will be amused.

CHAPTER 46

"Mr. President, the hot line is ready."

"Thanks. Let me put my, uh, smoke down."

"Yes, sir."

The president stubs out his blunt and sits down next to the telephone. The direct line between Moscow and Washington is deliberately kept as an old-style bright red telephone to remind the two world leaders of how things had been in the past, hopefully never to be repeated. He picks up the phone.

"Dmitri, my friend, how are you?"

"Very well, Albert. I hear you have much to celebrate."

"We do, we do. We have those loose kleptrons taken care of…"

"It must be quite a relief."

"Yes, it is. My FBI boys and girls found 'em with the help of those aliens, and then those giant bugs ate 'em."

"A most unusual means of addressing their neutralization. I will have to keep it in mind for other situations."

"Dmitri…"

"Yes, Albert, I assume there must be something you wish to discuss, important enough to take you away from your duties."

"Dmitri, there is. We deported that fella Fekalov back to you…"

"Yes, I know. Some assistants of mine greeted him when he got off the plane."

"Uh, just how did they greet him?"

"Albert, there were some, how do you say, issues with Mr. Fekalov that predated his visit to your country that still needed resolution. We needed to consult with him about these outstanding questions."

"I see. Is he still able to discuss things?"

"Only with difficulty. I do not think he will trouble your beautiful nation again."

"Thank you, Dmitri. Now, the other question we had is a bit more delicate. Your friend, Mr. Devalov."

Khishchnik's voice sharpens. "Yes, my friend Mr. Devalov. What of him?"

Moorehead sucks in a breath before continuing. "Dmitri, our friend Fekalov indicated to us that he did much of his mischief under the direction of Devalov. We…"

Khishchnik cuts him off. "I had not heard such a thing. He is quite a good friend, you know."

"Yes, Dmitri, I know. Perhaps you had not heard because your consultations with Mr. Fekalov ended prematurely?"

"It is possible. How did you find out about Ivan's, I mean Devlov's possible involvement in this, as you say, mischief?"

"He leaned on his niece, who gave him up when we were able to identify her as the source of the loose kleptrons. He threatened her parents, her brother, and even killed her cat."

"Family is very, very important to Russians, and you know I love cats."

"Yes, Dmitri, I do know you love cats, and I know how important family is in Russian culture."

"Thank you for telling me about this, Albert. Sometimes friends act in ways you do not expect, which can damage the relationship."

"I know, Dmitri. It can be most distressing. It is hard when a friend acts in a way that hurts a friendship, and when it is left to you fix that friend's errors. I would like to lessen the hurt, if I may. That favorite bourbon distillery of yours in Tennessee has just released a marvelous batch aged for 20 years. I'd love to send you a couple of cases."

"Albert, yes, that would help soften the blow. I would be indebted. I must confess that your American bourbon is the only thing that can stand up to our best vodka."

"I am sure you will enjoy it."

"I am sure I will. I would like, my friend, to end this conversation with the offer of a gift to you in return. I am told you have enjoyed one of our carefully cultivated strains, Siberian Sunrise…"

"Dmitri, I love that stuff. Knocks those silly California hybrids right on their fancy asses."

"A kilo?"

"I'd love it. Thank you."

"Albert, take care. You will not need to worry about these things."

"Dmitri, I knew I could count on you. Thank you."

The line is disconnected. The Prez relights his blunt.

******

From the New York Examiner-Journal:

Bizarre Accident Claims the Life of Russian Oligarch

A bizarre accident claimed the life of Ivan Devlov, 58, three days ago. The well-known industrialist had retired to his dacha 100 km outside Moscow for the weekend. Police say that he entered his private steam bath and that the thermostat failed, raising the temperature in the room to 80 degrees C. The door was found jammed, which had prevented him from escaping. Russian police investigators theorize that the abrupt rise in temperature in the room buckled the lock, as the door lock mechanism appeared physically damaged with the striker wedged into the doorframe; it took rescuers over an hour to secure entry into the room. Devlov's condition, when found, distressed the attending first responders. One investigating officer, speaking on the condition of anonymity, described the body as "as if he had been cooked sous vide."

President Khishchnik, known to be a good friend of the oligarch, has promised a full investigation of the manufacturer of the steam bath unit. "I am sure this happened from an unfortunate, strange concatenation of events," he said. "But if improvements to the manufacturing process can prevent this from happening to some other poor soul, we must identify them." Khishchnik expressed his optimism that the investigation would "likely wrap up in a day or two" and voiced his expectation that the inquiry would confirm that what had occurred was a series of unpreventable coincidences. "Nonetheless, we must make certain of this," he said, "so that there are no concerns about foul play."

Devlov, known for his extensive and diversified holdings in Russia and abroad, was one of the wealthiest people in Russia. Although he maintained that all his business activities were legal and above board, rumors persisted regarding his connections with the Russian and US underworld. During one interview, he admitted that some of his import-export activities "pushed the envelope," but he denied ever breaking the law. When all was said and done, he had never been arrested or indicted and was lauded for his activities as a philanthropist. Memorial plans are not final. He leaves his wife, two grown children, and his brother and his beloved niece, both of whom live in the United States.

CHAPTER 47

Penfor landed without fanfare. She left the plant specimens on her ship while awaiting further instructions from Lattern and consultation with Reldap and the humans. Reldap greeted her at LaFleur, and they stayed with Helen and me that night.

They were quite somber over breakfast the following day and didn't say much. My concern finally got the better of me. "Okay, folks, what's wrong?"

Penfor looked up from her pancakes. She had been pushing pieces around on her plate rather than inhaling them as per her usual. "We have some problems," she said.

"We gathered that," said Helen. "Tell us what's going on."

"It is complicated," said Penfor. "I have told you about how biobots are recycled or destroyed at the conclusion of their task?"

"Yes," I said. "Has Lattern Mission Control changed their mind? I thought you had been given permission to live on as you were nearly a year ago! Have you been asked to recycle yourselves? That would be terrible!"

"No, no, Dr. Gilner. It is not as bad as that. Mission Control feels that the e-Fleks have completed their work."

"And they want to kill them? But they aren't biobots. They aren't clones."

"They do not wish to kill them outright. The term we use is "life cycle acceleration."

"What does that mean?"

"We can reprogram them to complete their life cycles in four to six Earth months rather than their ten to twenty Earth years. Sometimes they live longer, infrequently shorter. They typically live about as long as a dog or cat."

"What's wrong with just letting them live out their normal life cycle?" said Helen. "I'm sure we could set up a safe old age home for giant beetles. 'The Edward and Helen Gilner Home for Aged Giant Alien Beetles,' or something like that." Penfor frowned at her. "Uh, sorry. That was in bad taste. I'm just unhappy."

"Yes, Dr. Helen, so are we," said Reldap.

"Reldap, they are not biobots. They are unique and original. They are crazy as anything, but they are harmless," I said. "I think there would be considerable resistance from humans to accelerating their life cycles."

"Would Lattern Mission Control consider human opinion?" asked Helen.

"Perhaps," said Penfor, "if there were a show of strong support. However, it would be unprecedented."

"Isn't this whole situation unprecedented?" I asked.

Reldap nodded.

I thought for a moment. "From everything you have said and told us, Lattern Mission Control respect the authority and the governmental proceedings of its partner civilizations, does it not?"

"Oh yes," said Penfor. "Very respectful. Government and the rule of law are paramount. Dr. Gilner, as you humans say, I see the wheels turning in your head. What are you suggesting?"

"Let's get our friend The Prez to hold a referendum."

"Ah," said Reldap. Penfor giggled. Helen gave me that look that I get from her when I start stringing wires between rooms for an experiment.

******

The Prez was intrigued. "Jeez, I get to tick my box as the champion of the little guy and defender of the democratic process against weirdo aliens. Let's do it." Consultation was held with other world leaders, and it was decided that since the e-Fleks were confined to the U.S., the referendum would be held exclusively in the U.S. The mere prospect of America having a hand in any international political activity panicked potential partners, who were more than happy to leave us to our own devices. As Penfor had predicted, after a considerable back and forth on the matter the Latternites agreed to be bound by the voting results, provided that the balloting was "free and fair." I think the subtext was good riddance, and don't tell us we didn't warn you.

Town halls and debates were arranged throughout the country. Vid ads proliferated, as did sagely worded opinion pieces in all the "serious" publications. What should have been a simple question—whether we let these critters live out their natural lives or not—became impossibly convoluted and deeply intertwined with every theory of law and philosophy currently in vogue.

The Prez rattled on and on about the e-Fleks' value and how they were a precious commodity and should be protected and nurtured. "I love the little guys," he said. "They've worked hard for us and solved a big problem.

Besides, they haven't found that stasis chamber. I'm really excited about that; it would be very cool-- I just wish they would stop spitting." He made it clear that the New Independent Party (of which he was supposedly the head) was dead set against life cycle acceleration and would continue supporting the trilobite venture.

In some respects, FOTLA presented the most straightforward argument. As far as they were concerned, life cycle acceleration (LCA) was out of the question. The e-Fleks had not achieved their primary goal. The trilobite stasis chamber had not been located. The Earth would benefit from their efforts and be a better place. FOTLA was particularly vocal, with raucous rallies and torchlight parades. It was quite something.

PETAl, People for the Equal Treatment of Aliens, also presented a simple argument. e-Fleks were intelligent beings, albeit not at our level. They deserved to live out their lives in peace and safety.

An opinion piece on one of the more conservative websites was more cautious. Fearful of setting a precedent of indiscriminate government handouts, the author favored letting the e-Fleks live out their lives, providing they generated their own financial support and contributed to the common good. How that would occur was to be determined.

Religious input was fascinating. Zealot Group A held that humans had been given dominion over all creatures on the Earth, and since the e-Fleks were on the Earth, humans would call the shots. ZGA was further subdivided into pro-Life Cycle Acceleration and anti-Life Cycle Acceleration camps, depending upon preexisting views and prejudices. Zealot Group B parsed the language of various religious tracts in greater granularity and held that since the Lord had given Man dominion over the Earth and not the Universe, the fate of extraterrestrials was not in our hands; we needed to follow the wishes of the Latternites.

The ACLU weighed in, holding that the referendum itself was not constitutional because the traditionalist interpretation of the Constitution (which was now in vogue, even with the ACLU) did not address the possibility that there were space aliens, and thus the Federal government couldn't intervene. It was up to the states to decide. I had trouble following all that stuff, so we won't go into it in too much detail.

The euthanasia lobby, still fighting an uphill battle for Federal laws and guidance, wisely kept silent.

The most robust support of Life Cycle Acceleration came from several Earth-first organizations. The rallying cry of a surprising number of people, "If you don't kill 'em, we will," was not humanity putting its best foot forward.

How about the bugs themselves? It was hard to know. Despite their occasional startlingly moving speeches, when all was said and done, they were pretty primitive. And delusional. Their sense of time was limited. My take was that they fundamentally didn't understand the question, and they didn't understand the consequences of the decision in either direction.

How did I feel? Like everyone else who had spent time with them, I had experienced a mix of amusement and frustration. The marching, the delusions, and the untimely and inappropriate interjection of British police slang into serious work and serious conversations were at times drop-dead hilarious but also sometimes felt like grounds for a quick squirt from a bottle of Raid. Most of all, I think we all felt they had said or done nothing to suggest that they had any understanding of mortality. Helen and I advocated hard for them to live out their lives in peace, marching and digging to their hearts' (or circulatory systems,' to be more precise) content.

For an American election, the results were remarkable. Fully 80% of the eligible population voted. Seventy-five percent of the voters voted against Life Cycle Acceleration. Reggie Rancourt, the dad of Waterville's police chief, owned a dairy farm and said he'd be happy to take them on. An epidemic caused by a novel feline retrovirus had dispatched his barn cats, and he needed some help with rodent control. We warned him about the marching and the flags, and he said he didn't care. It was a perfect solution. Latternite Mission Control was not happy but agreed not to interfere. The e-Fleks were all male, so there would be no more e-Fleks when these little guys were gone. It was a good solution. Reldap, Penfor, Helen, and I drove the e-Fleks to Reggie's place and dropped them off. Thrilled with the prospect of hectares and hectares in which to hunt and graze, they formed up into a straight line, saluted, and marched to the barn.

Resolution of the kleptron and e-Flek problems set the stage for resurrecting the information exchange. Reldap and Penfor had arranged for us to chat with Mission Control. We'd do that tomorrow.

CHAPTER 48

The four of us went to LaFleur the following day. We used Penfor's ship for the call since it was more spacious. The connection to Lattern Mission Control was straightforward. Ventak, Zeftan, and Genthor greeted us. All of them were smiling, which I did not view as auspicious; they would obviously make some giant ask. I was very surprised that no one from the US or UN alien relations offices had been patched in or had joined us in person. I was positive we were being set up.

Ventak started. "So, my human friends, you have resolved the kleptron problem and used your democratic processes to resolve the e-Flek issue. Most impressive, most impressive. It is time to move forward with the cultural and technological exchange, is it not?"

Helen looked at me and nodded, signaling me to answer. I decided to address my concerns head-on. "My Latternite friends, it is good to see you again. I trust you are all in good health." They nodded and mumbled thanks for my good wishes. I continued. "I am surprised you wish to discuss the exchange with Helen and me. We hold no positions in government; our roles have been, at best, advisory. We became involved with Reldap and Penfor by accident, not by design. How can we possibly represent the Earth in such serious negotiations?"

Zeftan answered. "Ah, my human comrades, a fair question. You might say we are just testing the waters, evaluating the opinions of the 'man on the street' to use a human term."

"An anachronistic, sexist term," said Helen.

Zeftan was not used to getting rebuked. He grimaced for a moment and then forced himself to smile. "My apologies, Dr. Gilner. English has subtleties that are sometimes not well-conveyed by our translators."

Horseshit.

"No apology is needed, Zeftan," I said. "However, Dr. Gilner appreciates your gracious comments. Please continue with your proposals."

"I will let Genthor speak. You have not met him previously. He is our technology exchange specialist."

I paused the conversation. "Before you start, Genthor, let me interrupt. I am going to record this conversation from now forward. I wish to convey your presentation to the appropriate individuals precisely and without error."

"That is fine," said Genthor.

"Good. Please go ahead," I said.

"As I am sure you are aware, we have examined your culture and technology in detail; the presence of the quantum communication station has facilitated our study of Earth. We greatly appreciate your reformulation of our rocket fuel. While minor, your changes to our cell culture techniques have been helpful. We have been amused by duct tape and folding chairs."

I was getting impatient. "Please, continue."

"We have found several other technologies and processes to be quite intriguing. Your software for non-quantum computers is excellent. Your communication systems for non-quantum communication are far better than ours. It appears you have pushed alternatives to the limit absent our quantum technology."

"Genthor, you have brilliant scientists and engineers on Lattern. Now that you know our techniques, these simple strategies can be reproduced without much effort. What is the real ask?"

Genthor looked at Ventak and Zeftan. They muted their microphones and had a short but intense conversation. Genthor spoke again, choosing his words carefully. "We are intrigued by some of your advances in materials science." *Ah, now we're talking.* "Your ceramics science is considerably advanced over Latternite knowledge in this area."

"I wasn't aware of that," said Helen.

"Yes. Your scientists and researchers have developed processes for bonding rare earth metals, as you call them, to ceramics, dramatically reducing the amount of the metals needed for catalytic functions and similar."

"Yes, we have," answered Helen. "I have had an interest in this research. Many of our most advanced medical imaging systems depend on rare earth metals. Without metallo-ceramic bonding, the availability of life-saving equipment would be severely limited."

"We have learned little about this technique and would like to know more."

"Genthor," I said, "this is very valuable information to the companies that have developed this technology. Electronic information storage is sequestered in such situations, and the most valuable notes and instructions remain on paper under lock and key. I take it that the real problem is that your monitoring and eavesdropping haven't been successful in getting what you want."

Zeftan got all huffy. It looked like I had hit the nail on the head, and I was pissed. Helen spoke, trying to calm things down. "Genthor, I thought your relationship with the Flektanians offered you almost unlimited access to rare earths. Why is this metallo-ceramic technology so important?"

Zeftan could not restrain himself. "Because if we had it, we wouldn't have to deal with the Flektanians any more. Do you think this Flektanian Delusional Syndrome is rare? It most certainly is not. They are so sensitive to broad-spectrum radiation that it is laughable. Just put one of the things out in the sun for three or four of your Earth days, and they are crazy. The normal ones? Hah! There's no such thing as a normal Flektanian, e-Flek or otherwise. They are all half-mad, to begin with. If we had your technology, we could abandon that planet and mine our own rare earths, and we'd have plenty."

I was shocked. "But then what happens to the Flektanians?"

"I don't care," roared Zeftan.

"Father…," started Reldap.

"Shut up! You are a traitor! You've been humanized! This is a disgrace!"

"Ventak," said Reldap, "I think my father is overwrought and may wish to reconsider some of his statements in the future. We will put them aside and not take them to heart. Perhaps the fate of the relationship between Lattern and Flektan can be subject to negotiation. It might be useful for the humans to know what we offer in exchange for this information."

"Yes," said Ventak. "Wise comments, Reldap. Genthor, can you provide this information?"

Genthor spoke. "We believe that you would benefit from understanding the design of our non-ionic rocket motors."

"Go on," said Helen.

"Your civilization would derive great pleasure from full access to the entire collection of fiction and music held at our central library."

I nodded. "Keep going."

"We have some biological samples of interest for you. Your DNA analysis techniques are as advanced as ours. Your computers would have no difficulty doing the necessary nucleic acid substitutions. These samples include various grains and vegetables highly resistant to pests."

"Latternite pests."

"Yes, Latternite pests."

"How about Earth pests?"

"We'd have to see."

"Genthor," I said, "how about quantum communication? Quantum computing? Ion rocket drives? Those amazing systems you use to protect your interstellar spacecraft from debris and radiation?"

"We do not feel that you are ready for these technologies. We will not make them available to you."

"So," I said slowly, "Lattern wants to give us details on making slight improvements on rocket engines that are already pretty good. You want to give us access to cultural materials and plants that might offer us no incremental benefit. In return, we give you one of the most valuable discoveries in materials science that we've made in the past 50 years. And the good stuff is off the table. I want to be clear about what we present to the people with decision-making capacity."

"I am sorry that you put our proposal in such a negative light. However, by and large you have accurately portrayed our negotiating position, Dr. Gilner."

I was about to end the conversation when Zeftan spoke. "Human Gilner, consider this offer carefully. We will get the information we need, one way or another. You might as well get something in return, even if it is not exactly what you hoped for."

I was shocked. "Zeftan, are you threatening us?"

"No," he said. "I am making suggestions and predictions."

"Goodbye," I said. I turned to Reldap and told him to close the communication circuit.

CHAPTER 49

My emotions were a mess. I was enraged. I was heartbroken. I was frustrated. Helen's eyes were brimming with tears. The four of us sat in the communication cabin on Penfor's ship.

I was just so mad. "So this whole exchange thing has been a scam, hasn't it, Reldap? You and your cronies back on Lattern have just been playing for time, sucking all the information you can out of us before you even start negotiating. How many times have your emissaries pulled some crap like the escaped kleptrons on another planet to slow down serious negotiations while you poke into every nook and cranny? We were all so thrilled to have you. It was going to be a new day for the Earth. We'd finally come together and work as a single civilization. We'd find our place in the universe. But here we are. Give us what we want, or we'll take it. Fine. Let's get the hell off this ship. I'll call Maria and Joe and explain how the 'exchange' is going forward."

Reldap looked at Penfor. They spoke urgently, in Lattern, without translation. Reldap looked at us and then turned on his translator. Penfor did the same. "My human friends," began Reldap.

"I am not sure the word "friend" is applicable anymore," I said.

"My human friends," repeated Reldap, "you are right to be angry, but hear me out. Part of this is my father's doing. I have seen him behave this way once before. It is the Flektanians. He despises them. Their irrational behavior and complete disregard for Latternite norms drive him mad. He cannot understand their indifference to Latternite standards of behavior. He wants nothing to do with that planet and will do anything to end the relationship, including jeopardizing this exchange.

"But it is also true," he continued, "that other exchanges with other civilizations have become testy."

"Testy?"

"It is true that our quantum communication station monitors your broadcasts. We have learned much and have relayed that information back to Lattern. But as Genthor has said, the real prize on your planet has eluded us. In the distant past, in similar situations with other trading partners, we have been stern."

"Stern? What are we? A bunch of little kids?"

"To some Latternites, yes. They see you like children with a chemistry set or a building set. In the course of playing, you have, by chance, created something wonderful, and we want it, and we will get it. If you do not give it to us willingly, we will take it.

"However, I would not worry too much. The last time Lattern was stern with a trading partner was many Earth years in the past. In the modern era, we have always been able to negotiate a reasonable agreement. Many things have changed on Lattern in the last 200 of your years. We are much more understanding and respectful of our partner planets' independence. We are taught no coercive techniques in our emissary training. Most importantly,

Penfor and I do not share this view and will not assist our home planet in taking what is not offered in fair exchange. Trust us."

He was about to continue when I interrupted him. "I have a question."

"Yes, human Gilner. What is your question?"

"Why in hell should I trust you or believe anything coming out of your Latternite biobot mouth?"

Penfor spoke. "Unfortunately, it is a fair question. Reldap and I have lived here for almost one of your years. There is much about your civilization that is insane, but much that is good. The best part is that we are free. We do not live under the rigid system of rank and nobility. Your species has a sense of humor and experiences joy more easily than we do. We like it here. This is our home, not Lattern.

"I ask you to trust us. Actions will speak louder than words. If you wish, don't believe anything that comes out of our biobot Latternite mouths, and do not trust our intent. But please, let us prove ourselves."

Helen and I looked at each other. "All right," she said. "Let's see what happens." I nodded my agreement. "You are on very thin ice. You know that, don't you?"

"Your skepticism is fair, human Gilner. Please be patient."

CHAPTER 50

Reldap transferred the video recording of the meeting of the humans and the Latternites to my PDD. He and Penfor returned to their home in Portland; Helen and I were not going to be good hosts, and they knew it. We cooked dinner together and talked over the events of the last several hours. What was going on? The Latternites had never before made any sort of even remotely threatening statements. We felt we did not have all the information needed to assess the situation accurately. I had a strong sense that we humans would get the raw end of the deal and that there was little we could do to change the trajectory of events. Helen was more optimistic. Right now, the best we could do was present the video to the powers that be and make the best decisions possible.

The following day, I called Joe Stein. He and Maria showed up in the late morning. I set up our vid screen so the four of us could watch a replay of our meeting with Lattern Mission Control. We watched in silence. "This is bad stuff," said Maria. "We are in serious trouble."

"Yes, it is possibly awful," said Helen. She recounted the conversation that had taken place after the dialog with Mission Control.

Joe looked at Maria and smirked. "Do we do it by the book or the right way?"

"The book will be more amusing," answered Maria. "At least we'll get an hour or two of comic relief before the shit really hits the fan."

"What are you guys talking about?" I said.

"By the book," Joe said, "means we have strict instructions to run stuff like this by The Prez before doing anything else. You know, optimize political optics, maximize the opportunity for personal gain, avoid criminal charges, that kind of stuff. The right way is to make a general announcement, publicly disclose the discussion, and get some of the wiser heads on the planet working on a response."

Maria grinned. "Yeah, definitely. Doing it by the book will be entertaining. A couple of hours of presidential antics, then everybody else gets down to business and we do what needs to be done. What do you think will be his reaction?"

"I don't know," said Joe. "Depends on how stoned he is."

With that, Joe got on his PDD and made a couple of calls. When finished, he turned to me and Helen. "I'm sorry, but I need to commandeer your afternoons. You two were the humans involved in the two conversations. The Washington folks want you there in case there are questions. Again, I apologize, but this is not a request. You will accompany us to Washington for the afternoon."

We ensured plenty of food and water was out for Tigress and Euphrates. In an abundance of caution, we both packed a light overnight bag. A small government vertical takeoff and landing ramjet awaited us at LaFleur. Given the urgency of our mission and with all sorts of government airspace clearances, our flight was given a straight shot to Washington, and it was only 90 minutes before we landed on the White House lawn. The trip itself was very cool.

Beefy Guy A and Beefy Guy B (we still didn't know their names, but they were friendlier with each encounter) checked us over and brought us to one of The Prez's offices. Vicki Nguyen, now promoted to Director of the Office of Alien Relations, was there along with The Prez and a few people we didn't know. They remained anonymous (this is George; that's Harry, and Anne is over there in the far seat kind of anonymous) and were introduced as technical advisors.

As usual, the room reeked of cannabis. A thin curl of smoke arose from The Prez's ashtray. He smiled and had a distant look in his eye. He looked at us. "You two again. What's it this time?"

"Mr. President," started Nguyen, "now that the kleptron problem has been solved and we've housed the e-Fleks, the Latternites have proposed starting the more formal technical and cultural exchange. This…"

"I thought we had started that. You know, L.L. Bean chairs, duct tape, shit like that."

"Yes, Mr. President. As I said, this is Lattern's initial proposition for a more formal exchange of culture and technology."

"Why the hell was it presented to these two jokers rather than me? No offense, docs, but you guys got no skin in this part of the game."

"No offense taken," said Helen. "Mr. President, my first response after this conversation was, 'Ed, we need to bring this to President Moorehead.'"

"Good girl. Hey, did you guys vote for me?"

"Of course, Mr. President. Who else could we vote for?"

"Yeah, they did take Senator Hepatitis or whatever the hell his name is off the ballot three days before elections…If he'd just kept his mouth shut, dumbass." He paused for a moment. "Oh well," he said brightly, "no matter. Bring it on."

The video was transferred to the president's computer and projected on the room's back wall.

The conversation had taken only about 30 minutes. Moorehead watched in fascination, absentmindedly taking an occasional hit on his blunt. When the video finished, he turned to us. "Holy shit. Those motherfuckers. Tell me about this conversation you had with the two aliens later, the one that supposedly made everything better."

"Mr. President, it didn't exactly make everything better. Reldap and Penfor…"

"Those two turtlehead robots, or biobots, or whatever the fuck they are?"

"Yes, sir. You've met them, I believe. They've asked us to trust them and not act hastily or emotionally."

"You think those Lattern bug wranglers are gonna rip us off?"

"Sir, I think they will try, and we will try and stop them."

"We have to negotiate with these assholes?"

"I believe we do."

The Prez shook his head, looking like he was trying to clear his head. "You tech people, any comments at this point?"

The tech named Anne spoke. "Sir, I think the Gilners have summed it up. Our metallo-ceramic technology is very valuable, and they are offering nickel and dime stuff in return. We negotiate hard, and we don't take no for an answer. Otherwise, we walk away from the table. I don't know what to say about the Latternites potentially stealing the technology. If the negotiations fail, we will cross that bridge when we come to it."

Vicki Nguyen spoke up. "Mr. President, maybe it's time we just ask them to leave. This brings the issue to a head. They haven't given us anything but trouble. Kleptrons, e-Fleks, and precious little else. Reldap and Penfor are sweet enough, but in the end, what's in it for us? So far, not much. If they threaten to take what we don't want to give, asking them to leave may not make much headway, but it is something to think about."

Sometimes, a bunch of people will be presented with a problem, and everyone is talking and thinking and not getting anywhere. Then, one person will say something or make an observation that makes everyone involved look at the problem differently. Asking them to leave was one of those "change the ground rules" ideas. As soon as she said it, the suggestion made sense. The people around the table were quiet and thoughtful. Except for our fearless leader.

The Prez had been following the discussion with difficulty and reverted to his transactional baseline. "Sweetie, if there are no aliens, you'd be out of a job 'cause there'd be no need for an Office of Alien Relations. Your dad would be so pissed at me I can't even begin to think about it."

Vicki, to her credit, didn't bat an eye. "Sir, I suggest that we arrange a more thorough discussion. Let's get Mr. Caldoni of UNARA, the United Nations Alien Relations Agency, in on this, and let's think about how we can best use what leverage we still have. We can have Reldap and Penfor set up a conference with Lattern Mission Control, start serious negotiations, and see what we can work out. We'll also develop a backup plan for keeping what's ours."

"Sounds good. Make it happen." He pointed at us. "Then get these guys back home. They are nothing but trouble and I'm tired of looking at 'em."

CHAPTER 51

As I thought back to that first revelation of Lattern's darker side, the meeting with the two biobots and Latternite Mission Control, I felt like I had been duped. All of Lattern's blandishments, all their assurances—rubbish. Lattern was on Earth for Lattern, not for mutual benefit. Giving the aliens our ceramics technology was not a big deal. In fairness to their scientists, now that the idea was planted, they'd probably figure it out eventually. Taking our technology would save them a decade or so in the most pessimistic projection. It was the principle of the thing.

As a species, were we so immature and volatile that we could not be trusted with spacefaring technologies? Was it Lattern's decision? After the exposure of their true nature, were they any better? They hopped happily from planet to planet, taking the good stuff and offering almost nothing in return. Should *they* be allowed interstellar flight?

In that instant, though, philosophical questions did not matter. We had to meet and negotiate, but also brainstorm in case negotiations failed.

The gravity of the situation required international participation, and top-level representatives of the G-36 countries were invited to attend, along with Mario Caldoni of UNARA, the UN Alien Relations Agency. Preparation for the meeting necessarily ended all secrecy, and word spread rapidly of Lattern's bad faith. Many humans, both private citizens and government functionaries, were angry and hurt. Difficult negotiations were anticipated. Nonetheless, we needed to attempt continued communication.

Reldap indicated that it would be simple to set up a conference link that did not require fifty or so humans to crowd onto one of the Latternite ships. He was asked to do so, and a meeting was arranged. Technical advisors were not needed. The issues were political, not scientific. Minor points regarding the relative value of various Latternite baubles were not on the agenda. They wanted what we had, and we wouldn't give it to them unless we got something in return.

I had not anticipated an invitation to the meeting. However, Reldap and Penfor requested that Helen and I attend; I think we were the only humans who might still harbor positive feelings toward them. This trip to Washington threatened to be much longer than the last, so this time we set up multi-day automatic food and water dispensers for Tigress and Euphrates.

The meeting took place at the U.S. Office of Alien Relations (OAR). They had a conference room that could accommodate the 50 planned attendees and the room had excellent connectivity. Reldap and Penfor, with the help of OAR IT techs, had already arranged a projection monitor and audio pickup that linked back to Penfor's atmospheric entry vehicle.

All the human representatives took a few minutes to settle into the room. These people were used to giving orders, not taking them, and there was a certain amount of arranging and rearranging of seats as the mysterious pecking order in such situations evolved. Vicki Nguyen was the American envoy.

The connection was initiated, and we saw the Latternite delegation. It was small compared to ours, with just Mission Control, Zeftan, Genthor, and one Latternite that was new to humans. Pleasantries were limited. Both groups introduced all attendees. We learned that the unknown Latternite was Feldant, a high-ranking official in Lattern's Office of Interplanetary Affairs. Even Zeftan was deferential to him. We learned of his previous involvement in decision-making only later.

Feldant started the discussion. "Thank you all for your introductions; knowing everyone's name and function is helpful. I have heard and seen many of you when we have watched your newscasts. It is good to finally meet you all, although it is unfortunate that it is under these circumstances. I wish our cultural and technological exchange with you were proceeding more smoothly. Reldap and Penfor, it is good to see you both."

Mario Caldoni of UNARA was the first human to speak and answered Feldant in a similar diplomatic tone. "Feldant, as you know, this is my first direct contact with your civilization. It is my pleasure to meet you all as well. Again, as you say, it is unfortunate that we must meet under these circumstances. Until now, our American friends in their Office of Alien Relations have been able to represent the interests of the people of Earth without UN Alien Relations Agency participation. I am afraid, however, that the issues have become so complex that all shades of human opinion must be represented."

"Good," said Feldant. "I believe we share similar goals of open, effective, and hopefully productive discussion."

"I agree," said Caldoni. "May I begin?"

"Certainly."

"Feldant, we are in a most difficult situation. We welcomed your outreach…"

"To be wholly accurate, at least two of your countries tried to destroy our quantum communication station."

"A regrettable error in judgment. Let me continue. Your emissary foolishly released several thousand kleptrons into our environment, causing great harm to many thousands of humans. Only now have we finally gotten this problem under control."

"As you described Earth's missteps, a regrettable error in judgment on the part of our emissary." Feldant glared at Reldap over 25 light-years. "However, your scientists-- I see one at the table, Dr. Gilner-- were able to make use of the kleptrons to provide a novel new psychiatric treatment. If I may digress for a moment, Mr. Caldoni, may I congratulate Dr. Gilner and her colleagues on the brilliant exploitation of an otherwise catastrophic situation."

"Thank you, Feldant," said Helen. "I do wish that the discovery of kleptron-assisted selective memory ablation (KASMA) had been discovered in a more controlled fashion."

Zeftan started shifting in his seat. "Please, let us keep going," he said.

Feldant looked irritated and stared at Zeftan, who stopped making eye contact with the camera. Feldant continued. "Of course. Mr. Caldoni, do you wish to continue?"

"Thank you, Feldant. To clean up the kleptron issue you brought to Earth, might I add, without human permission, giant beetles that suffer from Flektanian Delusional

Syndrome. We are grateful for their assistance, and we find them mildly amusing. Ultimately, however, they provide no incremental benefit for our planet."

"Aside from kleptrons and e-Fleks, you have only given Earth is the company of these two biobots." He gestured at Reldap and Penfor, who were sitting together. "You have intriguing technologies. We wish to learn how you have leveraged quantum entanglement for long-distance instantaneous communication. Tell us about how you have developed quantum computing. We want to learn about your ion rocket engines. The particle protection systems that permit your interstellar craft to travel safely also interest us.

Caldoni continued. "We have given you improved rocket fuel. Please don't deny that some of your medical scientists have been curious about KASMA. On the less technical side, we have shown your emissaries the glory of good food and communal eating. They have learned of duct tape and folding chairs. You have given us nothing."

Both sides were silent for a minute. Feldant then spoke. "As my colleagues indicated in the last conversation, we are prepared to offer more. We can provide you with a better chemical rocket motor. We have biological samples that would be of great interest to you. We will give you unlimited access to all of our cultural heritage.

"But the things you speak of? Ion engines and quantum technology? Particle protection systems? Let us consider these requests individually but in the context of your societal maturity." Caldoni looked angry but said nothing. Feldant continued. "The most benign request would be your desire to use quantum entanglement for communication. By itself, it is a reasonable request. However, we have studied your civilization in detail. You,

Mr. Caldoni, and your colleagues at this table are sensible individuals. Many of your species are not and would spew rubbish all over the galaxy. We cannot be responsible for that."

Caldoni interrupted. "What makes you think we cannot police ourselves? That we can't keep this technology out of the hands of fools?"

"Do you keep your current communication tools out of the hands of fools?" Caldoni did not answer. "I see," said Feldant. "Your silence is your answer. Let me continue.

"As to quantum computing, you do not need our help." Caldoni looked surprised. "I am serious; you do not need our help. You are almost there. We do not think you are ready for the computational power of high-end quantum computing, so we will not help you get there, but quantum communications will be yours within the decade.

"We hesitate to give you ion engine technology for the same reason we will not give you quantum entanglement. You will use it to travel, and you will be bad visitors. You will spew lies and misinformation in person, not only through broadcasts, and figuratively leave trash on the side of the road. We need you to remain in your solar system for the foreseeable future.

"If you will not be using ion engines, you will not need particle protection systems; these are only required when you travel at a significant fraction of the speed of light. Our hesitation here is straightforward. You are a violent, destructive species. As Reldap has said in the past, the technology that protects our ships when traveling at half the speed of light can also destroy planets. We do not trust you. You are an intriguing but immature species. You cannot have this technology."

I think, on some level, we humans were all ready for this speech. We'd heard it before from Mission Control. Even Reldap had expressed his concerns. The Earth delegation's response was muted.

"You have made your position clear, Feldant," said Caldoni. "You have told us before, but tell us again: what do you want from us?"

"We have an interest in your non-quantum computing software. Your non-quantum communication systems are better than ours, and we would like to understand that technology better for local transmissions. Most importantly, we wish to have access to your metallo-ceramic technology." Feldant looked at Zeftan. "Zeftan has already explained why."

"Your rocket engine is of marginal interest," said Caldoni." You know already that our technology in this area is good. Your designs will provide only a tiny increment in efficiency. If you wish to discuss biological exchanges, your biobot technology and neural imprinting hold much more interest than a bunch of plants that might or might not grow on Earth. As for your…"

Zeftan exploded. "If we teach you to make biobots, you will only make zombie armies!" He was irate. Feldant shushed him. "Continue, Mr. Caldoni."

"As for your cultural offerings, I am sure they will be of interest in the future if we continue our relationship. However, we do not understand your society. We do not understand your sense of aesthetics or how you hear music. We were shocked that, as a civilization, you did not see shared flavorful meals as an essential part of life, love, and social interaction. I offer that only as an example of the gulf between us, not a criticism. Yes, we will want access to your cultural offerings in the future, but only after we understand each other better.

"Here is our offer," said Caldoni, "local communication technology for the rocket technology, non-quantum computing skills for biobot technology, and metallo-ceramics for quantum communication. Regrettably, I must concede your points about particle defense systems."

Feldant answered. "I see. We anticipated such a response. It is not acceptable. We will not give you quantum communication, and we must have the metallo-ceramics. Biobot technology is out of the question."

Caldoni answered. "We recognize your technical superiority in many fields, but you are not superior beings. The differences between our civilizations are due to Lattern having perhaps a one or two-thousand-year head start on us in evolution. Maybe your planet experienced one less Ice Age? Those are rounding errors in the life of the universe. You may hold a technological advantage over us, but as beings, we are equals. We deserve respect, not threats. You are not welcome here if you do not treat us as partners."

The Lattern delegation suddenly looked very alert. "You said what?" said Zeftan.

"You are not welcome here if you do not treat us with the respect to which we are entitled," said Caldoni.

Feldant spoke. "I am choosing my words carefully, human Caldoni. In all of our years of outreach, not once have we been threatened like this. Other civilizations have known their place in the galactic hierarchy and have behaved as such. Please arrange to deliver the relevant information about metallo-ceramic technology to Reldap or Penfor.

Once we have that data, we will give you what we promised."

"No," said Caldoni.

"What?"

"No."

"Reldap," said Feldant," please explain to these ridiculous creatures what happened on Rheatus 200 years ago. We don't want to repeat that if we don't have to."

"No," said Reldap. "The humans are right, and I will not help."

"Nor will I," said Penfor. "The humans are right. This is disgraceful behavior, and I will not be part of it."

"The two of you," screamed Zeftan, "humanized! Disgusting!"

"Humans, this conversation does not close the matter," said Feldant.

"It does, Feldant." Caldoni was furious. "Please arrange with Reldap and Penfor to self-destruct and decide what you will do with the quantum communication station. We'd love it if you'd like to give it to us. Otherwise, ship it home or send it into the sun. We don't need another piece of space junk floating around."

"Goodbye, Feldant." There was a deadly silence in the room as Reldap terminated the connection and turned off the projector.

CHAPTER 52

I was surprised at Reldap's and Penfor's stance. It was unthinkable for a Latternite to refuse to follow the orders of a superior. Were they really going to rebel?

Caldoni had made a valiant but doomed effort to stand up to pressure from the aliens. Vicki and Mario approached each other and embraced. Representatives from the other countries crowded around Caldoni, complimenting him on his fortitude and thanking him for his efforts. At length, they quieted, and all eyes turned to Reldap and Penfor.

"Do you truly wish for us to self-destruct?" asked Penfor. Nguyen hesitated for a moment, as did Caldoni. "No," I said. I turned to the other humans. "Dr. Gilner and I know these two better than anyone else on the planet knows them," I said. "We also know Latternite culture, to the extent that any human knows Latternite culture. What these two just said in there, that they would not follow those orders, has severed their relationships with Lattern. They are with us." I suddenly found myself embraced by a weeping 2.5-meter-tall green-brown alien female biobot. It was totally weird.

"Thank you, human Edward. You truly have been our friend. Thank you."

"What now?" asked Nguyen.

"We will return to Waterville with the Gilners," said Reldap. "We must speak with Mission Control. We will try to reason with our colleagues. If we are unsuccessful, we must let a less favorable scenario play out."

"Will Lattern even listen?" I asked.

"Human Edward, you overstate the consequences of our actions, although not by much. Our relationships with Lattern are damaged but not severed. We still serve a practical purpose for Mission Control, and my father may believe that in time we will come around. We are the only representatives of Lattern on Earth. They must talk with us."

"Reldap, you mentioned a less favorable scenario. What scenario is that?" asked Caldoni.

"It is complicated," said Reldap. "Leave it to us." He motioned to Penfor and himself.

Caldoni was not happy, but nodded assent. "Very well. We are in your hands."

******

A government plane took the four of us back to Waterville. We stopped at Rancourt's farm to see how the bugs were doing vis a vis the rodent problem. Reggie was ecstatic. "Ten times more efficient than those damn cats," he said. "They don't play with them, they don't chase them, they don't throw them up in the air and see where they land. They don't leave 'em in my bed as a gift. They just eat 'em. No more problems in the grain bin."

We went over to the barn where the TLA had established their headquarters. The walls were festooned with the "Galactic Arthropodal Council" flag and the Trilobite Liberation Army pennant. "They wanted them up there," said Reggie. "I was happy to help." I shrugged.

Bizarrely, there was also a desk and computer connection in the room. A young man wearing a FOTLA T-shirt sat at the desk, busily reviewing the results of exploratory digs worldwide. He looked up. "Sorry," he said, "can't talk right now. Klak wants an update when we stand to this afternoon."

"Understood," I said. "Keep up the good work."

"Thank you," he said. "I spit in your presence," and laid a globber on the floor. Klak saw us and skittered over.

"Humans Gilner and Latternites, welcome. The TLA has a true friend in farmer Rancourt. A place to work and many tasty rodents. It is good."

"I am glad you and the rest of the TLA are well, Klak."

"We are, human Gilner. Why do you visit? Is there another investigation? A bank job? A bent copper? A body in the Thames?"

"No Klak, everything is fine. We just came to say hello."

"Disappointing. However, the TLA appreciates your support. I am sorry, but we have work to do." With that, he scuttled off.

"Thanks, Reggie," I said.

"It's fine, doc. A small price for no rats in the feed bin."

******

Helen, Reldap, Penfor and I went to the airport the next day. "Are you ready for this?" Helen asked of Penfor.

"I think this will go better than you anticipate, my human friend," said Penfor.

We gained access to Penfor's AEV and powered up the communications module. A grim quartet of Latternites greeted us: Zeftan, Ventak, Genthor, and Feldant. Zeftan forced a smile.

"Reldap, my son, perhaps we all were hasty in our words yesterday. Our experience on Earth has been most unusual. We have never had an exchange with such an unusual civilization."

"It is true, father. Nothing we (*he nods his head at Penfor*) were taught at university prepared us for this Earth exchange. They are a most exotic species."

"Indeed. 'Exotic' describes them well." Zeftan took a deep breath and let it out slowly. "However, it does not excuse them from following the laws and customs of interplanetary commerce and discovery."

"I'm sorry, father, but can you refresh my memory? Who or what is the authority behind these laws and customs?"

"Lattern, of course. Why do you even need to ask?"

"How can you unilaterally decide that Latternite law applies to Earth?"

"You are impertinent to ask such a question."

"That may be, but you did not answer it."

It was apparent that Feldant was growing impatient during this exchange and finally broke in. "Reldap, let us be honest with each other. The exchanges that we undertake with other civilizations are primarily for our gain. If our partner also benefits, so much the better, but it is of little matter if they do not."

"That is colonialism!" sputtered Reldap.

"Let me finish. We harm no one. The humans lose nothing if they part with their metallo-ceramic technology. We deprive them of no physical thing. They do not lose their knowledge. They have simply shared it, with more or less willingness."

"On Earth, this is not considered a fair exchange."

"That is of no matter. How can you obtain that technology?"

"I have not considered that question. We were not taught how to steal in our cultural exchange classes at university."

"We can remedy that. Can you subvert a human? Have you tried the active ping data scrape technique?"

"Feldant, I will not use the active ping data scrape. We use that at home to collect evidence of criminal behavior. These beings are not criminals."

"They are in our eyes," grumbled Zeftan.

"Quiet, you old zark," said Feldant. "Enough of your side comments. This is serious business."

Zeftan fumed but was silent.

"I will not do this thing," said Reldap.

"Nor I," said Penfor.

"Very well," said Feldant. "I give you one Earth day to settle your affairs, such as they are, and then you will deactivate yourselves. Your brains have been poisoned, and you will not upload your neural profile for integration into your original selves. We will activate biobots on the quantum communication station who are willing to further the interests of their home planet."

"No," said Reldap.

"No," said Penfor.

"Please rethink this, my friends. You will bring great shame on your families."

"We are biobots," said Penfor. "You are willing to deactivate us, yet you say we are still part of Latternite society? We do not accept this."

"As you wish," said Feldant. He terminated the connection.

CHAPTER 53

The connection to Earth ended. Lattern was a society of order, hierarchy, and obeisance. The words of Penfor and Reldap were the utterances of criminals and the insane. Perhaps they were both? They must be, thought Feldant. If they were criminally insane, that would justify what he was about to do. Yes, they are criminally insane, and they must be stopped. We will end them. They are damaged biobots that simply must be taken off line.

Feldant turned to Zeftan, who was still present. "I am sorry, Zeftan. I know it is difficult to see this. However, remember that your real son is safe on Lattern and has not been corrupted. This brings no shame on your family. We all misjudged the Earth project."

"Thank you," said Zeftan. "Your good wishes mean much to me. I agree that this insanity must be stopped. Do what you need to do."

"Good." Bolstered by self-justification and the reassurances of his subordinate, he asked Ventak to summon his best remote operations technician. The Latternite appeared shortly.

"Nentor, I wish to activate two biobots on the Earth project's quantum communication station and send them to Earth," said Feldant. "We must deactivate the two biobots that are currently active on Earth. They are compromised. Their behavior is that of the criminally insane, and they are dangerous."

"One moment, my lord," said Nentor. He quickly scanned the status board of the quantum communication station. All looked well. "My lord," he said, "I have two questions before we begin. First, I can activate the biobots, but how will we convey them to Earth? Both AEVs are on the planet."

"That is easy. We will use the escape pods. Once on Earth, they can use the two AEVs."

"Ah," said the technician admiringly. "An excellent solution. My second question: whose neural profiles shall we upload?"

Feldant looked grim for a moment. "We will use one of our generic dangerous task profiles." Even Zeftan looked shocked. "Yes," repeated Feldant. "We will use one of our dangerous task profiles. No independent thought. No independent action. No backtalk.

"No more diplomacy, no more making nice on the humans. Brute strength and raw computing power controlled by us and us alone. We get what we want. Then we put the biobots on the two AEVs and leave the planet. We deprogram all four of them when they get to the Q station and put them back in stasis. There is another candidate contact twenty light years from Earth. We can send the station there. The humans don't want us on Earth? Fine. We leave."

The tech took a long look at Feldant. "Now?"

"Now."

The technician put on his headset and looked intently at the two screens before him. He started tapping keys and speaking into his headset and then paused. He frowned and repeated the sequence. He waited a moment and tried a third time.

"What is the issue?" asked Feldant.

"The station refuses to respond to our biobot activation commands."

"Let me see," said Ventak.

He put on the headset and tried the same sequence of commands as the technician. Again, the system refused to respond.

"Give me a moment," said Ventak. He entered the highest-level access authorization codes for the system. He typed in several more commands and then several more verbal commands. He turned to Feldant with a rueful smile.

"They thought ahead," said Ventak.

"What do you mean?" asked Feldant.

"We have no control over any of the biobots."

"What???"

"We have no control over any of the biobots from Lattern. Remote control over the stasis chambers has been disabled. We cannot activate biobots in stasis. Remote programming and reprogramming of active biobots have been deactivated. Active biobots can only be turned off locally. I think that little expedition to fix a QCS malfunction was cover for a trip to the station so that the remote control of the biobots could be blocked. Almost certainly, there was nothing and is nothing wrong with the QCS station. Yes, the intrusion system can only be controlled locally on the ship, but the monitoring systems are a different story. Function of the station was fine, but all our readings were pure fiction. In the final analysis, none of that matters now. We are locked out."

"Can we turn the remote control back on?"

"No, my lord. Both the "malfunction" and the biobot lockout are skillful bits of programming done with thorough system knowledge. The lockout can only be reversed locally."

"I see. This complicates things, doesn't it…"

"Yes, my lord, it does."

CHAPTER 54

We were driving back to my house from the airfield when Penfor's PDD chimed. She looked at the screen and grinned. "Edward, please turn around. We need to get back to the airfield."

Reldap smiled as well. "Is this what I think it is?"

Penfor giggled. "Yes, it certainly is."

"Hmm. I'm surprised it took this long."

"I'm not," said Penfor.

"What in heaven's name are you two talking about?"

"Helen, bear with us. I don't want to spoil it. Please, let us return to the airport."

I turned the car around, and we went back to LaFleur. We quickly entered Penfor's AEV and established a communication link with Lattern.

It was just Feldant and Ventak. Feldant was smiling, but it was obviously forced. "Penfor, we seem to be having trouble communicating with the Q station."

"Really? What kind of trouble?"

"The stasis chambers are rejecting our commands."

"Hmm. So it's not really a problem of communication, is it? You're asking, and the ship is replying, so it's not a communication issue."

"I suppose not…"

"You really should be more precise in your language."

Feldant gritted his teeth. "Stop this nonsense. You have locked us out of the Q station."

"Correct. You wanted to deactivate us and steal from the humans. We didn't, so we did something about it. On Earth, that's called using one's initiative. It's an enjoyable component of Earth's culture. Are we done?"

"This is unacceptable. You are a disgrace."

"No, we are not. This is one of the best things I've done in my life, either on Earth or Lattern. It would be good if you and your cronies take a gort or two to think things over and get back to us."

Feldant sputtered but said nothing. Reldap closed the communication connection.

"Holy shit," I said. "You guys are something."

"Nice work," said Helen. "I am seriously impressed."

My PDD went off.

CHAPTER 55

We didn't have time to savor this victory. Something was up with the e-Fleks; Reggie Rancourt had texted "Get over here, now," and did not elaborate.

We got to the farm and immediately walked to the barn. The FOTLA kid we had seen the other day was pacing back and forth, thrilled. The bugs were so excited they were just clattering and turning in circles. I grabbed Klak and made him stop. "Klak," I said, "what is going on?"

"Human, this is a great day. They have found it."

"Found what?"

"The stasis chamber. It is a great day for arthropods. A great day for Earth. We have achieved our quest."

"Reggie, what on earth is going on here?"

"Doc, I dunno. I heard all this chatterin' and this crazy kid yellin', and I figured you and Doctor Ed would figure it out."

We swung around the desk and saw the screen. There was a live feed from an excavation site. "What am I looking at here?" I asked the FOTLA guy.

"Okay, we started digging a couple of days ago. You know how the e-Fleks said only to use hand tools, but some of our guys used excavating equipment. The crew got down about 15 meters when the bucket hit something. It wouldn't move. So they started digging around it."

I looked again at the screen. A one-meter silvery metal cube sat in a deep pit, still partially embedded in the rock. The metal was strange. It was unscratched despite being buried and hit multiple times with an excavator bucket. It gleamed so brightly that it looked like it was glowing.

"Where is this?" I asked.

"Nevada, about 200 kilometers east of Reno."

"That's in the middle of nowhere. Why would anybody be digging out there? There's absolutely nothing there. It's not even in a fossil bed."

I paused. "Is this a hoax?"

The kid got indignant. "Sir, absolutely not. This is alien technology. This is it. This is the stasis chamber."

I had to think quickly. The excavator crew needed to stop what they were doing until we could get some technical and scientific types out there. I hated bullshitting these guys, but I was going to need to approach them from within their reality, not mine. I asked the FOTLA kid in the barn to let me talk to Nevada, and he handed me the headset. The Nevada contingent looked at me through the video connection and started talking among themselves. Knowing that I had been working with the TLA, they decided it was OK to talk with me. I was working on coming up with an opening line when, conveniently, one of the people at the other end of the line asked me for my general take on the excavation and the findings. "Listen," I said. "We don't know exactly what we are dealing with. First priority, we must get the TLA out there before we do anything else." This statement was met with vigorous assent.

I continued. "This is the TLA's investigation, and we must prioritize their participation. On behalf of the TLA, I will ask you to stop exposing the artifact until Klak and his boys are out there. They need to oversee this." Again, vigorous agreement. The FOTLA types agreed to stop excavating and not touch the cube.

"I promise I'll do everything I can to get the TLA out there as fast as possible," I said. Then, making it sound like an afterthought, I continued. "We'll also bring along some scientists and engineers who may be able to facilitate the trilobite reanimation process." The FOTLA thought that was brilliant planning and agreed to that as well. I finally ended the conversation. "I don't know what you've discovered out there, but we'll figure it out." I handed the headset back to the kid in the barn.

Helen looked at me and smirked.

I shrugged. "Sometimes ya gotta do what ya gotta do."

I got out my PDD. "Joe, you are not going to believe this; no way, no how…"

******

To make a long story short, the Feds sent a drone out and confirmed something was there. Half a dozen Homeland Security folks, including Joe and Maria, were flown out and cordoned off the area. A science and engineering contingent from the Office of Alien Relations arrived half an hour later. FOTLA was not expelled, exactly, but they were safely marginalized. We (Reldap, Penfor, and the two Gilners) were invited to shepherd the TLA to the site. A government ramjet met us at LaFleur, and we landed in Nevada at the dig site just six hours after the first PDD call.

The bugs were ecstatic, waving flags and turning in circles. Some scientists and Homeland agents, unfamiliar with the chaos intrinsic to any goings-on involving the e-Fleks, got nervous, but Joe and Maria reassured them that the situation was under control and unfolding as expected.

The excavation continued until the cube was free from the surrounding rock. FOTLA's auto-crane grasped the object and deposited it next to the pit. Unable to restrain themselves, the TLA ran over to the cube despite the warnings and protestations of the bipeds. They nudged and fondled it and started marching and dancing around it. It looked like it was a quasi-religious experience for them.

Until this point, no living thing had touched the cube; a combination of fear and prudence had kept everyone at bay, and the device remained inactive. However, physical contact between the e-Fleks and the cube must have triggered some form of sensor: maybe an organic molecule sensor? Who knows. The device activated. A low-pitched hum arose from the box, and the e-Fleks were gently pushed back from the cube. It reminded me of the force field that protected the Latternite ships. A thin rod rose from the top of the cube, and what was obviously an antenna deployed. After about five minutes, a slot opened at the top of the cube, and a screen appeared. A synthesized voice announced in perfect, grammatical English, "Please stand by. We are gathering the necessary information to communicate effectively." The same message was displayed on the screen.

About 30 minutes later, a second slot opened at the top of the cube. An apparatus that looked like the periscope on a World War II submarine, like you see on the history vids, popped out. The hologram of a human-looking creature was projected out of the lens. "Hi there, you're about ten thousand years ahead of schedule. Let's chat."

This was not a hoax. Boy, was this ever not a hoax.

CHAPTER 56

No one spoke. The humanoid projection smiled. "Hi, call me Harry. The first thing we need to do is sort out these different organics here. You, what's your name?" He pointed to Joe.

"Joseph Robert Stein."

"Joe. Great. Joe, come over here and put your finger in that little opening on the cube's right side. I need a tiny tissue sample. It won't hurt, no permanent damage, don't worry. Yup, that's it."

Joe walked over and put his finger in the opening as requested.

"Great. Thanks. Are you guys the dominant life form on this planet?"

"Uh, I think so."

"Good. Now you, the tall green fella. What's your name?"

"Reldap."

"Super. Reldap, please do the same."

Reldap did as he was asked.

"Thanks. Uh, hold on here. There's a little bit of an anomaly. Are you natural or a construct?"

"I am a biobot based on the neural profile of a real Latternite."

"Okay, got it. Now, the data makes sense. You're not from around here, are you?"

"No, my home planet is about 25 light-years from here."

"Right. Final sample. Can one of you bipeds help an arthropod put a leg into the slot?"

Maria picked up Klak and brought him to the cube. Klak put a leg in the opening.

"Thanks. Wow, little guy, you got nailed, didn't you? Lots of DNA damage. And you aren't from around here either, are you? A little bit more like Reldap."

"I am from the same solar system as the Latternites, but I am not like them."

"Yeah, well, whatever. Species pride is good." The projection paused. "Okay, what is everyone doing out here?"

Before anyone else could respond, Klak spoke. "We are on a quest for the stasis chamber protecting the last of the trilobites. We will reanimate them and make arthropods great again. This box, this cube-- this is the stasis chamber, is it not?"

"And all you folks buy into this?"

The bugs and the FOTLA crew agreed vigorously; the rest of us were silent.

"Okay, a little bit of disagreement here." The hologram paused and gestured toward the box. "Sorry, no trilobites in stasis here. It's a little far-fetched, don't you think?"

"But we had done our own research," said one of the FOTLA crew.

"That doesn't always work out well," said Harry. "Look, I need to understand this better. I'd like to do a deep brain probe on a few of you. It is painless, harmless, and non-destructive, and then I'll know everything you know, and I won't sell it to third-party marketers. If I don't get volunteers, I'm gonna volunteer someone." An arm shot out of the side of the cube. The tip was a hand with a beckoning finger. If nothing else, this thing had a sense of humor.

I looked at Helen. "Among the humans, I'm probably the most conversant with everything that's happened," I said.

"Are you sure you want to do this?" asked Helen.

"I don't exactly feel like I have a choice…"

"Great. Come over here and sit on the ground. It will only take a minute or two."

I did as requested. Another appendage came out of the cube and gently encircled my head. I sat there, waiting for something to begin.

"See doc? All done. Just like you used to tell your patients, the anticipation was worse than the procedure. Who's next?"

Reldap was next. The probe took almost no time for him as well.

"Geez, dude. You are one piece of work. Lots of water under the bridge since you landed here. You've really risen to the occasion. Nicely done."

Klak was last. Even though he had the most primitive nervous system, he took the most time because the probe needed to move around among the ganglia that collectively formed his brain.

Harry was gentle when he spoke to Klak. "I'm sorry to disappoint you, but I am glad you and your friends are happy on Reggie's farm. It is a good place."

The hologram looked around at the collection of creatures in front of him. "Okay, I think I have enough information to tackle this. I am going to explain the situation as best as I can. It's a little complicated."

"I am a Venid construct. Think of me as a kind of super AI. It doesn't matter where my builders come from, and it doesn't matter what we look like. My holo appearance has been chosen so as not to upset you. The Venid have been a spacefaring race for millions of years. We visited Earth one hundred thousand of your years ago and buried this cube. It is a ceptronic wave emitter…"

"A what?" asked Helen.

"A ceptronic wave emitter, the ceptron particle being the product of the artificial fusion of a photon and graviton. It's pretty heady stuff, and therein lies the utility of this baby." Harry points at the cube.

"A civilization's understanding of theoretical physics is far and away the best indicator of its overall maturity, not just its scientific sophistication. More than literature, more than chemistry or biology or political structures, more than anything, really. It's quite interesting, and we're not entirely sure why. In our experience, though, only truly mature societies have generated or detected ceptronic waves. So, when a civilization achieves detection capability, it gets an invitation to the party." Harry smiled for a second but then became serious again and continued.

"Think of this cube as a test. Here's the way it's supposed to work. We plant the cube. Your civilization grows and learns. You develop an intellectual and societal infrastructure that can support the level of research that leads to ceptronic wave theory. Your scientists detect a ceptronic wave emitter buried out in the middle of nowhere. You find it and dig it up. I get activated and have a conversation with an advanced, sparkling society ready to go to the next level."

"Except that hasn't happened here. We buried our cube deep, where no one in their right mind would be doing deep excavations. The beacon is never supposed to be found by chance or accident. Thanks to this crazy trilobite stasis chamber delusion, people are digging where no one in their right mind would be digging. The emitter has been found before it was supposed to be."

"What do you mean by 'before it was supposed to be'?" asked Maria.

"I did not expect to be activated for at least another ten thousand years. This is all happening way too early. You see, the issue isn't just physical science sophistication. By the time another ten thousand years passed, you would have discovered and fixed your genetic defects and your society would have had a chance to catch up. You aren't ready. This screws everything up."

"What do you mean?" asked Helen.

"You humans have all sorts of wretched behaviors you have carried down through the millennia. Hoarding, greed, exploitation, tyranny, and the willingness to settle differences with physical force, to name just a few — maybe survival advantages for half-starved, pre-human hominids living in small groups and communicating in grunts, but for the here-and-now, not so much. Those traits have never gone away. They are still there. They are baked into your DNA. They rise up and bite you, both individually and societally, time and time again. You can't get to the next level until those faults are mitigated."

"Attitudinally, you and your Latternite guests are not ready. You may consider yourselves advanced, but I assure you, you are not. You humans still have much to learn about yourselves and the physical world. Latternites consider themselves more advanced than you, but by galactic standards, it is only by a little. Neither species is ready for long-distance, faster-than-light travel. Neither of your species has the cultural maturity to interact with beings profoundly different from yourselves. Until you have that maturity, it is best not to fly faster than you can see. You cannot, will not be good galactic citizens until those genetic defects are repaired."

"Can we be repaired? Can we get better?" I asked.

"Oh yes. Once the genetic defects are mapped, they are easy to fix."

"What do you mean 'fix'?" said Helen.

"The genetic defects in your DNA are easily located and altered. Fundamentally destructive behaviors can be softened without making humans something other than human. You don't all become vegetarians. You'll still argue with your friends and partners. Competitive sports don't melt away. There are still leaders and followers. There will still be employers and employees. There will still even be occasional criminals. But the species-wide instinct to grab and hoard is gone. Armed conflict disappears. Vicious, narcissistic leaders are a thing of the past. The less fortunate in society are treated with greater compassion.

"The biology part is simple. Constructing a safe virus-based delivery vehicle that will fix the genetic problem is straightforward. Most civilizations we've encountered have used an airborne spray delivery system. Takes a few years, but eventually, everyone on the planet gets inoculated. The genetic change is permanent; only one generation needs to be treated.

"The hard problem is changing your civilization to take advantage of your new sanity." I looked puzzled; so did Helen. He smiled and looked at us.

"Okay, you're doctors. Let me give you a medical analogy. Suppose someone has a mental illness. Not a devastating one, not one with hallucinations and delusions, but enough to make them unhappy and see the world through a faulty lens. Despite this, they do their best with what they have." I nodded in agreement; any doc had seen it a million times. "Now, let's say that person finally comes to treatment at the age of 30 or 35 and starts effective medication. That is a good thing. The illness itself has been brought under control. The faulty lens has been removed. However, this person has spent their entire life and formative years navigating the world using the wrong assumptions and distorted facts. It takes time for that person to learn new, healthy habits. Civilizations are the same."

"You humans are interesting. Despite all your flaws, I have a good feeling about your species. You have made many wrong turns and done many terrible things, yet you still manage to retreat from the brink. It is telling to me that it is almost two hundred years since you detonated nuclear weapons in anger, yet you have managed not to immolate your planet. That is better than many, many others."

"Can you help us?" I asked.

"We have never done so, but I see no reason we cannot. Your situation is unusual. Ten thousand years too early. We might as well make the best of it."

"What about Lattern? Can you help us?" said Reldap.

"Hmmm. Interesting question. Give me a moment." The arms on the box withdrew, and the antenna's position on the cube changed ever so slightly. The holo (or whatever it was) tapped its foot, looked up at the sky, grimaced, and caricatured the behavior of an impatient human waiting for an answer. After a few minutes, the arms reemerged, and the antenna returned to its original position.

Harry sighed. "I did a little digging and got myself up to speed. You Latternites are a joyless, rigid race. Your home planet is full of cranky, irritable, condescending beings. Your view of yourselves as a superior civilization is wholly unwarranted."

Reldap looked mortified, but Harry continued. "Your arrogance and rigid hierarchy are downright poisonous. You have a different set of problems that need repair. But yes, we can help your species. The logistics are a bit different, and I'd need to remember where we buried the ceptron emitter on Lattern. DNA's a little different… Yeah, but it's not a big deal. We can figure out the details later."

"So, let me just roll this around in my head. Both of your civilizations have a lot to learn. Your flaws complement each other. You Latternites have to loosen up and be more tolerant, and you humans need to learn how to build some healthy structure and tolerance into your societies and stop blowing each other up if you disagree. Working together, my guess would be that you can rid yourselves of those faulty lenses I was talking about more quickly than each species working alone. We've never tried this two-civilization thing, much less accelerating the maturation process. What do you think? Is this totally off the wall, or should we pursue it?"

No one said anything for several minutes. It was a lot to swallow. Eventually, Joe spoke. "With your permission, Harry, I want to bring your cube to our capital. I would like…"

"Yes, yes, of course. Meet your national leaders, meet the world leaders, talk to the relevant scientists, connect with Lattern, blah, blah, blah. Sure."

"Then let's do it," said Maria.

CHAPTER 57

The implications of the offer were staggering.

Word of the Venid encounter spread like wildfire through all the news outlets on Earth. The offer promised literally to upend life as we humans had known it for hundreds of thousands of years. Predictably, some nut cases didn't want their aggressive tendencies bred out, and many others were rightfully suspicious of this unheard-of technology. As of this writing, some of the world's best scientists are collaborating with Harry to figure out the details and then do testing of safety and efficacy. Even Harry admitted that we couldn't take him at his word; we humans needed to do our own research. He's a wiseass; he couldn't help but phrase it that way.

The pundits and experts are having a field day, as are the conspiracy theorists. Will we be a better species? Are we just being softened up for an alien invasion in 100 years from now, after we've been robbed of our instincts to defend ourselves? What do we want the new society to look like? These are hard questions that deserve thoughtful answers. However, the overwhelming majority of people who've expressed an opinion on the matter—expert or civilian--want to move forward and get The Fix, as it's been branded in the popular press. I'll leave it at that, because that story is far from ready to be written.

Returning to the immediate consequences of the discovery of the ceptronic wave emitter, it was hard to tell how our e-Flek comrades were taking this. Arthropods would not be great again, and there was no secret stasis chamber full of trilobites. The bugs had Reggie take down the flags and pennants in the barn. The FOTLA crew moved on to the next popular conspiracy theory.

The e-Fleks look like they are okay with living out their lives helping the farmers of central Maine. Reggie lends them out to his buddies for rodent control as needed, and the critters don't complain. It's almost as though they shrug their nonexistent shoulders and said, okay, no trilobites, let's move on. Maybe they are happy rather than just resigned; It's hard to say. I know we did the right thing by not accelerating their life cycle.

As for our Latternite friends and The Fix— Helen and I got a call from Reldap and Penfor the day after our trip to Nevada. Reldap invited us to the Waterville airport to be present when he and Penfor called home. By this time, Helen and I were sure that the Latternites knew about the Venid encounter from monitoring our newscasts. I was dying to know what they had to say.

Reldap spun up the communications module. The faces of Ventak, Zeftan, Feldant, and a new Latternite were visible. Reldap and Penfor immediately stood and beckoned for us to do the same. Reldap and Penfor then bowed deeply. "My sovereign, I am honored," said Reldap. Old habits die hard, I guess.

"Drs. Gilner," said Reldap, "this is Henuthorn IV, the reigning monarch of Lattern and its dependencies." I dipped my head out of respect, but I was too much of a democracy kinda guy to do much more. Helen bowed, although not deeply. Henuthorn looked at us and nodded, acknowledging our presence. He must have been briefed on how nutty Americans can get about this monarch stuff and did not take offense at the lack of obsequy.

"I understand you have news for us," said the king.

"The humans have a saying, my king," said Penfor. "The facts on the ground have changed."

"Indeed, they have," said Henuthorn.

"Your Majesty," said Reldap. "Let me begin…"

ACKNOWLEDGEMENT

I tried to sit down and write some short, witty comments on editing and being the foil to a writer. Nothing came out right.

So, I will simply say thank you, as sincerely as I can, to my infinitely patient wife who edited for me and was my creative partner. She spent hours looking at my manuscript instead of doing something else that probably would have been more fun and less hassle. She listened to me prattle on about aliens, Russian bad guys, and giant beetles without batting an eye. On top of it all, she did a great job. Her editing filed off rough edges and filled in nicks and gouges. Her suggestions about the story line and characters made the tale more understandable and flow smoothly. For all of this, I am grateful.

Eileen, thank you. I could not have written this book without you.

Made in the USA
Middletown, DE
08 April 2024